Titanic Sailing Again

An epic Novel

Lilly Setterdahl

NORDSTJERNAN
Förlag, New York

Nordstjernan Förlag, New York 2019

Titanic Sailing Again
Copyright © Lilly Setterdahl, 2019
Cover photo: iStockphoto
Cover design: Nadia Marks Wojcik
ISBN: 978-0-9968460-6-6
First Edition, May 2019
Printed in the USA

Nordstjernan Förlag
Book Services
PO Box 1710
New Canaan CT 06840
www.nordstjernan.com

Acknowledgments

A novel is not finished by the author alone. My sincere thanks go to John E. Norton for his proofreading of the manuscript, to my critique group at the Midwest Writing Center for offering advice, and most importantly, to Nordstjernan Förlag, for final editing, creating the cover, and publishing the book.

About the author

Lilly Setterdahl is a native of Sweden. She knows the subjects of the Titanic and the Swedish emigration especially well. So far, she has had 16 nonfiction books published about Swedes in America, and two more are on the way. Previously, Nordstjernan has published two of her books, *Not my time to die: The Titanic and the Swedes on board*, and *Katrin, almost American*, a Swedish emigration novel. In addition, Lilly has authored two historical novels about the Titanic and one contemporary novel. She has received numerous awards for her research and writing.

Table of Contents

Prologue

"My name is Anna Whitmore, and I'm a Titanic survivor. Today, it's 40 years since the beautiful ship sank. After that frightening experience, I learned that Martin and Ellen Olson had adopted me at birth in 1890. Papa Olson was the gardener at the Addison Estate. As a child, I played with my younger sister Christina and with Lydia Addison. I was 12 years old when my parents decided to return to Sweden to start a nursery business. Christina and I loved living in Sweden but spoke English to each other for a long time, thinking that someday we would like to live in America. I was 19 when I returned to Boston to work for the Addison family as their lady's maid.

"Every winter for three years, I sailed with the family to Genoa on the Italian Riviera. While we were in Genoa that last winter, Lydia took sailing lessons with the Italian lifeguard Roberto Cosentino. By the time the family and I were ready to leave Genoa for the French Riviera, Lydia was in love with Roberto and gave him money to sail with us to New York.

"At one time, when I accompanied Lydia to a party at Cap Martin on the French Riviera, my future husband, John Whitmore, asked me for a dance. He assumed that Lydia and I were sisters. I told him I was her companion, but he still wanted to date me. John was an architect, and his father had sent him to Europe to study old-world architecture. We fell in love and agreed to meet again in the U.S."

Chapter 1

Anna Olson Whitmore, 1890-1955

Beacon Hill, Boston, April 12, 1952

The Addison family and I sailed on the brand-new Titanic from Southampton, England. Never before had I sailed on such a grand ship. It was four city blocks long and eleven stories high. First Class had wall-to-wall carpeting, crystal chandeliers, and plump sofas. The Addison stateroom had a private bathroom and promenade deck. I traveled in Second Class with Lydia, and our accommodations were as luxurious as First Class on other ships. My sister Christina had decided to join me in Boston and traveled in Third Class.

On the night of the sinking, I sat at my small desk and wrote the last entry in my diary when I heard a scraping sound. I went out to investigate but was told to go back to my cabin because there was no danger. I had unpinned my hair to retire for the night when a steward knocked on my door and shouted, "Put on your life jacket and hurry to the boat deck!"

I worried about Christina in Third Class and decided to go there first. The door to steerage was locked and passengers pounded on it from the inside. I found the key and opened the door. The people surging out pushed me down, stepped on me and injured my head and one ankle. Christina saw me and helped me to my feet. Roberto and Lydia joined us on our way to the boat deck, but when we arrived, all the lifeboats were gone. I remember hearing screams, and then everything went black.

Mr. and Mrs. Addison and Lydia perished in the tragedy, and sadly, so did my sister. More than 1,500 passengers and crew died that tragic early morning of April 15, 1912 when the Titanic hit an iceberg and sank on its maiden voyage to New York.

Lydia's boyfriend, Roberto, rescued me from the sea, but I have no memory of it because I was unconscious then, and still in a coma when we arrived in New York. I had been identified as Miss Lydia Addison. Roberto went along with the misidentification and told the authorities that he was my beau. As Lydia's future husband, he would be well cared for, and as Lydia Addison, so would I.

The Addison family's lawyer arranged for Roberto to come with me to the mansion. I had a nurse who took care of me. In a way, it was good for me to have Roberto there, but I never felt close enough to him to believe that I was his fiancée. As I slowly began to regain my memory, Roberto left the mansion in the middle of the night. He had saved my life, so I couldn't be angry with him. He performed another good deed when he identified the bodies of Lydia and her parents.

John sailed to New York after the Titanic disaster. Frantic with worry, he searched all the survivor lists hoping to see my name but found only Lydia's. When his sister met him in New York, she told him about the article in the paper headlined, "The Princess is a Pauper." The pauper was me. John found me and helped me recover from the tragedy. When he proposed to me, I said yes, because I truly loved him.

Before I could marry him, I had to get used to my new life because by then I had learned that the pauper really was a "princess" after all. At least that's what the newspapers wrote about me. Tom, the butler, had revealed the family secret about my paternity. Before the Addison funeral and the reading of the will, he told me I was Mr. Addison's out-of-wedlock child with a woman who had worked in the Addison household. It came as a shock to me. Mr. Addison had always been kind to me, but I was surprised to learn that he was my father and he had included me in his will. I also inherited Lydia's share. I researched my birth record and verified what the butler had told me. Lydia and I had the same oval face and build because we were half-sisters. When I met my Swedish biological mother, I realized my Nordic look came from her genes. She was married to a Swedish carpenter and they had three children who were my half siblings. I came to love my blood relatives as much as my adoptive family.

As the new main shareholder in Addison Enterprises, I was expected to attend board meetings, but not knowing anything about running a corporation, I had to rely on the employees. I can still remember my trepidation as I entered the boardroom. Women had no voting rights in America at the time although the suffrage movement had begun. The company owned many properties in downtown Boston and invested in new ones. After John and I were married, he took over running the business. He also loved to restore dilapidated Victorian homes. We still live in the former Addison mansion that I inherited. Our first child, Henry, was born in 1913 and our daughter Kristina was born in 1918 after America had entered the war and while John served as an officer at the Food Department in Washington. I had learned to drive and was thankful for the freedom it gave me while our chauffeur and John were in the service. Kristina had a slight birth defect, a drooping eyelid. She underwent two surgeries that almost completely remedied the defect.

I had vowed that I would never again cross the Atlantic on a ship, but after World War II, John and I flew to Sweden for a visit. It was exciting to see my former home and old nursery, where I had lived as a young girl. While in Sweden, we also visited my relatives on my biological mother's side. Finally, we went to Cap Martin on the French Riviera where John and I had met.

Anna Whitmore

Chapter 2

Henry Whitmore

Boston, New Year's Day, 1960

I'm Henry William Whitmore, born in 1913, the son of Anna and John Whitmore. Like my father before me, I earned a degree in architecture. As a teenager, I learned to fly small airplanes and came to maturity at the dawn of aviation. My fellow flyers and I barnstormed and nearly killed ourselves. One day in 1936, I flew my small plane across the border to Canada. I thought I had enough fuel to reach an airfield in Montreal, but when the engine began to sputter, I aimed for a farm field to land. Coming in low, I saw the barbed wire fence but could not avoid it. I heard the scraping sound as the wire scratched the underbelly of my plane and the tip of one wing. The hard landing sent a sharp pain up my left leg. Hoping that I hadn't killed any livestock, I looked around and saw a bolting horse with a female rider. I used my arms to hoist myself out of the plane before slowly lowering myself to the ground on one leg.

"Are you alright?" the woman on the horse yelled from a distance.

"Stay away," I yelled back, gesturing to her to back up. "The plane might explode."

Seeing no other people or animals around, I limped away from the wreck as fast as I could toward the rider. The closer I came to the girl on the horse, the more I appreciated her flaming red hair and lithe appearance. She still worked at holding down her horse.

"I'm Henry Whitmore from Boston," I said. "Sorry, I scared your horse."

"I'm Sharon Stanton. My parents own this farm," she said. "I don't think you can walk all the way to the house, so I'll dismount and let you climb up on Thunder here."

I had never been on a horse and didn't trust one named Thunder, so I said, "Thanks, but I'll walk." When Sharon saw how I struggled, she said, "I need to check your leg." My eyes followed her movements as she jumped off the horse with ease and bent down before me. She tried to pull up my pant leg but it was too narrow. Instead, she took off her bandana and tied it tightly above my knee.

"If you could get up behind me on the horse, it would save you a lot of pain," she said.

I had to admit that she was right but wondered how. She solved the problem by walking me close to a fallen tree. I got her point and pulled myself up on the tree trunk. From there, I could ease down behind her on the horse. The best part was putting my arms around Sharon to steady myself. We rode to the farm, where a hired man helped me off the horse. Sharon told me to sit down on a hay bale so she could take a closer look at my leg.

"I'm a nurse and I can clean your wound and bandage it," she said. "I'm sorry but I have to make a slit in your pants." I gave my permission because I didn't want to take them off in front of her.

"Oh, this looks bad," she said. "The skin has come off along with some muscle. I can see the bare bone in one place." She began to talk more rapidly. "You need stitches. I can bandage it temporarily, but then I'm taking you to the hospital. You can't lose any more blood than you already have."

I was beginning to feel faint and assumed that Sharon was right. She went to her car to get a first aid kit. "This will sting, but it's necessary," she said. I remembered the scratches from my childhood and my mom's treatments that always stung and made me cry, but I was a man now and made no sound. "I'll get you a couple of painkillers before we go to the hospital," she said after having bandaged my leg.

Sharon flashed me an encouraging smile as she returned with the pills and a glass of water. She promised me it would make me feel better. She came around with her car and we were on our way to the hospital. When I tried to get up after the procedure, I felt wobbly. A nurse came to my rescue with a wheelchair. Without my pants, I worried about going home in my underwear with Sharon. Luckily, she had anticipated my problem and pulled a pair of sweatpants from her bag and handed them to me.

"Thank you. That was very thoughtful of you."

"You can thank my brother."

"Where is my wallet?" I asked.

"I have it in my purse," Sharon said. "Do you want it now?"

"Yes, please." Warily, I grabbed it and held on to it while the nurse wheeled me to the checkout. Another nurse wheeled me out to the car and put a pair of crutches in the back seat. Seated in Sharon's car and feeling weak, I spoke slowly. "If you hadn't rescued me, I might have bled to death."

"Someone else would have seen your plane go down."

"Perhaps, but I'm very glad it was you. I need to send a telegram to my parents." Sharon took me to Western Union, and to save me from the trouble of getting out of the car, she picked up a pad for me to write my message. Considering that Western Union charged per word, I thought carefully about what to write.

"Landed safely farm field near Montreal. Well cared for. Need money. Henry." The operator would insert a "Stop" between each sentence. I handed the pad to Sharon along with a few American dollars. "Perhaps they can be exchanged," I said.

The next morning, I got a call from Western Union saying that money had arrived for me from Boston. Again, I had to ask Sharon for a ride, but she didn't seem to mind. Thanks to my dad, I now had enough money to buy a train ticket home to Boston.

Sharon changed my dressing every day. She was my heroine and I think I fell in love with her at first sight. Working as a visiting nurse, she went on her rounds in the morning. Canada had organized a visiting nurse program in 1898 to alleviate the need for doctors in rural areas, she said.

I read books and newspapers and listened to the radio. As soon as I could, I hobbled around in the farmyard leaning on my crutches and looking at the livestock while talking with Mr. Stanton, his son Fred, and the hired help.

"I suppose you have a job to get back to, Henry," Mr. Stanton said.

"I work as an architect for my dad, but business is still slow after the Depression."

"We feel it here in Canada, too," Mr. Stanton said.

I told them my mother had survived the Titanic, and they told me about passengers whose destination was Canada but never made it. One family had intended to take a homestead in the Winnipeg area.

When my stitches had been removed, I asked Sharon if she would take me out to my plane so I could inspect the damage. This time, it was easier for me to mount her horse. I was relieved to see that the damage to my plane wasn't as bad as I had feared. We sat on the wing for a while and enjoyed our time together. I twisted her long, red hair around my fingers until I couldn't' resist pulling her closer and kissing her. She stroked my wavy hair that I had inherited from my father.

"So, you're leaving?" she said.

"I'm well enough to go home on the train."

"I'll drive you to the station, but I'm glad you're coming back."

"Next time I come, I'll be driving my car and bringing my tools. My friend Rick might come along to help me. We'll stay at a hotel in town."

Hugging her tightly, I looked into her green eyes, saying, "I definitely want to see you again."

"I want to see you too, Henry." Our love was new but we could both feel it.

Fred lent me a pair of slacks. "I'll help you with your plane when you come back," he said. I thanked Mr. and Mrs. Stanton for their hospitality and said I would pay up when I returned.

"That won't be necessary," Mr. Stanton said.

"We enjoyed having you here, Henry," Mrs. Stanton said. I wondered if they suspected that their daughter and I had fallen in love. At the train station, I kissed Sharon again and thanked her for taking good care of me. She waved to me as the train rolled out, and I waved back.

Dad met me at the terminal in Boston and said it was irresponsible of me to fly as far as Canada. He wanted to know the extent of the damage to the plane and I told him. He had contacted the insurance company, which I had neglected to do.

"Your mom and I are thankful that you weren't badly hurt, but Mom wants you to quit flying."

"I know," I said. "She has told me that many times."

Rick and I took turns at the wheel of my 1935 Hudson convertible roadster as we drove the 500 miles to Montreal. I had to hire a man to work on the plane. He and Rick worked from the inside of the plane to reinforce the belly. Meanwhile, Sharon and I took rides in my roadster and stopped often to embrace.

With the repair completed, I told Sharon that Rick and I had to leave but that I would be back for my plane. Before I left, I told her I had fallen in love with her. When she said she felt the same way, I asked if she would come to Boston and meet my family.

"Not in that small plane."

"I don't expect you to. I'll pay for your train ticket." I had never been in a relationship before, but with Sharon I felt I was ready. I didn't want to leave her, but as long as I was coming back, the wait would be bearable.

Before long, I was back at the farm. I took a test ride to make sure the flight would be smooth. My gas tank was full when I put on my leather jacket and fastened my aviator cap under my chin. I felt the stiffness in my leg as I climbed into the cockpit. Sharon sat on her horse and waved to me. Taking off from a grassy field was not ideal, but it worked. Up in the air, I tipped one wing to Sharon and headed for home. She had promised to visit me in Boston.

One month later, I met her at the Boston Terminal and welcomed her with a discreet kiss. She seemed nervous when I took her to our house to meet Mom and Dad. We had a butler and it was a shock to her. My parents saved the day by being gracious as usual, and Sharon began to feel at ease. I told Mom and Dad that the next time she came to Boston it would be as my bride. I hadn't proposed yet, but I was sure she'd say yes.

"She'll have to get her proper papers before she moves here," Dad said. I hadn't thought about the legal aspects.

Sharon accepted my proposal provided I would stop flying the small plane, and I surrendered. We were wed in her parents' home on the farm in the presence of her family, my parents, and my sister Kristina. I had taken a big leap but had no regrets.

As a wedding present, my parents gave us one of the Victorian homes that Dad had restored. Sharon and I began what we hoped would be a long and happy life together. We welcomed two sons, Bill and Norman, both born before World War II.

After Pearl Harbor, I answered the call to serve in the Air Corps. As a married man with two children, I was stationed in Alaska. It felt good to be able to fly a plane again. I didn't know anything about the Aleutian Islands until I got there. It must have been the most desolate place on earth. Japanese forces had occupied Attu and Kiska, populated by Aleut people.

The U.S. Army soldiers lived in tents as they fought the summer battles of 1942 and 1943. In the battle of Attu, the Japanese lost 2,000 men while we lost about 1,000. It was the only battle fought on U.S. territory during World War II. We flew air raids, and in 1943 we bombed Japan's Kuril Islands located between Japan and Alaska Territory. It was less dangerous than flying bombing raids in Europe. Sharon was alone with our children, except for the domestic help. Since my parents lived nearby, my mom visited often and enjoyed our children.

After the war, I concentrated on designing and building high-rises. Dad and I benefited greatly from the post-war building boom. My sister Kristina earned a medical degree and practiced family medicine in downtown Boston. She never married and preferred to live in a flat in one of our high-rises along the shoreline. Mom died in 1955 and Dad in 1957. I will always miss them.

Henry W. Whitmore

Chapter 3

Bill Whitmore

Boston, New Year's Day, 2000

I'm Bill Whitmore, born in 1938, the grandson of John and Anna Whitmore, and the son of Henry W. Whitmore and his wife, the former Sharon Stanton, originally from Canada. When I was a kid, I used to hang around the yacht club, waiting for a chance to go sailing with friends. I could handle sails and riggings from the time I was 10 years old. If I saw someone scraping or varnishing the bottom of a boat, I offered to help. I often lost track of time and had to run home.

I remember one day when I pushed open the back door, hoping that I would have time to clean up before dinner. No such luck. My family had already gathered at the table. My hands were dirty and my clothes muddy and torn. Mom told me to go and take a bath and then eat in the kitchen. Dad grounded me for a week. Worst of all, Mom had me sit at the piano and practice scales.

Having reached my teens, I went to the deep harbor and watched freighters load and unload. It was even more exciting to see all the immigrants from war-torn Europe coming ashore. I dreamed about sailing to distant ports. Contrary to my father and grandfather, I chose to study engineering.

My brother Norman never cared for sailing. He took flying lessons at a small airfield. In high school, he fell into the wrong crowd and started to smoke weed.

"You've got to get off that stuff," I told him. "It's illegal."

"You smoke cigarettes all the time. I only smoke pot once in a while," he said.

"I'll tell you what," I said, "I'll quit the cigarettes, but then you have to stop smoking marijuana." Only one of us kept that deal, until later. Norm didn't want to go to a regular college. He wanted to learn to fly like Dad had done, but in bigger planes. To get into the Air Force Academy he had to be clean and that made him quit pot. Four years later, we attended his impressive graduation ceremony in Colorado Springs, a proud moment for us all. Norm wanted to continue in the Air Force. We didn't know that it would be during wartime.

My college graduation gift from my parents in 1960 was a ticket on a passenger liner to Europe to visit our Whitmore relatives. To save money for other things, I chose a third-class ticket. Before I left, I went to the barber and asked for the trendy crew cut that would last for a while. My brown locks fell to the floor.

While enduring storms and seasickness on the Atlantic, I remembered what Grandma Anna had told me about her voyage on the ill-fated Titanic, and especially about what had happened to a large immigrant family. The mother had no way of supporting five children if the father had to stay behind on the sinking ship. I pictured the four little girls in white dresses and a toddler boy holding hands with their parents and jumping overboard. It was only one of the tragedies that Grandma told me about the Titanic sinking.

Dutifully, I visited the Whitmore relatives in London. Having seen how stiff-lipped and formal they were, I took a quick farewell and went down to the harbor, hoping to get a job on a ship heading to Europe. My best chance was as a deckhand on a small freighter headed for Holland. In the nearest thrift shop, I traded my fancy leather suitcase for a duffel bag. The North Sea can be as stormy as the Atlantic. Grandma had told me that many European immigrants suffered from seasickness on the first leg of their journey to America. I didn't dare to eat for fear of getting sick and being unable to work.

In the port city of Rotterdam, I managed to get a temporary job cleaning up scraps on the floor of a shipyard and didn't need to speak Dutch. Looking for my next adventure, I foolishly signed on as a stoker on a ship headed for Germany before I realized I didn't have any work clothes other than a pair of jeans with torn knees. My mother would have protested if she had known I packed them, but now they came to good use. Luckily, the furnace radiated so much heat that I could shed all clothes except the jeans. Shoveling coal was hard work and I planned to jump ship as soon as we came to Bremen. I thought about the stokers on the Titanic, who kept on working to keep the lights on while the ship sank. They had no chance of survival.

Having reached land in Bremen, I was black from top to toe and went straight to a bathhouse to clean up. No hotel would have accepted me. First, I discarded my jeans and worked hard at cleaning my sneakers. After a hot shower, I dressed in leisure clothes from my duffel bag and was ready for my next adventure. I stayed close to the shipyards but was stopped at the gate. At six feet with broad shoulders, I couldn't crawl through a hole in the fence like I used to do in Boston as a boy.

I wanted to visit Sweden and looked for a ship with Swedish flag. Having found one, I caught up with the Swedish sailors heading for the bierstube. I spoke to them in English, and surprisingly they understood me. We had a good time drinking beer and dancing with cute German girls dressed in short skirts. When the Swedish sailors heard I knew how to sail and wanted to go to Sweden, one guy said, "Come along, if someone has jumped ship, there might be a job for you."

I approached the Swedish skipper and asked if I could sign on as a crewmember. He looked at his watch and said I might have a chance. When a deckhand failed to return from his shore leave, the skipper hired me to sail with them to Gothenburg.

I was in my favorite element. We had good weather and didn't have to work all the time. During a break, I showed my shipmates the journal that my grandma Anna had kept during her visit to Sweden with my grandfather.

"I wonder if you can make out the names of the places she went to see?" I asked.

One guy by the name of Staffan leafed through the journal and said he saw town names such as Karlstad and Skara. I learned to spell them later. "You can locate those towns on any Swedish map," he said.

"How come your English is so good?" I asked.

"I go to the university. This is only a summer job."

"I see. Have you been on a boat before?"

"Yes, I went on a ship to England, and I've been on smaller fishing boats."

I told him I had just graduated college. "This is the first summer I'm not sailing for pleasure," I said. Thumbing Grandma's journal, I asked if he knew of a nursery near Gothenburg that grew and sold flowers and plants.

"There are many in the area, so I wouldn't know where to begin looking. Why are you interested?"

"I would like to see where my grandmother lived."

"I can take a look at the journal and let you know if I find the name of the place."

"I would appreciate that very much. May I call you Steve?"

"Sure," he said. "That's what everyone called me when I studied in England."

While on the boat, I learned some Swedish swear words, but I don't want to repeat them here. My favorite expression was *Oj då* - that sounded like oi dah. It could be used as a reaction to either something bad or good, sort of like "Oh boy."

I planned to stay in Sweden for a while and travel to all the places my grandmother had described in her journal, but I was also interested in sailboats and asked Steve if he knew of any shipyards that made sailboats.

"I know of the Hallberg Shipyard on the island of Orust. It makes quality sailboats," he said.

"Is it far from Gothenburg?"

"No, it's not. It's up the coast. When we get to Gothenburg, you can buy a map of Sweden, and I'll show you."

The next day we saw the enchanting coast of Sweden with red-roofed houses, white churches, green pastures, lakes, and forests. I described it in my journal and vowed to write something every day.

Chapter 4

By the time we anchored in Gothenburg, Steve and I were friends. He thought he knew which nursery I was looking for. The skipper paid me in Swedish money, and I promptly bought a map. Steve pointed to a spot and said, "This might be it."

"How is driving in Sweden?"

"We drive on the left side of the road like they do in England."

"I didn't think of that."

When Steve saw my hesitation, he said, "How about I drive you to your grandmother's place? You might need an interpreter. People in the countryside don't speak much English. I have a couple of days off before I go out again."

"That's a nice offer. I'll pay you for your trouble."

"You might get a chance to pay me back when I come over to the states."

We shook hands on the deal while waiting for a streetcar to take us to Steve's home. On the streetcar, I told Steve that my grandmother had survived the Titanic.

"Oh, really. I think I had a relative who was lost on the Titanic," he said. "My mother knows more about it."

She did. Steve translated for me and said the man was from Gothenburg and had been engaged to a young woman from Skara. He perished and so did the woman's brother. Skara was a place name I had heard before. My grandparents had visited there in 1950. We talked until 10 o'clock in the evening.

"It's still light," I said.

"That's how it is here in Sweden in the summertime. You'll see. It gets light at about 3 o'clock in the morning. In the winter it's just the opposite, dark mornings and dark evenings."

Steve's family offered me a bed for the night and I thankfully accepted. As far as I could tell, they were of working class, kind, and hospitable. The parents didn't speak English, but Steve's younger brother asked me many questions about America, using his school English.

The next morning, we got into a Volkswagen Beetle that Steve said was his, and we drove south toward the Mölndal area. I don't think I could have handled the manual transmission. I saw many Volkswagen cars on the road, but also Volvos and American cars. It felt strange to meet cars on the right side.

"Where are we going?" I asked.

"If I'm not wrong, your grandmother's place was the Olson *Plantskola* in Mölndal. We'll go there first and talk to the owners."

"Olson was my grandmother's maiden name."

"That's why I think it's the right one."

"What does *plantskola* mean?"

"It means that the plants are being "schooled" to become better plants."

I understood what he meant.

"Mom asked me to buy some rosebushes."

"I'll be glad to buy them for her."

After we had driven for a while and I had seen a lot of butting rock along the way, Steve said, "I think we're close. I'll turn off the highway here."

"There is a sign that says *Plantskola*," I said excitedly. "Martin Olson was the master gardener on an estate in Boston. The family moved to Sweden when my grandmother was 12 years old. Mrs. Olson died here, and Mr. Olson and their son, who was born here, moved to Boston."

"Then we can probably find Mrs. Olson's grave at the Mölndal cemetery."

"That would be fantastic. Does it say anything about it in the journal?"

"I think so." Steve drove down the dirt road and we saw another sign at the gate that said, "Olson Plantskola."

"I think we've come to the right place," I said.

A soon as Steve parked the car, we met a man wearing high rubber boots carrying a spade. "*Goddag*," the man said.

Steve returned the greeting, pointed to me and explained that I was from Boston and that my grandmother Anna Olson had lived there, adding that he wanted to buy rose bushes.

The man's last name was Bloom and he had heard about the Olson family but didn't buy the business from them. There had been another owner in between.

I extended my hand and said, "Bill Whitmore from Boston."

Herr Bloom wiped his hand on his pants before shaking mine. Then he walked ahead of us toward the rose garden.

"Is there anyone around here who would remember the Olson family?" Steve asked in Swedish.

The man pointed to a yellow house up the hill and said something about an elderly woman named Viola, who lived there. I took pictures of Bloom and Steve in the rose garden and photographed trees and bushes standing in neat rows. Steve selected two rosebushes, and when Bloom dug them up, I saw that the soil was loose and fine as potting soil. I paid for the rose bushes, and we said adieu to herr Bloom.

"Wait, Steve," I said. "I have to take a picture of the greenhouse and the main house." I wondered if it looked the same when my grandmother lived here. Then we began walking up the hill to see if we could find Viola. Standing on top of the hill, I turned around and took pictures overlooking the *plantskola* in the valley. What a beautiful, peaceful sight. I could see why Grandma liked it there as a girl.

We knocked on the door to the yellow house, and an elderly woman wearing a striped apron opened it. I was glad Steve was there to explain my errand in Swedish. Viola asked us to sit down on her veranda. Then she went inside the house and came back with a thick book.

Steve said that Viola had a picture of the nursery as it used to look. She also said that Anna and her husband had visited her after the war when many Swedish Americans came to visit. Viola had talked to my grandmother!

"*Här är det* (Here it is)," Viola said, pointing to a black and white picture of the *plantskola* in the big book. I snapped a picture of the page while Viola held it up for me. The book featured businesses and farms on every page. I heard Viola saying something about the Titanic, except she pronounced it differently. Steve explained to me that Viola knew that Anna had been on the Titanic and that Christina had died in the sinking. Viola looked at me, shook her head and wrung her hands to show her sympathy. I felt like hugging her but didn't dare. Instead, I said *tack* (thanks) and adieu while holding her hand.

We returned to the car and drove to the church. Steve said we had to find the cemetery keeper and ask for directions to the grave. It didn't take long before we spotted a man pushing a wheelbarrow filled with garden tools. Steve explained that my grandmother had been on the Titanic and asked if he knew where Ellen Olson's grave was. As soon as the man heard the word Titanic, his eyes lit up, and he motioned for us to follow him. The grave had a headstone with both Martin and Ellen Olson's names, even though he was buried in Boston. A smaller marker had Christina's name and dates. The inscription said she had died on the Titanic, and it explained why it was easy for me to find the grave.

"Oh yes, I remember," I said. "Grandma said she paid for this marker. It was meant as a memorial to her sister." I photographed the grave with its two headstones and the church. The door to the church was unlocked and we walked in.

"This is where the funeral for Ellen would have been held," Steve said. I took in the sight of the church with its high ceiling and white-painted walls. Although Ellen was not my biological grandmother, I felt a connection with the family. The woman had raised Anna and that was all that mattered.

"Your grandmother was probably confirmed in this church," Steve said. Now, I had yet another connection to the Mölndal Church. I was quiet as we drove back to Gothenburg contemplating what I had seen.

"You should be able to go by boat to Orust," Steve said. "The shipyard ferries sailboats to the harbor. I'll call tomorrow and ask."

"I don't know what I would do without you, Steve."

Chapter 5

Steve used the map to point out Gothenburg, which was spelled Göteborg, and said I should learn to pronounce it in Swedish with a soft G. With some practice, I got it almost right. Then he pointed to the rather large island of Orust on the map. I bought a dictionary that had one section translated from Swedish to English, and the other section from English to Swedish.

Steve had arranged it so I could sail to Orust on the freighter that had ferried new sailboats from Orust to Göteborg. The skipper conversed with me in English, because like so many other Swedes, he had lived in America for a few years. While we sailed north, he showed me brochures about the wooden sailboats they made at the shipyard. After a couple of hours, he treated me to lunch on board. We saw many sailboats on the water as well as freighters. When we had passed the island of Tjörn, the skipper pointed to the forested island of Orust. "This is Ellös where we make the boats," he said. As we approached the town, I saw the masts of many sailboats in the harbor, and my excitement grew. The owner, herr Hallberg, gave me a tour of the shipyard.

"I love these boats and I wish my father would buy one," I said.

"Do you want to go for a sail?" herr Hallberg asked. He was tall and skinny and had a thin and sunburned neck.

"Yes, but I couldn't impose."

"I have a customer here from England who wants a trial run, so you can come along."

"Really? I would love to."

"I understand that you're an experienced sailor, Bill."

"Yes, I learned to sail when I was ten years old."

"Come along then, and you'll get a chance to sail in Swedish waters."

Luckily, the sun would be up for many more hours. I forgot all about needing a room for the night. When we returned to the harbor, the owner asked me if I would like to try my hand at building boats.

"I would love to. I can do it for free," I said.

"If you are a good worker, we can always tip you to avoid the payroll," herr Hallberg said with a wink.

"Then I need to rent a room."

"Rooms are scarce on the island during the tourist season, but if you're satisfied with sleeping in a boat, there is always room."

"I would be happy to sleep in a boat," I said.

I stayed on the island three weeks and learned a lot about building wooden boats until it was time to ferry new boats to Göteborg. I heard that three men from Orust had been on the Titanic and that one of them, a skipper's son, had survived. He returned to Orust and was still alive, living in a retirement home. It was located on the other side of the island, so I didn't get to go there, but it amazed me how much I was finding out about Swedes on the Titanic.

I wrote a long letter to my parents enclosing brochures and telling them I had the time of my life in Sweden. Before I left the island, I washed my clothes in a machine on the premises and dried them outside. They smelled good as I folded them and packed them in my duffel bag.

Back in Göteborg, I located the towns of Skara and Karlstad on the map and decided to take the train to Skara first, where I was supposed to have distant relatives. On the train, I studied my grandmother's journal and tried to translate some of it with the help of my dictionary. The young girl sitting next to me saw what I was doing and asked if she could help. I must say that her bare legs had distracted me for a while, and I had seen her tiny waist as she stretched and placed her bag on the luggage rack. I turned my head and looked into her beautiful, smiling face. Her skin reminded me of a rosebud. Her wide-spaced eyes were as blue as the sky, and she had the cutest nose. She parted her long, blonde hair in the middle. I introduced myself, and she said her name was Stella.

"Stella," I tried it and found it to be both melodic and easy to pronounce.

"My parents used to live in Chicago and wanted to give me a name that was easy to pronounce in both Swedish and English."

"They succeeded because even I can say it. You can call me Bill. It's short for William."

"You're American, Bill." She pronounced Bill like the last syllable in automobile.

"Yes, how did you know?"

"I saw it on your luggage tag." So, she was as curious about me as I was about her.

"I'm from Boston, and I plan to visit Skara where one of my ancestors was born." I showed her the journal and asked if she could translate the part about Skara for me. Our hands touched and I felt a spark.

"I live in Skara and work at the library," Stella said. "Many Americans visit us and want our help in finding their roots. You're lucky to have this journal." I loved listening to her accented English as I wrote down what she translated for me. I learned that Anna and John had gone to the cathedral office and asked to see the church registers.

While there, Anna had copied what she found. It would be easy for me to follow her lead.

"Could you translate the entire journal for me if I pay you?" I asked Stella. "If you have time, that is?"

"Let me read some more first," she said.

Stella continued reading until we arrived in Skara. Meanwhile, I had time to take in the landscape from the window. Fields and meadows surrounded the well-kept farmsteads. "What are those yellow crops? I asked.

"It's called *raps*, she said. It's used to make cooking oil and margarine."

I saw grazing cows and people stacking hay until the scenery changed to town buildings.

Returning the journal to me, Stella said, "Look me up at the library, and I'll see what I can do." I was overjoyed at being able to see her again.

Close to the railroad station, I spotted *Turist Information*, entered, and asked where I could find a room to rent. People in the tourism business spoke English. I wanted to stay for a while and Steve had advised me to rent a room in a private home. Skara looked like a quaint old city. Older buildings surrounded the cathedral. While walking the narrow streets, I made plans to find out more about the history of the town, but first I had to find a restaurant where I could satisfy my hunger. It wasn't hard because *restaurang* was almost the same in English. The food was tasty and wholesome. With that taken care of, I went looking for the nearest place that had a room for rent. I wanted to be as close to the library as possible. The homeowner smiled and we communicated by using hand gestures. From the brochure I understood that the price included breakfast.

Having slept on a boat for three weeks with my clothes in the duffel bag, I could finally unpack. I removed the suit bag that I had placed on top, took out my suit and hung it in the closet, smoothing out the wrinkles. I hadn't worn it since I was on the Atlantic Steamer.

If Skara hadn't been so keen on preserving old buildings, my ancestor's home would have been razed. My grandmother's grandparents had lived there a very long time ago. I stood in awe before the small house with the old-fashioned, six-pane windows hung with white lace curtains. Not wishing to intrude, I headed to the library to tell Stella about it and see if she could find out who lived there.

"Good morning, Stella," I said when I found her behind a desk, looking as lovely as the day before. "Thanks for all your help yesterday."

"You are welcome, Bill. I enjoyed reading your grandmother's journal."

"I found the house where my ancestors used to live. What do I do next?"

"If you want to know who lives there, the easiest way would be to knock on the door."

"They probably won't understand me. Is there another way to find out?"

"Yes, I can look it up for you if you have time to wait."

I was in no hurry and sat down to look at magazines that I couldn't read, but I recognized the pictures of Hollywood actors and actresses.

Stella came to my table with a paper in her hand. "No one lives there now. The place is for rent or sale. Do you want to rent it?" she asked with a wide mischievous smile that showed almost all of her even teeth. "Here's the realtor's address and phone number," she said handing me a slip of paper.

"Thanks, Stella. I owe you. May I treat you to dinner this evening?"

"Where?"

"Wherever you want to go within walking distance. I ate at a pretty good restaurant last night."

"All right. You can decide. You can meet me here at the library at six o'clock."

I left whistling a happy tune. If she said yes to dinner, she wasn't likely to have a boyfriend. I cashed another traveler's check and went to see the realtor. I told him that an ancestor of mine had lived in the house and that's why I was interested. He grabbed an old-fashioned house key hanging on the wall and we walked the short distance to the house.

"Are you planning to stay in town for a while?"

"Maybe," I said.

On the inside, the house looked dilapidated and definitely in need of renovation. The windows were low, the wallpapers spotted, and the kitchen showed peeling paint. But I could imagine that it once had been a nice place.

"May I take some pictures?" I asked.

"Certainly. The exterior cannot be changed on a house this old. The interior, of course, could be fixed up. Once that's done, I'm sure it would be easy to find renters."

"I see," I said in a noncommittal way. "Are there any records any-where of who lived here in the 1800s?"

"The old records are at *Landsarkivet* in Göteborg." I had taken all the pictures I needed for sentimental reasons and thanked the realtor for showing it to me.

While having lunch, I read the notes that I had made of Stella's translation. Anna had met relatives here in Skara and it was only ten years ago. I might be able to find those same relatives. I asked the waitress for a phonebook and she brought me one. It surprised me to see how many people had the same last names and guessed that's why occupations were listed. I came up with two or three possible relatives by the last name of Nilsson.

Chapter 6

As I entered the restaurant, I heard a man and a woman speak English at another table, so I went up to them and introduced myself. Their last name was Johnson and they were from Chicago. They invited me to sit down at their table, and we had a good time talking. When I told them about my Titanic connection, they mentioned several Titanic passengers with a connection to Chicago. The couple was in Skara to trace ancestors who had settled in Rockford, Illinois. I asked them if they had heard of the lady from Skara who lost her fiancéé and brother on the Titanic.

"Oh yes, Mrs. Johnson said. "The woman was headed for Rockford, but she stayed there only to recuperate before returning to her parents in Skara."

"So how do you go about finding relatives?" I asked.

"First, we went to Rockford and searched the membership records of the Swedish churches there, and that's where we learned the names of the parishes where our relatives were born. Most were from the countryside, but one relative had emigrated from Skara. We went to the cathedral office here in town and learned that the older records are housed in Göteborg. The records kept here are from after 1896."

"I was told the older property deeds are in Göteborg," I said.

"That's correct, but most of the immigrants were young and didn't own any property. In our case, the parents owned farms, and we visited one of those farms. It had been combined with other farms, and the old buildings were gone, except a little cottage that was used as a summerhouse. We loved to see the little *stuga* because my ancestors probably lived in it," Mrs. Johnson said.

"The area has good farmland now, but I've heard that years ago many fields were full of rocks, which they used for the building stone walls," Mr. Johnson said. I had seen the stone walls from the train and thought about the rocky land at home in Massachusetts.

"Have you learned anything about the history of Skara? It must be very old," I said.

Mr. Johnson said Skara is one of the oldest cities in Sweden. "It was an important town already in 1070. The cathedral dates back to the year 1000. Two convents were built during Catholic times before the 1600s. National congresses were held here in the 1300s and the 1400s. Skara has been burned and ravished by wars, but what is left of the old architecture is being preserved."

"Yes, I noticed," I said. "I've just seen my ancestral home. It's ancient."

"Have you seen the cathedral on the inside yet?" Mr. Johnson asked.

"No, not yet. I arrived yesterday."

"We can show it to you if you like."

"Good, let's go." I was glad for the company until I could meet Stella.

For my date with her, I dressed in my suit with a white shirt that was still in the bag from the cleaners. Standing before the mirror, I tied my tie and thought I looked presentable. My hair had already grown out some and I combed it to one side. At 6 p.m. on the dot, I stood outside the library and waited for Stella. I saw her approaching the door from the inside and held it open for her.

"Thank you, Bill. You're a gentleman."

"My mother taught me." I linked arms with her and adjusted my steps to hers.

"I know about your ancestors from reading the journal, but tell me something about your parents," she said.

"My dad was born in Boston and my mom in Canada. We live in an old house that my grandfather restored."

"How come you have time to spend your summer in Sweden?"

"It was my graduation present. I graduated from college in late May."

"Congratulations. What are you going to do with your degree?"

"I don't know yet. But I think it will have something to do with boats. I just spent three weeks on Orust making sailboats.

"Really? We're kind of landlocked here, but it's not far to Lake Vänern."

I took her to a restaurant that served the famous Swedish *smörgåsbord*. The waiter showed us to a table and offered beer and something like club soda that was included with the meal. Then he said we could go ahead and help ourselves. I looked at the array of dishes and was confused.

Nudging Stella, I said, "Please tell me what's in each dish."

She laughed and said, "The first ones are fish, many different kinds of pickled herring for appetizers."

"*Oj då!*"

"Did you say *oj då?*" Stella looked surprised.

"Yes, that's an expression I've learned." I didn't know there was more than the one kind of pickled herring that my grandma served. But I helped myself to a couple of pieces, bread, and cheese, and went on to the genuine Swedish meatballs and potatoes.

"There is dessert too," Stella said. "But we'll get to that later."

We balanced our plates back to our table. "It looks delicious," Stella said.

"*Bon appetite.*"

"Do you speak French?"

"No, not really. How do you say it in Swedish?"

"*Smaklig måltid.*" She had to repeat it twice before I could say it, and I knew I would forget it right away. She picked up the fork and knife and ate the European way. I tried to do the same but reverted to eating with the fork. I allowed time for her to finish her plate before I said, "Now, it's your turn to tell me about yourself."

"You already know that I'm a librarian. There isn't much else to tell. My family doesn't live here in town. This is where I found a job and I like it."

"So, you're on your own."

"Yes, I have my own apartment."

"Where did you go to school?"

"Here in Skara and in Gothenburg." I assumed that was all she was going to tell me.

"Do you think you'll have time to translate my grandma's journal?"

"I have a day off tomorrow, and I could do it then if you give me the journal."

"I have it in my coat pocket."

I told her about the Swedish-American couple I had met at another restaurant for lunch. It must have been tiresome for her to speak English all the time, so I did most of the talking. She had no problem understanding me. Her warm ready smile encouraged me.

After dinner, I escorted her home. We walked hand in hand until we stood outside her apartment building. "Thank you for spending the evening with me," I said. I took out the journal from my coat pocket and gave it to her. I didn't have a copy, and a warning bell rang in my head, but I ignored it. She took the journal and put it in her purse.

"What time can I see you tomorrow?" I asked.

She shifted her weight from one foot to the other and seemed uncertain. Then she looked up at me and said, "Can you come for lunch? My best friend lives next door, and she wants to meet you."

"Will she be having lunch with us?"

"Yes."

"I would love to have lunch with the two of you." Well, that's what I said, but I would have loved it even more without the friend. "What's the address, in case I can't find it again?" She scribbled it on a piece of paper and said that she lived in apartment number 2. I wanted to kiss her but thought it was too early. Perhaps tomorrow.

With a bouquet of mixed flowers in my hand, I tried to retrace our steps from yesterday, but made at least one mistake. When I stood outside apartment 2 on the second floor, it struck me that I didn't know Stella's last name. Anxiously, I rang the doorbell. The elderly woman who lived in number 2 opened the door at a crack and then slammed it shut. "*Oj då!*" Guess she wasn't expecting flowers. I must have been in the wrong building. They all looked alike. I ran down the stairs quickly and checked the number on the house. I was supposed to be in the next building.

Stella rewarded me with a big smile as she accepted my flowers and thanked me. I told her what had happened and she laughed. "I'm sorry I didn't tell you that my last name is Green," she said. She put the bouquet in a vase and placed it on the dining table.

Stella's friend, Eva, a school teacher, was a petite and pretty brunette, who wanted to practice her English by speaking with me. To give her a chance to do that, I asked her which grade she taught and which subjects. She, like Stella, and other educated Swedes spoke English with a British pronunciation similar to my Boston accent.

Stella had furnished her apartment with modern Scandinavian furniture. We sat on small but comfortable chairs around a glass-top table, set with placemats, colorful china, and stemware. Stella had made open-face sandwiches, one with sliced hardboiled eggs topped with shrimp and garnished with dill, a warm mushroom sandwich, and a piece of hardtack with a tasty cheese decorated with thin-sliced radishes. I enjoyed it all, but mostly I enjoyed looking at Stella.

She said she had finished part of the translation. "I takes a long time for me to write it in English, so I think it would be better if I just describe the rest of the contents to you, page by page, and you write it down yourself," she said. I didn't mind because that way I would be spending more time with her. She served strong coffee in dainty cups with a plate of cookies on the Danish-style table in front of the couch.

"Did you make these cookies, Stella?" I asked.

"Yes, I did."

"They are delicious."

Eva said she had to leave, which suited me fine. Stella and I sat down on the couch, and I had no willpower to resist when my arm curled around her shoulders. She turned her face toward me, and before I knew it, I had kissed her on the mouth.

"It was a thank-you kiss for everything you're doing for me," I said. "But your work is worth more than one kiss." Nice try, Bill, I told myself. I leaned into her again and enjoyed her lips a little longer. I knew I could fall in love with Stella and wondered what she was thinking. Evidently, she thought about work because she stood up and came back with the journal. We worked for two hours before we were done. Then I gave her another thank-you hug and kiss.

Chapter 7

Stella suggested we go for a walk. Swedes walk a lot to get fresh air and exercise. I told her I had the phone number and street address to people who might be my distant relatives. She said we could look them up. It didn't seem so important to me anymore, but since she would go with me, I would definitely go. I fished out my notes from my wallet and said, "Here's one address."

"I know where it is," she said, and steered me in the right direction. I tucked her hand into the crook of my arm and walked as close to her as I dared in the light of the day.

"How're you related to these people if they are the right ones?" she asked.

"I'm not sure. I didn't bring Grandma's family tree, but you could ask if they are related to Anna Olson Whitmore from Boston. If they are, they will know that Anna visited them 10 years ago."

Stella rang the doorbell, and when a man answered, she introduced me as Anna Olson Whitmore's grandson, Bill Whitmore from Boston. At once, we were invited inside to meet the missus. Out of three possibilities, we had reached the right one. My distant relatives with the last name of Nilsson lived in a modern house on a wide street. They took out a photo album and showed me pictures of Anna and John's visit. They also showed me old pictures of my great-great grandparents, Walter and Elsie Erickson, from the time they had visited Skara many years ago. Walter's parents were from

Skara. "His father was born in a little old house that is still standing," she said.

"I know, I've seen it," I said. "What was his name?"

"I think it was Erik Andersson," she said. "The surnames used to change with every generation."

Stella explained that the son of Erik would be named Eriksson, and the son of Anders would get the last name of Andersson. We couldn't leave without having a treat, and accepted a glass of delicious *saft*, which Stella said was made of fresh raspberries.

I understood a little about the conversation through gestures. Evidently, they wanted to know if Stella was my girlfriend because Stella blushed, and said something about being a *bibliotekarie* at the *bibliotek*. I recognized the word *bibliotek* as the place where Stella worked. I took pictures of my so-called relatives and their house, and they got out a camera and took a picture of Stella and me. We also had to write in their guestbook before we left. Our visit was well documented, and I wondered if Stella would be part of my future. The Whitmore men had a tradition of marrying women of other nationalities. John married Anna, who was half-Swedish, and my father married Sharon, who was Canadian, so why couldn't I marry a girl from Sweden. It was a hypothetical question.

Out on the street, I put an arm around Stella's back as we walked.

"People are so friendly here," I said, "even to strangers."

"You aren't a complete stranger since you are related to them."

"In Boston, they would have liked to see proof."

It was time for dinner, and we walked to the restaurant where I had met the Americans. The Johnsons from Chicago were there again and waved to me. "Come here and introduce us to your pretty lady," Mr. Johnson said.

"Why don't you two join us at our table?" Mrs. Johnson said, so we did. As unbelievable as it sounds, it turned out that Stella and the Johnsons were distant relatives.

"You must come and visit us in Chicago," Mrs. Johnson said.

"I might do that," Stella said. "I always wanted to see what it's like over there. My parents used to live in Chicago, and my uncle still lives there." It opened new possibilities that I hadn't expected. If Stella came to Chicago, we could see each other again.

When we said goodbye to the Johnsons, Stella exchanged addresses with them. I felt like an outsider and gave Mr. Johnson and Stella my card that had all the information they needed to contact me. It was still early, so I asked Stella if she wanted to see a movie with me. I had no idea what movies would be showing in the small town, but Stella did.

"Would you like to see a Swedish movie or a Hollywood movie in English?" she asked.

"Whatever you like is fine with me, honey." The little word 'honey' just slipped out.

"My parents told me that Americans call strangers honey," Stella said. "It's sound so funny to me. We would never go around and call people *honung*."

"A southerner might call a stranger honey, but in Boston we don't. I call you honey because you're so sweet and I like you so much. You're wonderful." I proved it with a kiss that tasted as sweet as honey.

We had a choice of two movies, *The Virgin Spring* by Ingmar Bergman, starring Max von Sydow in Swedish, and *The Alamo*, a Hollywood movie with Swedish subtitles.

Stella surprised me by saying, "I'd like to see both."

"Terrific. Then we can see one tonight and the other one tomorrow," I said. "Which one do you want to see tonight?" She surprised me again when she said, "*The Alamo.* I've read about it, but I think I can learn something from the movie. You probably know what actually happened there."

"I do, but it will be interesting to see the film." I flattered myself by thinking she wanted to please me. We were almost alone in the theater. It looked like everyone else wanted to see the Bergman movie.

"I've heard that Bergman movies are dark and difficult to understand," I said.

"They are, but we Swedes like a challenge. *Virgin Spring*, *Jungfrukällan* in Swedish, has been nominated as the best foreign-language film at the Cannes Film Festival."

We could have any seats we wanted at the Alamo film. I planned to enjoy Stella more than the movie and took her to a seat in the back, not that it mattered if we were going to be alone.

As expected, *The Alamo* had a lot of fighting and killing going on, so I put one arm around Stella's waist and kept it there. At times, she closed her eyes because she didn't want to see all the fighting, which gave me an incentive to kiss her. To me, it was the best movie ever. When Stella asked me about the ending, I just said, "The Mexican soldiers won." It was a safe bet.

The Bergman movie put me in an escalated romantic mode. Stella watched intensely, and I figured out what was happening by looking at the actors.

"I don't want to say goodbye to you," I said, as we stood outside her building.

"I might fly to Chicago and we could meet there."

"And then you could come to Boston." My hopes soared.

"It seems to me that Boston and Chicago are far apart."

"Yes, but it's a lot closer than Sweden. If you write me a letter, I'll write you back."

"I will." Her answer earned her an extra hug and kiss.

"Are you planning on a long-distance relationship, Bill?"

"Until we can arrange for something better. I have to settle down and decide on what business I want to pursue."

"When are you leaving?"

"I should have left already, but I can't seem to tear myself away from you."

"I'll miss you, Bill."

"Not as much as I'll miss you, honey."

To stretch out the time with her, I said, "Tell me something about your family?"

"My parents lived in Chicago and they planned to stay there. I could have been born there, except the Great Depression interfered. My parents decided to move back to Sweden and buy the family farm. They made the right decision because my uncle stayed in Chicago and lost all his savings and was out of work for a long time. When he and his wife couldn't pay their mortgage, they lost their home. They have recovered since then. My parents speak English that is influenced by their years in Chicago. Sometimes, their words have Swedish endings. I have a brother, Sture, who is 18. He's still in school and doesn't want to be a farmer, so I don't know what's going to happen to the farm."

"Maybe you are thinking about marrying a farmer," I said, but I hoped not. I already had some plans for her myself.

"No, I would never marry a farmer," she said. Good, I still had a chance. When I kissed her goodbye, she kissed me back and it felt both wonderful and reassuring.

When the unavoidable parting came, and I had to take the train back to Göteborg, I snapped several close-up pictures of Stella because I needed a tangible memory of her. It was crazy, but I felt like she was my future wife.

To make it to England before my ship departed, I had to fly from Göteborg. No time to go visit Karlstad either. The young and vibrant Stella was a much better connection to Sweden than my distant relatives.

It was the first time I flew, and I was only a little scared that we'd crash so I wouldn't see Stella again. I took a long look at Sweden from the air and thought it looked lovely. I couldn't wait to come back. On the ship, I spent most of my time thinking about Stella. I wrote letters to her every day, although they wouldn't be sent by airmail to Sweden until we had anchored in New York.

Chapter 8

I returned to Boston a changed man. Gone was the careless boy who had left. I had a long talk with my parents and told them that I had made up my mind about my future occupation. I wanted to build sailboats. "If we could order a boat from Sweden, I'll use my engineering skills to design the machinery needed to manufacture something similar," I said.

Dad raised his eyebrows showing his surprise. "You'd have competition from other sailboat builders in Boston," he said.

"They don't make boats as beautiful as they do in Sweden," I said with conviction.

"If you're serious about it, I could lend you the money. You'll try harder if you have to pay it back."

"That's alright with me. I also want my own apartment." Since Stella had her own apartment, I felt I should have one, too.

"I'm proud of you son for taking on jobs in Europe and supporting yourself over there."

Later, I told Mom that I had met a Swedish girl named Stella. "It was Grandma's journal that brought us together," I said.

"It sounds like you've fallen in love," Mom said.

"I am infatuated with Stella. She might come over next summer to visit her relatives in Chicago, and then I'll go and see her there." As soon as I had my pictures developed, I showed them to my parents. Mom agreed that Stella looked lovely and Dad whistled his approval.

I began to look for a suitable place to manufacture sailboats. My chances improved when a shipyard came up for sale because the owner would retire. The company manufactured yachts as well as smaller pleasure boats. I would have the machinery I needed but also an inventory that would be costly. I worried about taking on a large debt at the startup. On the positive side, the company already had a customer base. I could be in business right away and didn't have to wait. I talked it over with Dad and he asked to see the financial statements. We studied them together and he concluded they were sound. He told me to take accounting classes. "Otherwise, your bookkeeper can fool you," he said. I had some money of my own that I had inherited from Grandma and Grandpa Whitmore, and I could use it as a down payment and startup capital. Dad would loan me the rest. He said wooden boats won't be profitable for much longer and that I needed to prepare myself for making boats of manmade materials. I didn't like the idea, but it was probably unavoidable. Dad used that argument to make the seller reduce his price, and I signed the contract. The employees promised to stay on. I was in business one month after my return from Sweden.

I wrote a long letter to Stella telling her about my big purchase. She'd probably think I was made of money, so I explained that I had taken out a large loan. I also told her I would soon have my own apartment. "Do you think I should furnish it in Scandinavian design? They call it Danish here."

Wisely, she wrote back saying that I should furnish it the way I saw fit. She didn't think that Scandinavian design would look right in a country where everything is big. In a way, she was right. I loved her insight and I loved everything about her. In our letters, we discussed a range of issues. Stella asked me questions about the danger of the atomic testing going on in Nevada. In November, she was excited about the election of the young John Kennedy as president. She asked about the price of a television set, the price of clothes and other things. I hadn't paid attention to how much women's apparel cost, but I cut out ads from newspapers and mailed them to her. If she saw anything she liked, I could send it to her as a Christmas gift.

I asked when she would come to the U.S., and she said she would take a one-month vacation in June '61. She would fly all the way to Chicago to save time. Transatlantic flights were rather new, and I thought she was brave.

I took an evening course in accounting, and when that was finished, I signed up for a Swedish class. At work, I approved sales and purchases and always checked invoices. It frightened me how much money I spent. The workers expected the boss to sit in the office, but I preferred to be out on the work floor with them. When my boat from Sweden arrived, I proudly showed it to my employees. "Now we're going to make a line of these beauties, only a little bigger," I said.

The winter months passed quickly, and I realized that the lawns and trees would soon turn green. I had yet to move into my apartment that stood waiting for me. With no time to furnish it, I hired an interior decorator. Having approved of her drawings, I authorized her to buy everything according to her plans. It did get more expensive that way, but the result was stunning to me.

Stella would be in Chicago soon, and I planned to fly there to meet her. I called a college buddy in Chicago and asked if I could visit him. "Certainly," Mark said. "I'll take you sailing on Lake Michigan if you come on a weekend."

"Here is the thing, Mark. I met a terrific girl in Sweden, and she's in Chicago visiting an uncle, so I want to bring her if we go sailing."

"That's fine. Then I'll bring my girlfriend. You can sleep on my couch."

"I appreciate that."

"When are you coming?"

"I'll call you back and let you know. Thanks Mark."

I still hoped Stella would come and visit me in Boston. I would take time off to show her around. I wanted to take her sailing on my Swedish boat and to our beach house on the Cape if we had enough time. My parents usually didn't go there until August. I would take her to restaurants and movies. But everything depended on Stella and if she still liked me.

Mark met me at O'Hare Airport and drove me to his apartment. As soon as I was inside the door, I called Stella. She had arrived a week earlier. I loved hearing her voice as she described her trip.

"I'm staying with a friend, and he wants to take us sailing on Lake Michigan. Are you up to it?" I asked.

"It sounds like fun. Will you be picking me up?"

"Yes, I have your address. My friend Mark is bringing his girlfriend. We'll call you before we leave, so you can be ready."

"See you tomorrow then."

"I can't wait," I said.

When Mark said he would show me the Chicago nightlife, I told him we couldn't have a hangover the next day. "It will just be a couple of beers," he assured me.

We walked up and down the Magnificent Mile of Michigan Avenue with its many department stores, restaurants, and bars. Mark pointed out the best bars. He had a favorite one, and that's where we went, just him and me and no girlfriends.

We drank our beers, listened to the music, and looked at the crowd, while talking about our respective lines of work. Mark worked as an engineer in a factory. I told him how busy I was making boats. "I could use a good engineer like you in my shipyard," I said.

"Don't count me out. I might be interested."

I told him about Stella and how much I wanted her to come to Boston. If she didn't, I planned to go to Sweden and see her. "The problem is that I can't leave my business for very long."

"Are you serious about her?"

"I am. Wait till you see her. She's really something."

Mark told me about his girlfriend, Jill, who was born in Chicago to Swedish parents.

"Sweden sounds like a country worth visiting, and Swedish girls are worth the chase," he said.

"It was for me. I went there to find my roots, met Stella, and fell hard for her. I also worked for a while in a shipyard that made sailboats and decided that's what I want to do for a living."

"You're a darn lucky man if all that works out."

"I know, but it remains to be seen."

The next morning, I called Stella early and said we would pick her up in one hour. First, we had to go and get Jill. "I have a surprise for you," I said. "She's Swedish but born in a neighborhood called Andersonville."

"I'm looking forward to meeting her." Stella said.

"What about me?"

"Yes, I'll be especially glad to see you, Bill."

"Good, because I can't wait to see you again."

Jill looked very Swedish, tall and blonde, plus she had the American way of carrying herself with lots of self-confidence. She wore white shorts, a red top, and white sneakers. Sitting in the front seat with the window open, she let her long hair blow in the wind.

I wondered if Stella had changed. We pulled up in front of her uncle's house on Ashland Avenue, and she came outside looking as great as ever, dressed in blue and white. I jumped out of the car and kissed her on the cheek. She gave me a tentative smile as I took her bag and put it in the trunk.

"I brought a jacket and long pants in case it gets cold," she said, "Uncle Gus said that I might need it when we are out on the water." She was still my practical Stella.

I was as smitten as ever with her and couldn't stop smiling. Mark and Jill got out of the car and greeted her. The two girls were about the same height and seemed to hit it off from the start. I opened the door to the backseat for Stella and climbed in after her.

"Go ahead and kiss her," Mark said, as he backed out of the driveway.

"I will," I mumbled, "but you should keep an eye on the road, my friend."

Stella and I fell into each other's arms. I stroked her bare arms and thighs while kissing her neck and mouth. Mark and Jill talked in the front seat, but we hardly noticed them.

Chapter 9

Once we were at the Monroe Harbor Station, I helped Mark get the boat ready to sail while the girls sat on the pier and talked.

"You're damn right. She's a knockout," Mark said.

"Jill is a looker, too. You can't deny that."

"I'm not."

The wind was perfect for sailing. Life vests were not yet common, but we fastened belts around our waists, donned sunglasses and headed out with wind in our sail. After a while, we looked back at the skyline of Chicago. "It's beautiful," I said. There were other boats on the lake and Mark gave them plenty of room.

"The Chicago Yacht Club was founded in 1875, and the race to Mackinac began in 1898 and has been held every year except during World War I," Mark said. When I asked how long the race takes, Mark said it depends on the wind. For the benefit of Stella, he added that Mackinac Island is located in northern Michigan."

Sitting down beside Stella in the stern, I let her back rest against my chest.

"It's so quiet and beautiful. I love it," she said.

I watched her for signs of seasickness, but she seemed to be alright.

"My aunt and uncle asked if you could come and have dinner with us. Uncle Gus said he could pick you up."

"I accept. It would have to be tomorrow night. Then I have to fly back because I can't be away too long from my business. But I'd gladly pay for your ticket to Boston. Then we could be together a little longer." I looked at her hoping she would agree.

"I'll think about it. I went to a library and asked if they would hire a Swede with a library degree. They recommended that I try a historical library on Lake Shore Drive. I just wanted to find out if I could support myself in this country."

"Smart girl. We have libraries in Boston, too."

"But this is a special library that has some Swedish collections. There's also a library at a college founded by Swedes that has books and papers in Swedish."

"What else have you been doing since you got here, honey?"

"I visited the Johnsons we met in Skara, and they took me to a Swedish gift shop and a restaurant that had a Swedish waitress."

"It was nice of them to do that."

"They said hello to you, Bill. I think there are a lot of Swedish people here, even young people who have been here only a couple years."

"So, you think you'd like it here?

"I really do."

"Do your uncle and aunt have any children?"

"Yes, but they are older than me and married. I've been to their homes and seen their children. I would have many relatives if I settled here. How long did it take you to fly from Boston?"

"About three hours."

"It's that far?"

"Yes, unfortunately, but now that I'm here, I want to be with you all day tomorrow. I can take a cab to where you live, and then you can think of something for us to do until dinner time."

"Okay. I think we should go to the Museum of Science and Industry. You're an engineer and I'm sure you'd like it."

"As long as I can be with you," I said, kissing her ear.

"How're you two lovebirds doing?" Mark asked.

"We're doing fine," I said.

"Do you want to have lunch at the yacht club?"

"Sounds like a good idea. It's my treat."

"After lunch, we could go to the Shedd Aquarium. It's fantastic."

"I think they have everything planned for us," Stella said.

"As long as I can keep my arms around you, I'm happy."

After we had seen all the fish at the aquarium, I said to Stella, "I don't think I will eat fish for a while."

The time we had together went much too fast, but I enjoyed every minute. Stella and I went alone to the Museum of Science and Industry. We pushed buttons and competed for scores. We walked in the park, sat on the benches and kissed. Stella said that in Sweden, people would have gawked at us, but here no one seemed to care.

Stella's uncle and aunt were genuine Swedes, who spoke English with a Swedish accent. Gus said he could see that Stella liked me. "She has talked a lot about you, Bill," he said.

He asked me many questions. It was almost like he measured me up as Stella's husband. When they heard about my Titanic connection, Gus said he had read about a Chicago Swede who lost his entire family on the Titanic. He had saved money to send for them. His wife's body was found and buried in Halifax, but the children's bodies were never found except for a baby floating on the waves without a lifejacket. The grief-stricken father required hospitalization.

"That's one of the worst stories I ever heard about the Titanic," I said, "and I've heard several."

My feelings for Stella intensified, and I just had to plan to see her again.

"Would you let me buy you a ticket to Boston? I want you to meet my parents," I asked.

"Can I fly from Boston to New York?"

"Yes, you can."

"Then I think I should change my ticket to go via Boston," she said.

"I would be glad to pay the difference if it costs more."

"You'll have to give me a few days to arrange it and to say good-bye here."

"That's alright, as long as I know you're coming. I'll meet you at the airport. I'm falling for you all over again, sweetheart."

"I'm falling for you, too." That's what I wanted to hear.

I waited impatiently for Stella at Logan Airport. Her plane was 30 minutes late. When I finally saw her at the baggage claim, I ran toward her, swung her around, hugged, and kissed her.

"Welcome. I'm so glad you're here, darling."

"I'm glad to be here, Bill. Could you please help me with my suit-cases?"

"Of course. Point them out to me."

"How was your trip?"

"It was fine." We had talked on the phone after I left Chicago but being with her in person was so much better.

"I'm nervous about meeting your parents," she said. "What have you told them about me?"

"I told them you're the girl of my dreams and showed them pictures of you. Mom said you look lovely, and Dad said you are beautiful."

"But I'm a simple girl, and I grew up on a farm."

"That's a plus. Mom did too. You're here now, and it's a big step forward in our relationship."

"I know, Bill, but, but...."

"No buts." I silenced her with a kiss, and she kissed me back. I carried her suitcases as we walked to my new Volvo.

"You drive a Volvo!" she exclaimed.

"For you, I want to be as Swedish as possible. I even took a Swedish class. "*Hur mår du?*" (How are you?)

"*Tack, jag mår bra.* I'm impressed."

"I wanted to call you *älskling*, but it's easier for me to say darling."

As soon as we were inside the car, we kissed again and again until I became almost too excited to drive.

"Where are we going?" Stella asked.

"I'm taking you to my parents' place. They want you to stay with them at night, but I'll be taking you out every day. Mom and Dad aren't always home."

"If they are anything like you, I'll like them. I bought a present for them in a Swedish gift store in Chicago, but I didn't bring anything for you."

"You are my present, darling, and there is none better."

My parents were as gracious as they could be toward Stella and welcomed her to their home. I could tell that Stella was a little overwhelmed by the big house, her own bathroom adjacent to her room, the maid, and the serving girl in a black dress and white apron.

"Do I have to change for dinner?" she asked me.

"Not always, but this is a special evening."

Stella came down the wide staircase in a pretty baby-blue dress. The dining room table was set with linen napkins folded like ships on the plate, and several shining silver forks and knives, not to mention large and small stemmed crystal glasses. Stella looked at everything with a big question mark on her face. I whispered, "Just do like I do." The candles in the two candelabras, one at each end of the table, were lit and cast a shimmer on Stella's blonde hair. I pulled out the chair for her and sat down beside her. Discretely, I took her hand under the table and squeezed it to reassure her.

Chapter 10

The subject of the Titanic always seemed to come up when we had company. This time, Dad talked about a family of seven that lost their father and three sons. Only the mother, a daughter, and a small son survived. They lived in Worcester, Massachusetts. The mother had to take in laundry to support herself and her two surviving children.

"That's too bad," Stella said. I think she liked my parents.

"You're probably tired after your flight, so we won't keep you up, dear," Mom told Stella.

"Yes, I want to go to my room and write a letter to my parents."

"Tomorrow you can tell us more about them. They have raised a fine daughter."

I interrupted. "Before you go, Stella, I want to have a word with you." I took her into the study where we could be alone. She asked me if we dined like that every evening.

"My parents do most of the time, but you can rest assured that I don't in my apartment. I prefer to bring in takeout and eat in front of the television."

"That's a relief."

"My parents are leaving for New York in two days, and then you can relax."

"It's so different from in Chicago. There, everything was more like home."

"I know but don't let it scare you. Tomorrow, I'll take you sight-seeing in downtown Boston, and we'll eat at a family restaurant. I'll show you my shop and introduce you to my workers. They'll love you. Don't worry about anything, darling."

"If it weren't for you, Bill, I would run away," Stella said.

"Don't even think about it. I hope you'll sleep well. Take a warm bath and relax. I'll come for breakfast. It won't be served in the dining room. My dad leaves for work early, so it will only be Mom, you and me. It's very informal. Wear one of your miniskirts. I love to see your legs."

"Thank you, Bill. I feel so much better." I think I did a pretty good job of kissing her goodnight.

For breakfast, Mom came downstairs dressed in a white mini-skirt, almost as short as Stella's, and a white top. We went to the counter and helped ourselves to fruit, rolls, cereal, hard boiled eggs, and pieces of bacon. When we had eaten, Stella gave her gift to my mom.

"What do you have here?"

"It's just a piece of Swedish crystal that I bought in Chicago." I helped Mom unwrap the peace that was shaped like a ship.

"Thank you, dear. It's beautiful," Mom said. "We'll put it on the mantel in the living room." She kissed Stella on the cheek.

"You can call me Sharon. I was raised on a farm in Canada. You should have seen me when Henry brought me home to his parents. Anna and John lived in a mansion and had a butler. You can imagine how intimidating that was to a shy farm girl. Henry's mother made me feel at ease telling me that she had lived in the gardener's cottage when she was little. She was great. John was, too. When I heard about their love story and how Anna had survived the Titanic, I loved them even more."

"Thank you for telling me this," Stella said. I knew it was hard for her to call my mom Sharon, but she would get used to it.

"I'm playing tennis today. Enjoy your day. See you tonight. Ta-ta."

Stella looked at me and laughed. "Your mom is amazing."

"My dad is too, just wait until you get to know him better."

"What was that ta-ta your mom said when she left?"

"It's like bye-bye or see you later. Are you ready to spend the day with me, darling?"

"Yes," She stood up saying, "I wrote a letter to my parents last night telling them about this fantastic house. I want to mail it when we go out."

"Do you have stamps?"

"Yes, I bought stamps in Chicago. But I need to cash a traveler's check."

"It's not necessary. You're my guest."

"I want to use my checks. I'll go upstairs and get the letter and my purse. Then we can enjoy our day, like your mom said."

In the car, Stella asked, "Do you think your parents are worried about us getting too close?"

"They were young once."

"But they probably think you're too young to be serious about a girl."

"I know. I'm only 23, but I feel much older."

"I'm 24."

"You really need to get married before you're too old," I joked.

"Don't you have any brothers and sisters, Bill?"

"I have a younger brother in the Air Force. There's a picture of him in his uniform in the living room. He has the same color hair as

Mom. When I get married, I want many kids. How about you?"

"More than one would be nice. Where are we going?"

"First, we're going to my shop. I want to talk to my foreman."

As I walked in with Stella on my arm, the workers whistled their approval.

"Hello, everyone, this is Miss Stella Green from Sweden," I said.

"I've got to hand it to you, Bill," the foreman said, slapping my shoulders and grinning. I asked him if we got the contract I had been waiting for, and he said we did. Then I showed Stella the wooden boats we were making.

"Where's the one you bought in Sweden?" she asked.

"It's in the water. We'll go for a sail as soon as we can."

I told the guys to take care of the place because I was taking the day off.

"Have fun," they said in chorus.

Stella was impressed with my shop, as I called it, and the friendly atmosphere.

"I'm sure you're a good boss," she said.

"Now, let's go downtown. I want to show you the oldest house in Boston, the house of Paul Revere. It's not as old as the cathedral in Skara, but it was built in 1680. I don't know if you've heard of Paul Revere."

"Yes, I have read about him."

"Have you heard of Longfellow, an American poet? He wrote a poem about Paul Revere."

"Of course, I'm a librarian. Longfellow's poems are well liked in Sweden. Many of them have been translated to Swedish."

"I didn't know that. Anyway, Paul Revere was a silversmith, who worked mostly with gold."

"I know that, too. It will be interesting to see his house. Please tell me more about him."

"He wanted to warn the Americans that the British were coming, so he rode all night to tell the farmers and everyone loyal to the American side. That way the Americans were ready with their guns when the British came."

"Yes, I remember now. He was an American hero. Was that just before the United States became independent in 1776?"

"You know our history well. Yes, it was in 1775."

After driving through heavy traffic, we reached the bustling downtown, and I drove up a parking ramp a couple floors before I found an empty spot. That impressed Stella. The small town of Skara didn't have anything like that. She was afraid we'd have to walk down the same way we had come.

"Oh, no, we'll take the elevator down. I just have to remember where I parked."

I cupped her elbow and guided her out on the street. She looked at everything with great interest and stopped to peak into store windows.

It surprised her that the Paul Revere House was a two-story building. Evidently, she thought that Boston was still a shantytown in the 18th century. She took her camera from her bag and looked for the best place to get a picture. I had to pose in front of the house.

The house that was Revere's former home had opened as a museum the year before, so I hadn't seen it on the inside yet. As we walked through the rooms and looked at the displays, Stella exclaimed, "He had 16 children!"

"Yes, from two marriages. His first wife died after she had given birth to their eighth child. Then he had eight more children with his second wife."

"He really needed a big house."

"I don't think all the children lived here at the same time, but Revere bought this house in 1770 when he was 35 and lived here when he made the ride to Lexington."

"I see that his mother also lived here," Stella said.

"Yes, and nine of his children."

"It's interesting to see how they lived," Stella said.

A souvenir shop sold silver jewelry, and Stella wanted to buy a piece. She took a long time to decide while checking the price tags. Finally, she selected tiny earrings.

"I'll put them on when I get home," she said.

"Is that all you want?" I could have bought her more expensive earrings, but I didn't think she would let me.

"Yes, it's just a little souvenir." When we left the Revere House, I recited the first verse of Longfellow's poem, "Paul Revere's Ride."

Listen, my children, and you shall hear

Of the midnight ride of Paul Revere,

On the eighteenth of April, in seventy-five

Hardly a man is now alive

Who remembers that famous day and year.

"I love it even more in English," Stella said. "Do you know all the verses?"

"No, there are 15, and I never learned all of them."

"Now, I want to go to a bank," Stella said. "It's an awful feeling not to have any money to spend." I hadn't thought about that.

"That's much better," she said as she put the American dollars in her wallet.

It was time for lunch and I asked if she was willing to try pizza. I hadn't been able to find it in Sweden.

"What's pizza?"

"It's like a hot sandwich. The Italian immigrants brought it here. Boston and New York were the first American cities to open pizza restaurants."

"Alright, I'm willing to try it."

At first, she grimaced at all the tomato sauce, and bit into it carefully, chewed and drank water.

"It's actually quite good, but I'm not used to the spices," she said, as she wiped her mouth with the paper napkin.

"They have different kinds, and some are spicier than others," I said. She let me pay for lunch without an argument.

My aunt Kristina had come to have dinner with us, and Dad introduced her to Stella.

"I heard that Bill was here with his Swedish girlfriend, so I just had to come," Kristina said. She wore a black cocktail dress. Having retired as a physician, Kristina taught at the College of Medicine.

That evening, Stella wore a hot pink dress that ended well above her knees and her silver earrings. She looked just as beautiful as the night before. While we had drinks in the living room, the conversation became lively and Stella seemed to relax. She said she had enjoyed the visit to the Paul Revere House and Museum.

"Stella seems to know as much about Paul Revere and Longfellow as I do," I said.

"I'm not surprised," Dad said. "My mother impressed me many times with her knowledge."

I asked Dad to tell us something about Grandma that I didn't know.

"Have you heard the kidnapping story?" he asked.

"Kidnapping story! No, I haven't."

"I don't remember much of it, because I was only 3 years old when

Mom took me along on a train to visit my grandmother in Stamford, Connecticut. I called her "Mo-mo." When Mom put me down on the platform to greet Mo-mo, a man grabbed me and ran away with me. Mo-mo's husband ran after him but couldn't find us. The police came and Mom called my dad. I was so scared. The man took me on another train, and I screamed for Mama. Everyone assumed that the man was my dad, so they didn't pay attention, but it was hard for him to hide on a train. The kidnapper didn't have a car. From what I heard, he took me to Bridgeport, and then on another train back to Stamford. He told me he was going to take me to my mama. By that time, my dad had arrived, and he cooperated with the detectives. As soon as I saw Dad, I called out "Daddy, Daddy," and the detective tripped the man so Dad could grab me. We stayed the night at Mo-mo's house in Stamford, and all three of us slept in a double bed."

"Was there a ransom?" I asked.

"No, but obviously it was the kidnaper's intention to ask for a ransom in return for me."

Looking at Stella, I saw fear in her eyes. Would it scare her from marrying into a well-to-do family?

Chapter 11

My parents left for New York in the morning. Kristina would stay and keep Stella company until they came back. When Stella said she wanted to see my apartment, Kristina said that she also wanted to see it. What was a gentleman to do? I had to pick up both of them in the morning. As I opened the door to my apartment for the ladies, Stella looked around and said that I had good taste. Kristina liked it too. I confessed that I had hired a decorator. Then I escaped to the kitchen to make coffee while the women looked at everything—the paintings on the walls, the books in bookcase, and even my bedroom. I was glad I had made my bed.

"If you're done with your inspection, coffee is served in the kitchen," I said.

"I could live in a place like this," Stella said, and I was happy to hear it.

Tasting the coffee, she said, "You make good coffee, Bill."

"I learned it in Sweden."

"In Chicago the coffee was so weak that I asked for tea."

"My mom prefers tea."

"The cookies are good," Kristina said. "I shouldn't be eating them because I've put on weight."

"Are you doing any cooking, Bill?" Stella asked.

"On most days, I only eat breakfast at home, and I wouldn't call it cooking. I eat lunch at a restaurant close to my work, and whenever I have time, I eat dinner with my parents."

Kristina invited Stella to see her apartment, and I continued as their chauffeur. Kristina's apartment looked a lot more expensive than mine. Stella was in awe of the view of the waterfront. She asked if we could go for a ride along the shore. It took the rest of the day. We couldn't leave Kristina to have dinner alone at the house, so Stella and I ate with her. I thought that my parents interfered with my plans and acted like Stella needed a chaperone. After dinner, Stella walked with me to my car.

"I'm sorry we couldn't be alone today," I said. "But tomorrow we're going sailing, just you and me. Kristina doesn't like to sail."

"Good."

"Don't forget your sunglasses. I can bring a hat for you. Put your bathing suit on underneath your clothes, so you're ready to go for a swim any time."

"Can you handle the boat all by yourself? I don't know how to sail."

"Yes, it's not that big. We're not going out very far." As the sun set, I saw the red sky to the west. A storm would spoil our sailing day.

On the way to the marina, I asked Stella if she thought she could imagine living in Boston.

"I haven't seen much of it, so I don't know," she said.

"I want to show you more of my town."

"My parents would be very sad if I decided to emigrate," Stella said in a reflective mood.

"I understand that, but you wouldn't be the first Swede to do it."

"My aunt and uncle said they would sponsor me if I wanted to come to Chicago."

"I like that. How do you feel about going ashore on an island, darling?"

"I like that," she said. When other sailors waved to us, she waved back.

"This is fantastic," she said.

"There's a bucket close to you, in case you get seasick."

"I didn't get seasick on Lake Michigan."

"I know, but the sea might feel different." When the wind kicked up, I steered toward the nearest shore. Stella's face had turned white.

"It looks like we're alone at this spot, at least for now. We'll bring the picnic basket and a blanket," I said. Stella already felt better. We were not hungry yet, so we decided to swim for a while. It was wonderful to be close to Stella in the water. After rollicking in the sea, I put the basket in the shade, and Stella helped me spread out the blanket. Then we plunked down and held each other tightly.

"I love you, Stella," I said while running one hand up and down her back and kissing all the bare spots on her body.

"I love you, Bill." I looked around for a more secluded place. There were some bushes farther up the hillside.

"I think we should move out of the sun," I said, "or you'll get a burn."

I carried the basket, and we spread out our blanket on a bed of sand with bushes shielding us. We got closer to each other than ever before and reached the brink but didn't fall off the edge. Then we cooled off by swimming in the clear water. Afterward, we devoured the food and drinks that I had bought at a fast-food market. I kept a close watch on the sky. The clouds were rolling in and the sun disappeared. When it got cooler, we dressed quickly.

"I'm sorry, darling, but we need to head back before the weather gets bad." It began to rain as we lifted anchor. The rolling sea made Stella sick and she had to use the bucket.

"Don't worry, darling, it's only temporary. As soon as we are on dry land, you'll feel fine."

Having docked the boat, I walked her into the clubhouse so she could clean up. The rain poured down. I went back to the boat to get our picnic basket and snap on the tarp. The blanket had stayed dry in one of the compartments, and I left it there.

I worried about Stella and hurried back to the clubhouse. She had regained some of her color and smiled when she saw me.

"How're you feeling, darling?"

"I'm okay now, just a little weak."

"Do you want some hot tea or coffee?" I asked.

"Tea would be good." When I brought her a steaming cup of tea from the restaurant, she said we looked like two drowned birds with wet feathers.

"Sorry, you got sick," I said. "Next time, I'll make sure there are no storms in the forecast."

"Please take me home so I can change my clothes."

"Yes, and I'll make it up to you tomorrow." I joined Stella and Kristina for a late dinner. Both had dressed casually. I loved Stella more with every passing day and it was difficult to leave her and drive back to my apartment.

I sat my alarm to get up early so I could stop at the shop first. To my dismay, I had to work half day. I called Stella and said we could have lunch together and best of all, the whole afternoon. She said she had a good time listening to Kristina telling family stories. Stella looked radiant as she came outside to meet me.

"Did Kristina entertain you?"

"Yes, she told me she was named after Anna's sister who died on the Titanic. It must have been very sad for Anna to lose her sister. They were close, and Anna had arranged for Christina to come to Boston."

"You're right about that. I saw the memorial stone for Christina in Mölndal. I know that Anna had paid for it."

"Were you there?"

"Yes, I was at the *plantskola* that their parents owned. I also met a woman who remembered Anna and John from their visit in 1950."

"It sounds like they had a happy marriage."

"They did. All the Whitmore couples have had happy marriages, and I expect the same."

Stella put her arms around my neck and stood on tiptoe to kiss me. My arms surrounded her and I pulled her close. I didn't care who saw us, but we separated as Kristina headed to her car.

"I'll be back late. You two kiddos are on your own," she said. We didn't mind at all.

My parents weren't coming home until the next evening, so I called my foreman and said I didn't want to be disturbed. Stella brought everything she needed in a small bag and came with me.

"Finally, I can have you to myself," I said.

"And I can relax with you, Bill."

As soon as we were inside my apartment, my foreman called and said that I must come at once and solve a problem. "I'm sorry, Stella, do you want to come with me or stay here and wait for me?"

"I'll wait here." I kissed her goodbye with a remorseful, "See you soon, darling."

I didn't know that the problem would take four hours to fix. When I finally got back to Stella, she asked me to take her home. I could tell that she had been crying.

"I got hungry, and there's nothing to eat in this place," she said.

I apologized profusely. I was hungry too. I grabbed a box of crackers that we ate in the car. The cook had dinner ready when we came home, and we ate alone sitting quietly side by side.

"I have only one day left here," Stella said. "I don't want my stay to end like this."

"I don't want it to end on a sour note either. I love you, and I'm so sorry I had to leave you."

"Isn't that how it always would be if I lived here?"

"I hope not."

"I think it's best that we take a long break from each other."

"With you back in Sweden, it will be a long break."

"I know. We can always correspond, but I think we should see other people. It was foolish of me to think that our relationship would last."

It came as a shock to me. "You're breaking up with me?"

"I think it's for the best."

"But you said you loved me."

"I was then, but now I'm not sure."

"My feelings for you haven't changed." Except they were hurt.

"Bill, it's not going to work out. Tomorrow, I'll ask Kristina to take me shopping. I need to buy gifts for my family. You can go back to work."

The rejection hit me like a rock in the chest. "I still want to take you to the airport when you leave," I mumbled.

"If you can break away from work that is, or I can ask Kristina." That was another blow to my heart. My parents came back the next day, and they sensed something was wrong. Kristina and Stella were still out shopping. "Trouble in paradise?" Mom asked.

"Stella broke up with me."

"She did!"

"I still can't believe it. I was so happy with her."

"I feel bad for you right now, but you're young and you'll get over it," Mom said.

"There was a problem at work that took me all day to straighten out, and I left Stella alone."

"Once you're established in business, you should be able to keep a girlfriend," Dad said.

I had only one thought in my head. Maybe I could change Stella's mind, but I didn't get another chance to talk to her. Kristina treated Stella to dinner at a restaurant, and I ate with my parents.

Chapter 12

I worked hard in the shipyard and tried to forget Stella, but it was impossible. We wrote a few letters to each other, but they were not the love letters we had exchanged the previous winter. My Swedish friend Steve came from Göteborg to visit me.

"If you truly want to get Stella back, you should show it by going over there," he said.

In the summer of 1962, I took Steve's advice and flew to Sweden. In Skara, I looked up Stella's friend, Eva, while Stella was at work. It was earthshaking to stand outside Stella's door with Eva's door to the right. I rang Eva's bell.

"Hi, Bill. I'm surprised to see you. Are you looking for Stella?"

"Not yet. I wanted to talk to you first. Has she said anything about me?"

"Please come inside the door and I'll tell you," she said.

"I shouldn't be telling you this, but since you're here, you have the right to know." I looked at her intensely and wondered would come next.

"When Stella didn't want to go out with me and meet other young people, I asked her if she was still in love with you, Bill. She began to cry but nodded and said that she had made a terrible mistake by breaking up with you." My hopes soared.

"Thank you, Eva, for telling me this. I still love her and that's why I'm here."

I went to the library and waited until Stella came out at the end of the day. She stopped as soon as she saw me. "Bill, what're you doing here?"

"I'm looking for you. Eva told me that you're still in love with me. I hope it's true, because I'm still in love with you, Stella."

"I must be, because I can't get you out of my mind. I don't know how many times I have fantasized about you coming for me, and now you're here. I'm so sorry I broke up with you. Can you forgive me?"

"Of course, I can." We stood there outside the library with people coming and going, but I took her in my arms and wiped her teary face with my handkerchief.

"They are tears of happiness, Bill," she said.

We went to our favorite restaurant and made plans for our future. I asked the waiter to give us some privacy before ordering, and he smiled and obliged. Stella said she would ask her uncle to sponsor her to immigrate. We agreed it would be best to be married in Chicago. In Sweden, I wouldn't even understand the language.

"In Boston we'd have 300 relatives and friends from my side and the family, and only a few from your side," I said. She laughed at the thought. It felt good to see her laugh.

"In Chicago I might have more guests than you, considering my cousins and their families," she said.

"What do you think about asking Mark and Jill to come?"

"I want them to come."

"And I could ask Mark to be my best man, if we need one."

"I like that, but I have to get my visa, and have to give notice at the library. I also want to have my wedding dress made here in Skara."

"Knowing that you'll be my wife, I can wait, darling. Do you want to get engaged here or in Chicago? I brought my grandmother's ring for good luck, just in case."

"Oh, Bill. I'll let you decide."

"Then let's do it." Certain that she would say yes, I took the ring out of my pocket and went down on one knee.

"Stella, I love you so much. Will you marry me?"

"I love you, Bill, and yes, I'll marry you."

"I can buy you another ring later."

"Bill, it's an honor to wear your grandmother's beautiful ring."

People around us began to applaud as I put the ring on her finger and kissed her. The waiter brought out a camera and photographed us. I thanked them with a bow.

"It calls for a toast," I said.

"We don't have champagne," the waiter said, "but I could bring wine."

"That will do," I said while looking at my fiancée and kissing her again.

A man came up to me and said he was a reporter.

"Would you agree to a short interview, mister?" he asked. "It's not every day we have a proposal here, and surely never from an American."

Stella said it would be fun, so she told our story in Swedish, and I told mine in English.

It was in the paper the next day with our picture. I forgot to mention that Stella invited me to her apartment after dinner. Of course, we also had to visit Stella's parents and tell them the big news.

Her parents spoke Swedish-English and her brother spoke British English that he had learned in school. Her parents said they had noticed Stella's unhappiness since she came back from America and now, they could see she was happy again. They told me to call them by their first names, Elmer and Märta, and invited me to stay with them until it was time for my return to Boston.

I enjoyed learning how to grow grain. It was a science in itself. At that time, they still had a dairy herd, and Elmer rose early in the morning to start the milking machine. I borrowed his car to see Stella whenever she was free. It didn't take long for me to get used to the clutch and driving on the left side of the road. The family promised to come to Chicago when Stella and I were wed.

When my distant Skara relatives read about our engagement in the paper they came to the library to congratulate Stella. Other people sent cards and wished her happiness. I realized that she had many friends and that she sacrificed a lot by marrying me.

One day when we took a bicycle ride out in the country, Stella asked me, "What would you have done if I hadn't been interested in you anymore?"

"I had a Plan B to travel to Karlstad and look up my relatives there, but this is so much better."

"You could still go to Karlstad and I could go with you."

"Do you mean that?"

"Yes, we could borrow my parents' car. It's easier to drive than going by train."

"Are you sure?"

"Yes, why not. I think it would be fun. We can look up their address in your grandmother's journal. If they're in the phone book, I can call them in advance."

"I love you, Stella." We got off our bikes and kissed in the middle of the road. No cars were coming.

For our ride to Karlstad, Stella brought a picnic basket with a coffee thermos and sandwiches. I enjoyed being at the wheel of Elmer's

Saab with the free-wheel drive that let me coast down the hills. At first, we drove northeast on the highway through a pretty, changing landscape with farms, grazing cows and horses, and fields interspersed with wooded areas. The traffic was light. We saw cars pulling small vacation trailers.

"We'll drive along the shores of Lake Vänern," Stella said. Being used to driving long distances in the U.S., I didn't think anything of driving for several hours, but when we came to a place where we could see the wide expanse of Lake Vänern, Stella said it was time to stop for a coffee break.

"See the rest area over there? That's where we'll have our picnic and enjoy the scenery," she said. She chose a picnic table and began to unpack her basket. I watched in amazement as she put a colorful rectangular cloth on the table and then a basket with sandwiches and cinnamon buns on top before pouring coffee in our mugs.

"Please sit down," she said. I straddled the bench and said *tack*.

"Isn't this amazing," she said as she took a deep breath and looked out over the lake.

"Yes, it is," I said, "but you're even more amazing."

"I've been brought up to enjoy nature as much as possible," she said.

We saw other travelers, families with children running around to work off some of their abundant energy. After a short trip to the restroom, they were ready to take off again, and so were we.

Chapter 13

Having rounded the lake to the north, we came to the towns of Kristinehamn and Karlskoga, but continued until we reached Karlstad. We parked in the town square. Looking around, I saw a large building facing the square and asked Stella what it was.

"*Residenset*," she said. "That's where the governor resides."

"Really," I said. "He has the whole house to his disposal."

"No, the building also houses many county offices."

I noticed the big cathedral church and the merchants selling flowers and vegetables in the square. Stella bought flowers to take to my relatives. Then she asked a woman sitting on a park bench for directions. The woman pointed to a street and that's where we headed. Stella said it was close enough to walk.

My relatives lived in a family home with an open porch and an abundance of flowers in pots and flowerbeds and small trees in the yard. Stella knocked on the door and a plump elderly woman opened it. Her name was Dagmar. They talked Swedish while I stood back until Stella pointed to me and introduced me as Anna and John Whitmore's grandson. I took the woman's hand, bowed and said hey, which Stella said sounded the same as *hej* in Swedish.

"Hey, welcome to my home," Dagmar said in English, but after that she spoke Swedish. From Stella's translation, I understood that Dagmar remembered my grandparents' visit. Stella told her we were newly engaged and pointed to her ring saying it was Anna's. The woman smiled warmly, said *grattis* to both of us and asked us to come inside. The table was set for coffee. It was like teatime in England. I enjoyed the cookies and pastries while Stella and Dagmar talked. Dagmar's husband had passed away since Anna and John visited. After the coffee, Dagmar showed me pictures of our common ancestors. She also brought out a family tree and pointed to the descendants including my great-great-grandmother, Elsa Carlsdotter. I had never known her maiden name. Dagmar wanted me to update my family information, and I did the best I could, and she said *tack så mycket*.

Stella took a picture of Dagmar and me, holding the album, and Dagmar took out a boxy camera and photographed Stella and me. Our visit did not end there. In came a younger family with children in tow. "This is my daughter, her husband and children, and also some of my grandchildren," Dagmar said. More handshakes and smiles. "We'll take pictures outside," she said.

For the picture taking, Stella and I sat on chairs in the middle with the smaller children on the ground in front of us, and the adults lined up according to size behind us. They were all strangers to me, and still we were related somehow. I remember thinking that they all looked very Swedish. Thankfully, Stella carried most of the conversation. I was sort of an object from America. The younger people spoke English haltingly and said they would send me a print of the group picture with identification. I gave them my card so they would have my address, hoping they wouldn't all come to Boston and surprise us.

It was late afternoon before Stella and I could head back to Skara. Being mentally drained, I let Stella drive. It was amazing to think that I had so many relatives in Sweden.

"You might have more relatives in Sweden than I do, Bill," Stella said with a soft laugh. "They told me you have many, many more who couldn't come to see us."

Stella immigrated to Chicago, and after I had allowed a couple of weeks for her acclimation, I flew there to support her with the wedding arrangements. Her parents would host the wedding, and the ceremony would be at the Lutheran church, which they had belonged to while they lived in Chicago. Stella's parents and brother had come from Sweden a week before and stayed with Gus and Norma. My parents and Kristina flew in from Boston and took in at a hotel, where they hosted the rehearsal dinner. My brother came from Colorado Springs dressed in his uniform. He and I shared a room at the hotel, and I welcomed the opportunity for us to talk and share our experiences.

My bride couldn't have looked lovelier as she walked up the aisle with her father and Jill. Mark was my best man. He and Jill had been married the year before.

When Stella and I had boarded the plane to Boston as husband and wife, I put our tickets inside my coat pocket. Then, I heard Stella say, "May I see my ticket?"

"Sure," I said and handed it to her. She looked at it for a long time, so I had to ask, "Is something wrong?"

"No, it's just that I feel like I've lost my identity. Mrs. H. William Whitmore seems so strange to me. I love you Bill, but why can't I be Stella Whitmore?"

"You are. It's just that married women in this country go by their husband's name."

"But your mother is also Mrs. H. William Whitmore. I want to be my own person."

"You have a point, darling. When you get your new driver's license, it will say Stella Whitmore, and if you get a job for instance, you'll be Stella Whitmore at work."

"Then I want a job. I could work at the library if there's an opening."

"Don't you want a honeymoon first, darling?"

"What do you have in mind?"

"I want at least one week with you alone, Stella Whitmore. I suggest Cape Cod."

"I'm all for it, but after that I'm going job hunting."

"You're a spunky girl and I love you."

Stella worked at the library until she became pregnant and nauseated in the morning. When my parents heard the happy news, Dad said, "It's time you get your own house. Bill and Stella, you can go house hunting. It will be a gift from Mom and me. You'll need a bigger place when the baby comes."

"Dad, that's very kind of you." I knew their own home was a wedding gift from Anna and John, so I wasn't surprised. Stella looked at me like she couldn't believe it.

Turning to Stella, Mom said, "Of course, we want you to choose the house. Henry's parents chose ours. I learned to like it, but it was not my first choice."

"It's very generous of you," Stella said. She chose a contemporary house and I wondered how she would furnish it.

"Let's move everything from our apartment so we can see how it looks," she said. It actually looked great but the house was much larger than our apartment, so we had to buy more furniture.

"We have to furnish the baby's room, too." I reminded her.

"I would rather wait until we know if it's a boy or a girl," she said. "To begin with, the baby can sleep in our room."

Her friends at the library gave her a baby shower. She said she had never seen so many gifts for a baby. "I want to make some things for our child myself."

One evening when we had gone to bed, Stella said, "I think we should start talking about baby names. If it's a boy, what do you think about Michael, and Elisabeth for a girl?"

"Those are good names, but what about my names? We have a family tradition of naming the firstborn son Henry William."

"I think it's overdoing it. Where do the names come from?"

"William was my great-grandfather's name, John's dad. Henry was Anna's biological father's name."

Stella sat up, showing her surprise. "You mean the estate owner who made his servant pregnant?"

"Yes, but Anna must have liked him because she called her son Henry. I'm Henry William Whitmore, Jr. and our son would be Henry William Whitmore II." Stella jumped out of bed and stood facing me, flailing the air with her arms.

"The child that I'm carrying under my heart is not royalty and if it's a boy, it's not going to have a number." She paused and continued in a lower voice, "In Sweden we often give the children three names."

"Come back to bed, darling. I didn't mean to upset you."

"Not until you promise that our baby won't have a number."

"Alright, I promise. If it's a boy, we could give him a third name."

"That's better."

"We'll talk about it later after the baby is born. Elisabeth is a good name for a girl." I comforted my wife until I was sure that she had calmed down and could go to sleep.

Our son was born in 1965. I held him carefully in my arms at the hospital and thanked Stella for the precious gift. I had never paid much attention to babies before, but Stella and I had given life to this child and I considered him a miracle. We named him Michael Henry William, but called him William, although Stella sometimes called him Ville.

Our country had become more and more involved in the Vietnam War. In 1963, we had 15,000 troops in Vietnam, and in 1964, the bombings began. We worried about my brother Norm, who was stationed in Tokyo.

One day in 1968 when Dad answered the doorbell, he saw an Air Force officer saluting him. Mom came running and heard the words, "Mr. and Mrs. Whitmore, I'm sorry to inform you that your son's plane has crashed in enemy territory." Mom collapsed in Dad's arms. "We don't know if your son survived and we're searching for him and his gunner."

The news was bad either way. The officer said the Air Force would keep us informed, saluted and left. We were all numb but prayed for a miracle and clung to every possible sliver of hope. If they had survived the crash, they would have been taken prisoners by the Viet Kong, or shot on the spot, but I never said that aloud.

Two days later, we learned that Norm had been killed when his plane went down in the jungle. It was devastating news. I wished I had spent more time with my brother. Thanks to his fellow soldiers, his body was recovered, shipped home, and buried at Arlington Cemetery. My parents, Stella, and I were there. Mom tearfully accepted the folded flag. We received Norm's dress uniform with the captain's bars. Mom clung to it for a long time, and sometimes she wore his cap inside the house. We let her spend as much time as she wanted with our children, Will and Lisa, and eventually it helped her overcome her grief. Dad grieved too and showed it by being broody. I worked more than usual at the plant, but it was still difficult to go to sleep at night without thinking about Norm and missing him.

The draft lottery began December 1, 1969 for men born between 1944 and 1950. Being born in 1938, I was safe, but many of my men at the plant were not. When the war was over in 1974, 58,000 American soldiers had been killed and many more had been injured. We had seen and heard of many protests against the war. The servicemen who came home didn't get the respect or therapy they deserved. I had veterans in my shop who continued to relive the war in their minds. I helped them as much as possible because any one of them could have been my brother.

Stella and I both wanted more children. In 1970, we were blessed with another son, and we called him David. Five years later, Stella surprised me by saying she was pregnant, and we looked forward to welcoming our fourth child, but it was not to be. Little Christopher was born too early and had a serious heart defect. He received emergency baptism and died a few hours later. Stella never got to hold him. Everything had gone so well for us up to that point, but with Christopher's death we felt powerless. It was especially difficult for Stella. I sent for her parents to console her. We also visited Sweden many times, with and without our children.

Lisa went to Sweden to study and fell in love with a fellow student in Göteborg, married him, and stayed there. Our son David loved to sail as much as I did. He graduated from the Naval Academy in Annapolis and became a Navy officer. On one of his voyages, he met an Australian woman and married her, but they later divorced.

For the last few years, I have built boat motors and nothing else. My father Henry died in 1993 and my mother Sharon in 1998, leaving two empty spots in my life. I'm lucky to have my dear Stella and we're still happy together. I work part time and will probably retire in two years.

H. William Whitmore, Jr. (Bill)

Chapter 14

Will Whitmore

San Francisco, December 2013

I'm William Whitmore, born in 1965, the son of Bill and Stella Whitmore. My full name is Michael Henry William Whitmore. When I graduated from college in 1987 with a degree in engineering, my parents gave me a trip to travel around the world, all expenses paid. Mom wanted me to go to Sweden, but I was steered off that path while I was in London visiting our Whitmore relatives to find out if they had loosened up since Dad was there. The younger generation proved to be friendly. I don't know how many "second cousins removed" Daniel Whitmore and I were, but we got along just fine. Dan had the typical Whitmore features, an oval face and brown hair, while I had inherited my Swedish mother's light hair, blue eyes, broad face, and high forehead.

"Do you want to see Buckingham Palace?" Dan asked.

"Since I'm here, I probably should."

"Anything else?"

"The Tower of London."

"I'll take the sightseeing bus then. We can hop on and off wherever we like." There was a long line to get tickets to tour Buckingham Palace, so I saw it only from the outside. The Tower of London struck me as the most gruesome reminder of London's history. Two of Henry VIII's queens were beheaded there, Queen Anne and Queen Catherine. The executioner made several blows with his axe to finish the job. I had seen enough.

"I would like to visit Australia," Dan said. "Do you want to come along?"

"Why not? I'm supposed to travel the world. If you can do it, Dan, so can I."

"My family has money, so it's no problem."

"Let's go then."

We stopped at a travel bureau and got the airline tickets to Sydney.

"Convicts from the British Empire founded Australia, and I would like to see how their descendants have turned out," Dan said.

The flight to Sydney was long and tiring, but we slept part of the way. Talking to Dan made the time go faster. He told me that "sailing bums" from all over the world gathered in Sydney to take advantage of the year-round warm weather. If we could make friends with any of them, we might be invited to sail with them, he said. We both liked to be out on the water, but we would take one day at the time and do what came naturally. It was the fun part about being young and unattached.

At the airport in Sydney, we saw men in uniform wearing short pants. We stopped at a money exchange and were ready to spend our Australian dollars. Of course, we had our credit cards to pay for hotels and bigger expenses. I noticed that the English spoken was different than in London and sometimes difficult to understand. An airport bus took us to downtown Sydney. Large eucalyptus trees grew on the side of the road. The grounds looked dry with little greenery. In the downtown area, I saw many people that Dan called the Aborigine. Their skin was black as coal unless they were of mixed race. Dan told a cabby to take us to "The Rocks," an area that used to be shabby, with saloons and brothels frequented by sailors, but now was a popular area for tourists. He said we should stay near the Circular Quay, and we checked into a hotel overlooking the Harbour Bridge. We had arrived during the Australian winter, and the air was pleasantly warm and not too hot.

The jetlag got to us and we hit the beds in our hotel. "I'm so bloody tired that I feel like an old man," Dan said. I had to agree with him. We didn't wake up until after dark. Sydney was nine hours ahead of London. After a shower and change of clothes, we were ready for Sydney's nightlife.

We went to an international restaurant appropriately named All Nations at "The Rocks." As we entered, we heard several foreign languages spoken at the same time. "Are these the sailing bums you mentioned?" I asked Dan. "Let's find out," he said. He bumped into one of the girls in the crowd on purpose and promptly apologized. "Where're you from, miss?" he asked. "It's not your bloody business," she said and turned away.

"Better luck next time," I said.

We ordered steak. When I complimented the waitress on the food, she smiled and said, "You're American," sounding a bit like my mother.

"Yes, and you must be Scandinavian."

"How did you know?"

"My mother is from Sweden, and, by the way, you look Scandinavian."

"I'm from Norway."

"Oh, you are. Then I would like to talk to you some more, but you're probably busy."

"Yes, I am, but I'm working the afternoon shift again tomorrow."

"Hope to see you then. My name is William and this is my cousin Dan," I said, and gave her a generous tip." Her nametag said "Amanda."

She left to wait at other tables. Bill coughed and said, "Not bad Bill, but obviously, you don't know that you don't have to tip here. It's included in the bill."

"Well, this time it was worth it I said," feeling smug.

"I'm sure she's waitressing to make money to pay for her trip," Dan said. "In Norway, she might be a student."

"I'm planning to be here tomorrow afternoon and find out," I said.

"For Christ's sake, you can't hook up with the first beautiful girl you meet. There's plenty more if you take your time."

"My father met my mother when he was in Sweden, and they have lived happily ever since," I said.

Dan and I didn't always agree. He stayed out late and slept until noon. I didn't want to waste half of my first full day in Sydney, so I let him sleep and took a walk to the harbor. The large ships were anchored far out, but I was more interested in the sailboats. Walking up and down the piers, I spotted a boat with the Norwegian flag hanging from the stern. My mother had told me it had the same colors as the American flag, and all the Scandinavian flags had crosses.

"*Hej*," I said. "I see you're Norwegians. I'm 50 percent Swedish, and I'm a skilled sailor. My father makes sailboats in Boston." That got their attention. We talked about boats and one of the boys asked me, "Do you want to come along for a sail? We're going out for a while."

"I'd love to," I said, and hopped on board their boat. "I'm William Whitmore. My mother calls me Ville."

"Nice to meet you Ville. I'm Bjarne Iversen and this is my brother Olaf."

They were tall and fair like me and had let their beard grow.

"This will be the first time I have sailed in the Pacific," I said. "I arrived yesterday."

"Then you don't know how difficult it is to find fish in the restaurants."

"No, I didn't know that."

"We have heard that the Sydney Harbour is so polluted with chemicals that the fish is not fit for human consumption," Olaf said.

"That's too bad," I said. "Can you buy frozen fish from somewhere else?"

"Yes, that's what we do, but it's not the same as a fresh catch."

From the boat, I had a good view of the Sydney landmarks, the Opera House and the Harbour Bridge. The weather was perfect and the Norwegian boys were good company. By the time we came back to the dock, I knew that both brothers worked as geologists in the oil industry in Stavanger. They told me that their sister was also in Sydney and worked as a waitress to make enough money to rent a room.

"Is your sister's name Amanda by any chance?" I asked.

"How did you know?" both brothers asked at once.

"I met her last night at the restaurant. She had a nametag and she sounded Scandinavian. My mother is Swedish so I'm familiar with the accent."

"We have met people from many countries here, but no Americans," Bjarne said.

"Would you boys and your sister care to have dinner with me at the Bridge Hotel?"

"Yes, of course, but not tonight. We have already planned our dinner," Olaf said. "You're welcome to eat with us."

"What time and what can I bring?"

"Oh, at 1900 hours and you can bring any side dish or drink you want."

"Thanks, I enjoyed our sailing trip. See you later."

With determined steps, I headed for the bar and restaurant

where I had met Amanda and hoped she'd be there. It was still early for a crowd, so she came up to me right away and asked, "Hi Ville. How many?"

"Just me," I said. She took me to a small table. I expected her to serve water, but she didn't.

"May I have a glass of water?" I asked. Dan had ordered beer the night before.

"What kind?"

"Regular water with ice, please."

"We don't serve tap water. You have to buy a chilled bottle of water."

"Okay, a bottle of water then."

When she came back with the water, I told her I had met her brothers and gone fishing with them.

"You didn't?"

"Yes, Bjarne and Olaf. They invited me to dinner on the boat tonight. Are you coming?"

"Of course. What a coincidence."

"So, what time do you get off work?"

"6 o'clock."

"I'll come and meet you."

"I would like to go to my room first, so I'll see you at the boat."

"Great. What do you recommend for lunch?"

She recommended a meat dish and that's what I had. I scanned the menu and didn't see any fish at all. Again, I tipped her. It couldn't hurt.

Chapter 15

As I walked out of the restaurant, I met Dan, who had just gotten up. I told him what I had been doing while he slept. "The early bird finds the worm," I said, but I found more than that. I have to go shopping now because I'm invited to dinner on a boat, and I'm bringing the drinks and side dishes. You've to eat alone today." Dan gave me a stare and muttered, "It's a bloody shame, but have fun, cousin."

I wasn't sure what was available in the food stores, so I began browsing to get an idea about what to bring to the boat. With more time on my hands, I went to the hotel to read brochures and find directions to the museums I planned to visit the next day. After a short nap, it was time for me to leave. Grabbing my backpack, I went shopping. I bought two kinds of salads and bread before selecting a bottle of white wine, six bottles of beer, and sparkling water that seemed to be popular. I put it all in my backpack and headed for the small-boat harbor.

"Ville, wait for me," a female voice said. For a second, I thought it was Mom, but it was Amanda. She had changed into shorts. We both wore dark sunglasses, but I could see her white teeth as she smiled. She carried a bag close to her body.

"I have to be careful walking alone," she said. "There're many homeless in the area."

I had seen them myself and thought it was a "bloody shame," as Dan would have expressed it.

"When it's dark, one of my brothers walks me to my room," Amanda said.

"I'll be happy to walk you to your room," I said, and really meant it.

"Where are you staying?" she asked.

"At the Bridge Hotel."

"Your cousin came and had lunch after you left. He called it breakfast."

"Yes, I know, he slept late."

We turned onto the pier where the boat was anchored and I had to walk behind her. I didn't mind getting a better view of her well-shaped body, not to mention her legs.

Bjarne and Olaf welcomed us on board, and I unstrapped my backpack and unloaded my goods.

Bjarne said I had read his mind. Olaf watched something simmering on the small stove. We put the salads in the small fridge. Amanda began to set the table on the open deck.

"How about a drink before dinner?" I asked.

We sat down around the small table and toasted each other.

"Here's to Norway," I said.

"And here's to our friendship," they said, as we clinked our beer bottles.

"How long are you staying here?" I asked.

"We've rented this boat for a month and have ten days left. It's good to get all this sun, but one month is enough," Bjarne said. He was looking forward to working again.

Amanda said she had to do some research and write a paper before going back to the university. I was curious and asked where and what she studied.

"I attend the university in Bergen and my major is biophysics."

"I'm impressed," I said. "I just graduated as a civil engineer."

"What will you do when you start working?" she asked.

"To begin with, I'll help my dad in his shipyard. He makes pleasure boats and specializes in wooden sailboats."

We talked about boats of all kinds and how the Chinese had become big competitors in the manufacturing of boats and ships. Then it was time to eat. I liked the meal they had prepared from frozen fish and small potatoes. They served it with a delicious sauce. I added the salads and the bread. I had forgotten the butter, but they had some in the fridge. I had also forgotten to buy dessert, but we drank the wine, and munched on the grapes and cheese that Amanda had brought. We sat and talked until late.

"We're sleeping on the boat," Olaf said, pointing to his brother.

"My dad slept on a boat for three weeks when he was in Sweden working at the Hallberg shipyard," I said.

"Hallberg!" Bjarne exclaimed. "He makes the best wooden boats in Scandinavia. We have one of his boats at home in Stavanger."

"We have one in Boston," I said.

"We have much in common," Olaf said, touching my shoulder. We laughed at the similarities in our lives.

"After it had turned dark and all the food and wine was gone, Amanda said, "I would like to go to my room now."

"And I promised to escort you," I said, standing up.

I picked up my empty backpack and offered to treat them all to dinner at my hotel the next day if it suited them, and they accepted. Amanda would be working the afternoon shift again and be free at 6 o'clock.

She said *Ha de'* to her brothers, or something like that, and I said goodnight and "See you tomorrow." I could hardly believe my luck. A day of sailing, a terrific dinner, and a beautiful girl on my arm.

Amanda and I walked past "The Rock" until we came to a side street. "I live here," she said. I was sorry our walk ended so soon.

"Thank you for walking with me, Ville. Are you doing something interesting tomorrow?"

"I'm planning to go the Historical Museum in the morning.

"I haven't been there, so I don't know how it is."

"Would you like to come with me?"

"Yes, but I have to be back in time for my afternoon shift."

"It shouldn't be a problem. I think it opens at 10. May I pick you up at 9.30?"

She said yes. I waited until she was inside the door. The street showed signs of neglect. A little later at night, I wouldn't be surprised if there were homeless people sleeping in the doorways.

Dan stumbled in at midnight and woke me up. But I went back to sleep and dreamed of Amanda. Dan was still asleep when I left in the morning. I picked up Amanda and we walked hand in hand to the bus that would take us to the Historical Museum. First, we looked at the exhibits describing the original inhabitants all the way back to the Stone Age. The blacks were segregated from the white population for a long time. The original native people had to wear 'dog tags' until 1957, but the practice still continued in the 1970s. Amanda thought it was awful. I thought it was much worse than the segregation we had in America.

"You don't have any minorities in Norway, do you?" I asked.

"Oh yes, we do have the Sami people, originating in Lapland, and many thousands of their descendants, but most have integrated into the general population. It they wish, they can attend their own national Sami Congress, and we respect their traditions."

I enjoyed Amanda's company and asked if she wanted to have lunch with me. She accepted my offer. While we ate, I told her more about my family back in Boston and that my grandmother had been on the Titanic and survived.

"I never met anyone who had a relative on the Titanic before," she said.

"Weren't there any Norwegians on the ship?"

"There were some, but we had our own ships sailing from Norway to America."

"I imagine so. Norway has always been known for its fleets."

We talked about the discovery of the Titanic wreck the year before (July 1986).

"The bow is in one place and the stern in another," I said. "There could have been an explosion on board, just like some of the survivors said."

"There was nothing left of the bodies, but shoes and suitcases seem to be almost intact," Amanda said.

"That way, our bodies are inferior to a lot of manmade things."

"The Titanic discovery interests me since I'm studying both biology and physics. I'm planning to write a paper about it."

"You're a smart girl," I said. "You'll go far." I admired her immensely already.

I walked her to the restaurant, where she'd change into her waitressing clothes. I didn't think that a girl with her brains should be doing that kind of work, but it was not my business.

While I made a reservation for our dinner at the hotel restaurant, I looked at the menu and saw that it was meat, and more meat, just like Bjarne had said. The bar was well stocked.

Dan showed up in our room for a change, and we compared notes about our stay so far. He had befriended an English bar owner and had a good time, he said.

I dressed in my suit and went to pick up Amanda for our dinner.

She looked pretty in a navy-blue dress with white trim. Her hair was down, and she wore makeup. Very attractive, I thought.

Bjarne and Olaf wore dark blazers and slacks. They had shaved off their beards and didn't look like sailing bums at all. The food and the service were all good. I'm sure Amanda enjoyed being served for a change. She joined us men in accepting a glass of red wine, and I made a toast to our new friendship. That night, I kissed Amanda after walking her home, and we made plans to meet again.

Together, we visited the Taranga Zoo, where Amanda laughed at the funny looking kangaroos. We saw many colorful birds. The kookaburra shrieked at us from the trees. Another day we went to the art museum and saw George Lambert's large painting, Across the Black Soil Plains, depicting the many horse teams that pulled nine tons of baled wool in about 1899. The painting was valued at 1.6 million AUD.

"What're you doing tomorrow," I asked.

"I have a free day, and I'll probably go sailing with my brothers."

"As an alternative, I could take you to the beach."

"That would be so much better," she said.

"So how about I pick you up at 9 in the morning?"

"That's fine. I'm looking forward to it."

"Me too." While I kissed her goodbye, I pictured her in a bikini.

Chapter 16

The weather had been beautiful every day so far, and I hoped it would be just as beautiful for our day on the beach. Amanda wore a wide-brimmed, braided straw hat, and I bought one at the Quay. The ferry ride to Manley Beach took half an hour. When we got there, we saw a man raking up broken glass from the water. He told us to go to another beach. "Just follow the sound of the surf," he said. It wasn't far, and we were rewarded with clean water. I looked around and saw parents with children all around us. Amanda took out a beach towel from her bag and shed her shorts and top revealing her bikini. My eyes lingered on her.

"Aren't you going swimming?" she asked. I had forgotten to remove my shirt and shorts.

"Oh yes, of course." I was glad I wore my swim shorts underneath my clothes because there were no changing rooms. Having placed our valuables under the towel, we ran into the water hand in hand and dove into the surf. When we were out far enough, we rode the waves toward the shore. I caught Amanda and held her close. We kissed and laughed. It's strange how water can release people's inhibitions.

After our swim, we sat down on Amanda's towel. When the sun had dried our skin, she took out sunscreen from her bag and dabbed it on her legs.

"Would you please put some on my back?" she asked.

"Of course," I loved rubbing it on her skin. When she rubbed some on my back, it sent shivers through my body. Our fair skin needed it badly. Amanda ran a comb through her blond curls while I finger-combed mine. We were both thirsty but didn't find anything to drink until we boarded the ferry. Then we gulped a whole bottle of water each. The air was dry and we were dehydrated. A rain shower surprised us and chased us below deck, but when the ferry docked at the Quay, the rain had stopped. We bought hotdogs from a vendor and ate them sitting on a bench while looking at brown-skinned Aborigine descendants playing muted melodies on long horns. Onlookers tried it for a few coins but couldn't make a sound. We saw many Asians at the Quay. They weren't tourists but immigrants. Some of the Asian women had formed families with Aborigine descendants.

"What're you doing the rest of the day?" I asked Amanda. I didn't want the day to end.

"I thought I would go to the boat," she said. "Do you want to come along?" Her eyes looked invitingly at me.

"Of course. I would love to. I'll buy something to take along."

I didn't have my backpack with me, but Amanda offered to put what we bought in her roomy bag, and I carried it to the boat.

We surprised Bjarne and Olaf but they said we came at the right time.

"We brought ice cream, so we've got to eat it right away," Amanda said. She placed paper bowls, plastic spoons and napkins on the open-deck table, and Bjarne poured the sparkling water. Later in the evening, Bjarne brought out wine and crackers, and asked us to stay for dinner.

"Hope you like lamb chops."

"I love lamb chops," I said. "I've heard that Australia raises a lot of sheep."

"That's true, and it's true for Norway also."

After dinner, the boaters around us began to sing, first in English, then in other languages. Olaf played a tune on his harmonica, while Bjarne and Amanda sang the lyrics softly in Norwegian.

"I recognize that tune and some of the words," I said. "My mom used to sing it to me."

"It's about a little boy who meets a bear in the woods," Bjarne said.

"Yes, that's it. *Mors lilla Olle*," I recited. The song made me sentimental, and I decided to write a long letter to my parents and tell them about my new friends.

"My mom spoke Swedish to me when I was little, and I'm told I spoke it when we visited Sweden, but I don't seem to be able to speak it now," I said.

"It will come back to you if you give it a chance," Bjarne said.

"My dad learned some swear words from sailors when he was in Sweden, and he remembers those. Before he married my mom, he even took a class in Swedish."

As I walked Amanda to her room, I asked if her brothers had any girlfriends back in Norway.

"Not at the moment," she said.

"So why aren't they trying to find someone among all the boaters here?"

"There are very few women on the boats, and they are either wives or girlfriends."

"So that means I'm extra lucky to have found you before another boater did."

When Amanda and I stood outside her building, our kisses got hotter and deeper than before. I craved more of her. She lingered as if she didn't want to go inside.

"I saw a cockroach this morning in my room and I'm afraid of going inside," she admitted.

"Do you want me to come with you?" I hadn't expected the opportunity.

"Would you kill it for me, Will?"

"Sure." For her I would kill a roach. But the roach was in hiding. Amanda hunkered in her bed and looked frightened.

"Do you have a newspaper?" I asked.

"There's one in the waste basket."

I lay the newspaper on the floor to be ready when needed. Then I sat down on the edge of the bed and told Amanda to stop worrying about the roach. "I'm not leaving until it's killed," I said. To comfort her, I kissed her trembling lips. I had started to tug at her clothes when she froze.

"I heard something," she said. "It's the roach."

"It can wait," I said, but my momentum was gone, so I might as well kill the damned roach. It was sitting in a corner and was almost as big as a Louisiana crawfish. I had seen big roaches crossing my path outside. Pedestrians seemed to give them the right-of-way. No one wanted to step on them, hear the crunching sound and get them underneath the soles of their shoes. Bugs of all kinds thrived in the warm climate. I would eliminate only one. There would be millions more. I looked at the rust-colored roach and put the newspaper in front of it, thinking it would hop onto it, but it refused my offer, so I nudged it with one of my shoes. Quickly, I folded the other part of the newspaper over the roach and slammed down on it with my shoe. Crunch!

"Is it dead?" Amanda asked.

"Yes, where do you want to bury the remains?"

"Outside, please." My romantic evening ended with the dumping of the roach in a garbage can.

The next evening, I asked Amanda if she wanted me to check for more roaches.

"Would you please?"

"Happy to comply." When no roach showed up, I said I had better stay just in case.

The 'maybe roach' gave me a chance to spend more time with Amanda. Holding her in my arms, I assured her I was in love with her and didn't want our romance to end in Sydney.

"It's crazy to think we've fallen for each other so quickly," she said.

"Haven't you heard about love at first sight?"

"Yes, but it wasn't quite like that for me, maybe at second sight."

"Why do you think I have pursued you? I was smitten with you from the first time I saw you."

The day was fast approaching when we had to part. Amanda and her brothers were flying back to Norway, and I would fly to Shanghai to look at boats made in China.

"When are you graduating?" I asked Amanda.

"Next spring."

"May I have your phone number?"

"Yes, I can give you the number to my parents' home and my apartment in Bergen. I live with two other girls, and we share a phone."

"I wish I could carry my car phone with me."

"Maybe one day you can."

"It would have to be smaller. Here's my card with my address and phone numbers. I hope to have my own apartment soon."

Amanda didn't have a card but wrote her information on the back of one of my cards.

With that taken care of, I resumed stroking Amanda's irresistible body. It felt so right. I began to call her darling, sweetheart, honey or 'my love.' I needed all the words I could find to express my feelings.

Dan said he would fly back to London the next day. I apologized to him for not having spent more time with him, but he understood. He said he had a girlfriend in London and missed her.

"I'm flying to Shanghai to look at boatbuilding there, but after that I'll fly home to Boston. Come and visit us there."

"I might do that. I'll pay half the hotel bill as I leave," he said. We shook hands and wished each other safe flights.

Chapter 17

It was easy to say goodbye to Dan, but extremely difficult to part with Amanda. She had started to open up to me and tell me more about herself, but she still surprised me when she revealed her plans after graduation.

"I have applied for a research scholarship in the United States. I don't know yet at which university it will be, if I do get it."

"Really, that's wonderful news. Just think if it will be Dartmouth in New Hampshire. It's a well-known research university, and it's one of the oldest and most respected in the United States. That's where I got my engineering degree."

"How far is it from Boston?"

"It's about 200 kilometers from Boston, and it takes about two hours to drive there. It's located in a beautiful area close to the White Mountains. You'd love it. I could drive up there every weekend, if you're still my sweetheart."

"I'm not there yet, Will."

I had promised my father I would assist him in the shipyard, but now that I had a girlfriend, I might have to reconsider. Perhaps I should go back to Dartmouth and pursue a graduate degree.

Shanghai was a modern metropolis comparable to New York, except for all the signs in Chinese and the Asian population. I saw many westerners in the business district. The first shipyard I visited made smaller pleasure boats with aluminum bottoms. From Shanghai, I flew north to Shandong and saw several shipyards making yachts with fiberglass hulls.

Having collected a bagful of promotional material about the boats with price lists in U.S. dollars, I wrote postcards to my parents telling them about Amanda and a long letter to Amanda, addressing it to Stavanger.

I continued by plane to Beijing but didn't stay there, partly because I found the air to be unhealthy to breathe, and partly because I wanted to see the Great Wall of China. I reached it by taking a sightseeing bus to a place where all the tourists went to see the wall. The guide spoke English along with other languages in a monotone voice.

I learned that the Great Wall was designed to stop invaders, secure border control, and charge import duties. Soldiers and convicts began to build it as early as the 7th century BC, but most of the wall was built during the Ming Dynasty, 1368-1644. The wall is made of stone, earth, wood, brick, and other materials but has been rebuilt and repaired many times. It has watchtowers, troop barracks, and garrison stations. I walked the part of the wall designated for tourists.

Back in Beijing, I went to the airport and bought a ticket to New York. The only seat available was in business class, and I charged it. Flying time was about 13 hours. Leaning back in the comfortable reclining seat, I thought about my wondrous stay in Sydney and of Amanda.

Having landed in New York, I called home before catching another flight to Boston. Tired and weary, I stepped off the plane in Boston, where Mom and Dad met me. Mom asked me many questions about Amanda. Dad said I might have the Whitmore luck of finding a partner for life in another country. My suitcases landed with a thump inside the door. I opened one of them and gave Dad the bag of promotional material from the shipyards in China before going to bed.

While enjoying breakfast with my parents in the morning in the sunny breakfast room, I told them I wanted to continue my education and earn an advanced degree.

"Does this have something to do with Amanda?" Mom asked.

"In a way it does. She's incredibly smart and I don't want to fall behind," I said with a grin. It was hard not to grin when I thought of Amanda.

"We'll support you wholeheartedly. You shouldn't feel you have to continue in the boat business," Dad said.

"I'll help you for the rest of the summer, but I don't think I'm going to make it my career."

"That's alright. I looked at all the brochures you brought home, and I don't think we'll be able to compete with the Chinese for much longer."

"I don't think so either, Dad."

"I can't wait to see the pictures from your trip!" Mom said.

"I'm taking the rolls to be developed this morning, but first I want to make a call to Norway."

My brother David wasn't up yet, but my sister Lisa came to the breakfast room rubbing her eyes. Although she was only two years younger than I, she jumped into my arms. "Did you see any crocodiles?" she asked. "No, I'm sorry to disappoint you. I'll tell you more about my trip later, Lisa."

I went to my room to make my overseas call. First, I dialed 011 and then all the numbers that Amanda had given me. A man sounding like Bjarne answered the phone.

"This is Will Whitmore," I said.

"Hi Ville. Bjarne here." I could hear him calling Amanda's name and music in the background.

"She's practicing her violin, but she's coming," Bjarne said. Before

Amanda came to the phone, Bjarne and I exchanged a few words. He and Olaf were back to work at Statoil, the Norwegian Oil Company.

It was wonderful to hear Amanda's soft voice.

"I didn't know you played the violin," I said.

"Well, I started with the piano but liked the violin better. My mom is accompanying me on the piano. How was your trip to China?"

"It went well. How're you, precious?"

"I'm fine, Ville."

"I just got home and I miss you already."

"I miss you, too, Ville."

"Did you get my letter?"

"Yes, thank you. I answered it right away."

"Good, what are you doing these days?"

"I've started research for my paper."

"I'm going to look into doing graduate studies."

"Oh, good, maybe we can be at the same university."

"I hope so. I'll call you again at this time tomorrow. I love you."

"Me too," she said. We were both restrained, but I felt my body heating up. Having finished the call, I sat quietly and thought about what our lives would be like living apart. She had one year of college left in Bergen. I could do one year at Dartmouth before she graduated.

I hadn't driven a car for a long time and enjoyed starting my Corvette and taking off for the photo store with my film rolls. Then I drove to the shipyard and said hello to all the workers.

"When are you coming to work, Willy?" they asked.

"As soon as I get over the jetlag," I said.

Next, I wanted to see my grandparents, Henry and Sharon.

Grandpa had retired from Addison Enterprises, but he still provided occasional architectural drawings for the company. Grandma Sharon was active in charity work, something that was expected of a Whitmore wife. They still lived in their old Victorian home but traveled the world. I told them about my trip to London, Sydney, and the cities I had visited in China.

"Next, I want to see Scandinavia," I said. "Norway and Sweden."

"We heard your new girlfriend attends the University in Bergen. We were there a few years ago. It's the birthplace of the composer Edvard Grieg. We also went to Oslo, Copenhagen, and Stockholm. In Stockholm, we saw the 300-year-old warship Vasa that your father saw when it had been lifted from the sea floor. It was made of oak and well preserved. It's ironic that a ship made of oak could survive for so long, and a modern ship like the Titanic has deteriorated so badly."

"It shows how durable wooden boats can be. Did they find any artifacts on the Vasa?"

"Yes, lots of old coins and gold. But on the Titanic, they have found personal items that belonged to the passengers, and I don't think they should be brought up. My mother Anna would have called it disrespectful."

After the visit with my grandparents, I could feel the jetlag in my legs and drove home to take a nap. Tomorrow, I would call Dartmouth and ask them to send me literature for graduate studies in engineering.

Dartmouth admitted me to its School of Engineering, and I rented a small apartment that I hoped would be big enough for both Amanda and me should she join me. I concentrated on my studies and called Amanda once in a while to make sure we were still a couple. I hoped to visit her in Stavanger over my Christmas break, but she said it was a dark and gloomy time of the year and that I should wait until next summer.

After Christmas, she told me she had received a scholarship from

Stanford University in California, a top-notch research university. I was happy for her, but where would that leave me, I wondered.

Next time I called Amanda, I couldn't hide my newfound enthusiasm.

"Stanford has an excellent School of Engineering. Do you think it would be too much of a distraction for you if I moved out there?"

"No, I would like having you there, Ville."

"It would definitely be good for me. I'll apply and if I'm accepted, I'll transfer to Stanford. But I want to see you before then."

"Could you come to Stavanger in the last part of June?"

"Yes, but I don't know how I can wait that long."

"We can see each other in August as well, since I might stop in Boston on my way to San Francisco."

"That's good because my parents want to meet you."

"My family is looking forward to seeing you this summer." I could picture her sweetness as we spoke. "I love you, Amanda, take care of yourself."

"I love you too."

Chapter 18

The first 20 wind turbines in the world had been built in New Hampshire in 1980. I had seen them and hoped they would be followed by many more wherever the wind could generate the most power. I also hoped that I would get an opportunity to learn more about wind energy at Stanford. When I had secured the transfer from Dartmouth to Stanford, I called Amanda and told her the good news.

"That's wonderful," she said, "Congratulations."

"Best of all, I'm coming to see you in Stavanger."

"When are you coming?"

"Next week. I'll email you the details."

With much enthusiasm, I began my journey to be reunited with the lovely Norwegian girl I had met in Sydney. After a change of planes in London, I landed at the Sola Airport in Stavanger, where Amanda met me. I picked her up and swung her around while smothering her with kisses.

"Amanda, it's so good to hold you in my arms again."

The car that Amanda drove was a late model Mercedes. "It's my parents' car," she said. I don't have a car. I fly back and forth to Bergen or take the ferry."

I already had the feeling that her parents must be well off. The oil industry had created great wealth in Norway.

"I'm happy you're here, Ville," Amanda said, as I put my suitcase in the trunk. "Bjarne and Olaf will be glad to see you again. You're staying in Bjarne's apartment. He and his girlfriend are on vacation. Almost all of us Norwegians are on vacation in July."

"I hope it isn't far from where you are."

"No, it isn't. I'll do my best to make you feel at home. First we're taking your luggage to the apartment and then you're invited to my parents for dinner."

I wanted more time with her and looked at my watch that I had reset to western European time. "What time is dinner?"

"At six o'clock."

"Good, then I have time for a 'nap' with you," I said. Perhaps it was presumptive, but she didn't object. The outside air was refreshingly clean and crisp. Amanda drove along the shoreline of the bay and explained that the "Three Swords" stuck in the ground as a sculpture symbolized peace, unity and freedom. The grounds were green and the buildings well-kept and colorful. I didn't think Norway had any slums.

My accommodations made me extremely happy because Amanda stayed for two hours. I'm embarrassed to mention it, but I went to sleep in her arms. After a shower, we had a little discussion.

"How are the prospects of renting an apartment near campus at Stanford?" I asked.

"I've reserved one, but I don't know what it looks like."

"I could fly out there and have a look. I've got to go there anyway and make certain I can specialize in wind energy."

"Great, let's go and tell my parents that we're both moving to San Francisco."

"They won't object to us living together?"

"No," she said with a laugh. "Many couples cohabitate here in Scandinavia."

"It's getting more common in the U.S. also," I said, "especially in California."

"I won't have much time to keep house, so you'll have to do your share."

"I'll be glad to," I said. "My mom taught me to cook and do laundry. How did your research paper go?"

"I wrote about the Titanic. You know that the iceberg hit the forward side, and that's where the low-quality iron rivets held the hull together. Well, I believe if steel rivets had been used for the entire ship, the Titanic would not have gone down as fast as it did. I'm also wondering about the fire in the coal bin. Surviving passengers had heard an explosion and the ship split in two parts before it sank. Some think it came from the boilers exploding."

"If the fire continued to burn, it could have weakened the hull, but what about the human bones? Did you conclude why they dissolved completely?"

"Because we're biodegradable," Amanda said. "The pressure at 2,000 feet in the Atlantic made it happen so much faster," she said.

"How many Norwegians were on the ship?"

"There were 31, ten were saved and 21 perished. One of the survivors, Olaus Abelseth, a Norwegian American, testified at the Inquiry. He said he had jumped off the ship when the deck was only five feet from the waterline. He mentioned a shut gate, but an officer ordered it opened so the women could get through. Abelseth said a group of men had climbed out on a crane and over the railing to get around the locked gate."

"But the women couldn't do that in their long skirts," I said. "What else did you find out?"

"I thought it was interesting that a smaller Norwegian schooner, Samson, was in the area while the Titanic began to sink. An officer on board Samson, Henrik Naess, later said that both he and the captain had seen the Titanic, which would have put the Samson between the Titanic and the Californian. This fact strengthened Captain Lord's testimony that the ship he had seen from the bridge of the Californian was a smaller ship. He was criticized for not coming to the rescue of the Titanic but said he had been stuck in ice during the night, and in the early morning he had to proceed slowly through the ice. When he finally reached the place of the disaster, there were no survivors. Captain Lloyd died two months before the article was published in Trondheim in 1965."

"It all sounds so interesting, Amanda. What are you going to study at Stanford?"

"Bioscience."

"I'm so proud of you, darling."

Amanda's parents Iver and Marita lived in a sprawling home with a stunning view of the bay. Both spoke English; Iver, an engineer, was more fluent than Marita. Olaf was home briefly before going on a sailing vacation. Amanda took me through one room after the other, all with furniture arranged for groups of people. There was a piano in the living room. Amanda's violin hung on the wall. The covered patio had bamboo furniture and steps leading to the spacious lawn that slanted toward the shore of the bay.

The dining table was set with fine china and crystal. I saw no sign of hired help. We passed the food between us—big lamb chops, new potatoes, and homegrown vegetables. Very tasty.

Olaf asked the first question, "How're your studies going, Ville?"

"Fine, thank you. In fact, I'm transferring to Stanford University. It offers more of what I need."

Olaf smiled. "And that includes my sister, I suppose."

"I didn't mean it that way. What I meant is that I can study wind energy."

"It's a good subject. I think wind energy will gain in popularity. Bjarne is working on developing floating wind turbines for Statoil."

"Really, but Norway has oil and hydro power."

"The oil might be gone in 20 years. It's not renewable. Hydro is fine, of course, but we need to do more."

"I agree one hundred percent, and I would like to talk to Bjarne about it and follow its progress."

"He might be home before you leave."

As we rose from the table, Amanda said, "Ville and I are planning to live together when we come to San Francisco," to which Mr. Iversen replied, "You're both adults and it's your decision. We will miss you Amanda, but you're following your dream to study in America, and that's important. I'm sure you'll both succeed." Mrs. Iversen politely asked me about my family, and I told her about my great-grandmother who had survived the Titanic.

"I'll meet Ville's family when I stop in Boston on my way to San Francisco," Amanda said.

"You'll have some amazing stories to tell us," Mrs. Iversen said.

One day, Amanda took me on a commercial boat tour to see a high cliff that looked like a preacher's pulpit called the *preikestolen* high above the fjord.

"Some unhappy people have committed suicide by jumping off," Amanda said. "A few have come from other countries." I saw the water churning against the rocks. It was a sure way to die.

The family took me out sailing and we stopped at an island for a picnic. They let me take the wheel for a while, and we reached 10 knots. One time, we took a ferry to an island that looked subtropical. Palm trees, decorative scrubs, and lots of flowers made for an astonishing display. Everywhere I looked, the view was different. Amanda explained that the temperature stayed well above freezing in the wintertime. I knew winters were mild in Stavanger, similar to winters in San Francisco, only darker. Norway made up for it in the summertime when it was light almost all the time.

After we had moved to San Francisco, Amanda wrote a letter to my mom describing the city. She asked me to read it before mailing it.

"You could have written it in Norwegian and Mom would have understood it," I told her.

"But now you can read it as well," she said.

"I love the feel of San Francisco with its narrow, hilly streets, and old buildings that remind me of Stavanger. The Golden Gate Bridge is magnificent. We are close to the sea and not far from the Redwood Forest, or the mountains. We can take long nature walks on Sundays. The campus is beautiful. I think the "Quad" where the School of Engineering is located is the most spectacular. You should see the palm trees! I think the climate is perfect, not too hot in the summer, or too cold in the winter."

I told Amanda she wrote beautiful English and that I couldn't have written the letter better myself.

Chapter 19

Every year, we went to Boston to celebrate Christmas and New Year's Eve, and every summer we went to Norway. Since Amanda was in the United States on a student visa and wanted a green card in order to stay permanently, she contacted the American Consulate in Oslo and found out she had to have a sponsor and a place of employment. As her fiancé, I could sponsor her. The university verified that a position was open for her on the faculty. After two years in America, she became a permanent resident and obtained a green card. Two years later, we both graduated with doctor's degrees. We invited our parents, brothers, and sisters to attend our doctoral promotions, followed by our wedding in the interdenominational Stanford Memorial Church on campus. Bjarne was my best man. After the ceremony when we turned around as husband and wife, we faced the Tree of Life that embraced the virtues of love, faith, hope, and charity. Amanda was the first Whitmore wife to have a profession that she wouldn't give up as a married woman.

We packed our suitcases for our honeymoon trip that would take us first to the eastern states and then to the Scandinavian countries. We hiked in the White Mountains and waded barefoot in the shallow parts where water tumbled down from the higher elevations. Amanda loved being out in nature. Before we left New Hampshire, I showed her the wind farm and Dartmouth College. Following a few days in Boston with my parents, we went to New York City, stayed at a hotel, and went to see Broadway shows.

From New York, we flew directly to Stockholm to see the *Vasa* warship that both my grandfather and father had told me about. It's the only 17th century ship in the world that has been preserved, and it's unique in many ways. Amanda and I could see it in the newly built *Vasa* Museum at Djurgården. We took a quick ferryboat ride to the island and walked a short distance to the museum that received more than a million visitors annually. Visitors could choose among 13 languages to listen to the ship's history. Built between 1626 and 1628, it sank on its maiden voyage just like the Titanic but after having sailed only 1,300 meters.

We studied the displays and learned the reason for the sinking. With two decks loaded with 64 guns, 48 of them weighing 24 pounds each, *Vasa* was top heavy, and when a sudden gust hit the ship, it heeled to port and water poured in through the open lower gun ports, sinking the ship.

Most of the bronze guns had been salvaged in the 1700s, but the rest of the ship rested on the bottom of the inlet to Stockholm for 333 years until 1961 when new technology made it possible to raise it. *Vasa* was 69 meters long and four decks high. The hull made of heavy oak planks had fared relatively well, while nothing was left of the iron bolts. The large anchors and cannon balls made of cast iron had survived. Some human remains had been found, mostly bones held together by clothes and boots, but also human hair, fingernails and toenails and some brain matter. We found it interesting that human remains had been preserved for so long.

When we came to the stern of the ship and looked back on it, we were impressed by its height and beauty. It was decorated in blue and gold with 500 sculptures, the figurehead lion, the royal coat of arms, and a sculpture of King Gustav II Adolph near the top. It looked much taller than we expected. The preservationists were still fighting the deterioration of the ship. We hoped it would stay intact for the world to enjoy for many generations.

In Stockholm we rented a car and drove to my mother's hometown, Skara. The Swedish countryside looked just as picturesque as

I remembered. I wanted to introduce Amanda to my Swedish grand-parents Elmer and Märta. They had visited us in Boston, but I hadn't seen them for several years.

"Welcome, welcome, Ville and Amanda," Märta said, "I'm so glad to meet Amanda at last."

"Congratulations on your marriage and your doctoral degrees," Elmer added. We enjoyed lunch with them before driving back to Skara where we met my uncle Sture, who showed us some of the sights, including the library where Mom had worked.

"You have to come back and stay longer, so you can get together with my family," Sture said. "The kids are grown now, but they are still your cousins, Ville."

"I know, please say hello to them. Your mother showed us pictures of them."

"You're all welcome to visit us in San Francisco," Amanda offered.

"We might take you up on that."

We returned the rental car at the Arlanda Airport and flew to Copenhagen. While in the air, I saw the first offshore wind farm with eleven turbines built by Danes.

"We can't leave Copenhagen without seeing Tivoli," Amanda said, so we did. I had heard Tivoli was much more than just a huge amusement park. Copenhagen turned out to be another great honeymoon city for us.

In Stavanger, I spent several days at Statoil to learn about a prototype floating wind farm that would roll with the waves in the open sea. The governments of Norway and Denmark subsidized the development of wind energy that would reduce our carbon imprint in the world.

After a fantastic honeymoon trip, Amanda and I returned to San Francisco where we planned to make our permanent home. Amanda retained her maiden name at the university because she was already known as Professor Iversen.

I taught undergraduate classes and worked with Stanford on research to build offshore wind turbines in northern California like Denmark had already done in 1991. With the deep waters off the California coast it was a challenge. I also hoped for more land-based wind farms in California.

The discussions were lively in my class, pro and con.

"The United States has too much oil, gas, and coal to invest in wind energy," one student said.

"Norway has plenty of oil, natural gas, and hydro power, and still the government invests in new innovations," I said.

"In California, we need private investors as well as government money," the student said.

"The waters are too deep here for offshore wind farms," another student said.

"It's a problem that can be overcome by building floating wind turbines anchored to the ocean floor," I said.

One female student who was a protector of wildlife, argued that offshore turbines would disturb the whales.

"Don't you think the whales are smart enough to swim around them?" another female student said.

I held workshops and seminars to educate people and still hoped an offshore wind farm would become a reality off the California coast in my lifetime. The tourist people asked me if the wind turbines wouldn't disturb the view from the coast. "No, they would be 50 miles from the shore," I said.

Amanda and I bought one of the many tall, narrow houses that San Francisco is known for and we filled it with second-hand quality furniture. With the help of two of my students, who wanted to make money, I painted the house red like a Norwegian country home.

Amanda approached the birth of our first child scientifically. But after a few hours of labor, she admitted it was much harder than she had anticipated. Our son, Henrik William, was born in 1995. Amanda managed to do what my mother had not: remove the name of Henry from the Whitmore names for the eldest son. "We can't name him both Henrik and Henry," she said and that was it.

We traveled with Henrik as soon as he could sit by himself. But when Amanda was away on lecture tours, I stayed home alone with our baby except for the hours he was in daycare. I loved taking care of him and was rewarded with his smiles and recognition. At times, I even cancelled daycare and worked from home to be with him. When Amanda played in the symphony orchestra, I spent many evenings alone with our son.

We continued to travel to Boston to celebrate Christmas and to Norway every summer. While in Stavanger, I took the opportunity to check on the progress of the prototype floating wind farm. Being at home in Stavanger, Amanda relaxed and we could spend more time together, which was good for our marriage. While she worked and traveled, we didn't have much time for each other. When Henrik was 3 years old, I thought it was time to stop the birth control.

"Honey, I would like to have another child. Don't you?"

"I do, but not yet. I have too much work lined up."

"Henrik needs a brother and sister to play with."

"I know darling, maybe next year."

But it never seemed to be the right time for Amanda. It was the only thing we quarreled about. I thought about how much she had changed since I met her in Sydney, but no doubt, I had also changed.

"Do you remember when I killed the cockroach in your room?" I asked with a smile on my face.

"Me, a scientist, being afraid of a cockroach. That was ridiculous."

"I liked being your protector. Now, you don't seem to need me."

"Don't be silly, Of course, I need you, darling."

"For what? You can support yourself financially."

"You're my rock, a good father, and ... I can't make a baby without you."

"Well then, let's do it."

I tried my best for a long time, but it didn't work. I suspected that Amanda was still on the pill and searched the bathroom for the small round disc with the pills but didn't find it.

"What kind of birth control are you using, honey?" I had to ask because I had heard of more permanent methods.

"Hmm, the usual."

"You're still on the pill, aren't you?"

"Yes, but I'll stop soon."

"Henrik is asking for a brother or sister like the other kids have. I have a sister and a brother and you have two brothers. We have learned to share. Henrik will never know that."

"He's learning that in daycare."

Chapter 20

I was thinking that our child had spent most of his waking hours in daycare and not with us, but I didn't want to press the issue. I couldn't expect Amanda to be at home more than I was. She had applied for American citizenship and prepared for it by learning all the names of the American presidents in chronological order.

"I doubt that you'll be asked to recite all those names," I said. "Except for the latest presidents, most Americans could only name George Washington and Abraham Lincoln. I'm not sure I could name them all."

"It would be nice to know them regardless. Would you please check if I'm doing it right?"

"Alright, but you have to give me the list."

When Amanda had been sworn in, I asked which questions she got from the judge.

"He only asked if I knew the date of our Independence."

When Henrik was four years old, we both had to write research papers, but first we would spend the summer in Norway. We had borrowed an apartment and were on our own. Henrik played with Bjarne's children and often stayed overnight with them. He had learned to speak Norwegian and enjoyed playing with his cousins. I postponed my research on the wind farms, so I could spend quality time with Amanda. One evening, Amanda surprised me by saying,

"Here's your chance because I forgot to bring my pills."

"But won't they still work?" I hoped not.

"We'll have to let providence decide whether we'll have another child."

"I love you Amanda." I sent up a silent prayer for another love child and thought that providence was on my side because I had my wife to myself for the entire month we stayed in Stavanger.

Back in San Francisco, I waited anxiously for Amanda to say something about being pregnant. She didn't have to after I saw her vomiting in the bathroom one morning.

"Why didn't you tell me you're pregnant, darling?" I asked.

"I wasn't't sure," she said, rinsing her mouth and washing her face.

"You're making me extremely happy," I said, quickly adding, "Sorry about your nausea."

"I need to have it confirmed by a doctor. I'm a little worried since it will be five years since I gave birth."

"You're a healthy woman. You exercise and you're not overweight. I'm sure you'll be fine."

The test was positive and it pleased me tremendously. Amanda was anxious to get her latest research paper finished before the birth, and I gave her all the time she needed. When she began to show, we told Henrik he would have a brother to play with and it made him somersault across the living room floor. Everything went well and our child was born healthy in 1997. Amanda said I could name him.

"My first name is Michael and I was never called that, so now I want to name our new baby Michael," I said.

"That's fine. I like that name. But what else do you want to name him, dear?"

"As long as we can call him Michael, you can pick his second name."

"In that case, his name will be Michael Iversen Whitmore. How's that?"

"It's fine with me. I like your family name."

Henrik took one look at the newborn Michael and said, "I can't play with him."

"You were just as little."

"Oh, no. I was never that puny."

"He'll grow, you'll see."

"When is he getting up?"

"He can't get up by himself. We have to lift him up to feed him and change his nappy. You couldn't walk either until after your first birthday. You can hold your brother if you're very careful."

"Nope. I'll wait until he gets bigger," Henrik said, but he looked at Michael every day to see if he had grown.

Amanda had finished her research paper before Michael was born and mine was almost done. I had researched how many wind farms we had and their locations in the United States. Most of them were in the eastern part of the country. I predicted that by 2010, America would be the largest producer in the world of wind-based energy but emphasized that we could do so much more.

The year 2012 marked the 100th anniversary of the sinking of the Titanic, and it received a lot of publicity. We saw the movie Titanic, and although it was a fictionalized account, it was factual.

With her research paper as background, Amanda made up a power-point program about the Titanic to show to her undergraduate students. She called on me to tell the story of my great-grandmother's survival. First, she showed a picture of the Titanic while narrating.

"The Titanic was 109 feet high and 882 feet long. It carried 2,028 passengers and crew. Her gross tonnage was more than 46 tons and she was designed for a maximum speed of 23 to 24 knots."

I clicked the forward key, and a picture of the lifeboats showed on the screen.

"The lifeboats could carry 1,078 people only. It was still according to regulations.

Click! Pictures of items that had survived, such as suitcases, shoes, china, jewelry, coins. Amanda continued by explaining why those items had survived but human bones had not.

Click! Picture of Bruce Ismay, manager of the White Star Line.

"Some of the surviving passengers reported that the captain and manager of the White Star Line, Mr. Bruce Ismay, wanted the Titanic to reach New York in record time despite the icebergs in the water. The desire to break a record might have contributed to the collision. The ship had no radar, and the lookouts had no binoculars. One of the two lookouts sighted a berg and immediately contacted the bridge. The bow of the ship slowly began to turn to port, but the iceberg scraped the starboard bow.

Click! Picture of an iceberg.

"As you might have seen in the movie Titanic, some of the passengers heard the scraping sound and went out on deck to investigate. Ice had splattered up on deck and young boys were kicking it around. The passengers were told there was no danger and they should go back to their cabins. It was not until the captain had ordered an inspection of the ship that the passengers were told to put on their life jackets and come to the boat deck at once. The lifeboats were released and the call for 'Women and Children First' rang out. But when the officers loading the boats learned that water poured in on the lower decks, they knew they didn't have time to fill the boats. Many boats left the ship with empty seats. The women thought they were safer on the big ship and they didn't want to leave their husbands. One of the two collapsible boats didn't right itself and plunged into the sea as a flat raft. Men swam to it and crawled up on it. The people in the water died of hypothermia."

Click! Why did the Titanic sink so fast?

Amanda showed deteriorated iron rivets and explained the difference in the composition of iron rivets and steel rivets.

Click! Why did the waterproof compartment flood?

Amanda showed a picture of such a compartment and said, "Because the ship leaned forward." I looked at the students' faces and saw that they were totally engaged. When Amanda's presentation was over, she introduced me as a descendant of a Titanic survivor, and it was my turn to take the podium.

"My great-grandmother Anna was a lady's maid traveling with Mr. and Mrs. Addison and their daughter Lydia of Boston. Anna and Lydia shared a cabin in second class. Mr. and Mrs. Addison occupied a stateroom in first class. Anna's sister, Christina, traveled in third class. Anna said that Mrs. Addison would have been saved if she hadn't refused to go in a lifeboat without Lydia, but Lydia was with her boyfriend, and they ignored the warnings until Anna and Christina came to get them. Together the four of them made their way to the boat deck but couldn't find Mr. and Mrs. Addison among all the frantic passengers. Anna later said she had been thrown overboard when the forward funnel collapsed. The experienced lifeguard Roberto jumped overboard to save himself, but he also saved Anna. Lydia went down with the ship along with her parents, and so did Anna's sister."

"I can imagine the horror of the survivors in the boats closest to the ship when they saw the Titanic sinking lower and lower with 1,500 people on board. They heard the screams of the victims and saw them tumble into the sea, or go down with the ship. The survivors didn't think they would live through the cold night. Anna was unconscious and didn't see any of that, but she was the only female who survived having been in the cold water. Some of the survivors sat in the boats for six hours before the rescue ship *Carpathia* arrived at 4 o'clock in the morning. Thanks to the decision of *Carpathia*'s Captain Arthur Rostron to steam toward the Titanic from 58 miles away, 700 people were saved. By the way, Captain Rostron was born in England but his parents were born in Sweden. For his heroism, Swedish survivors presented him with a silver cup after the *Carpathia* arrived in New York."

After Amanda had given her program at the university, the fraternal organization Sons of Norway contacted her and asked her to give the program at one of their functions. Again, she wanted me to come along to tell my ancestor's story.

I, William Whitmore, recorded these memories in April 2013 after I learned that a billionaire in Australia planned to build a replica of the Titanic and sail it in passenger traffic. Dad said if the ship became a reality, he wanted to go on its maiden voyage. I wasn't sure I wanted to go. Amanda said, "No way."

M. H. William Whitmore

Chapter 21

Henrik Whitmore

San Francisco, March 24, 2017

I'm Henrik Whitmore, born in 1992 in San Francisco, the son of William and Amanda Whitmore. I have one brother, Michael, who is five years younger than me. He resembles the Whitmore side of the family while I look more like my Norwegian mother and Swedish grandmother. I learned to speak Norwegian from my mother and learned more when my parents and I went to Norway every summer. I grew up loving to sail in San Francisco Bay.

My parents were both professors at Stanford University. Dad worked with research and development of wind energy and Mom in bioscience. My parents are so perfect that I have a hard time living up to their ideals. My mom wanted me to take violin lessons, but I preferred to play the guitar.

One day I started a garage band. My friends and I made a lot of noise that our neighbors complained about. As I got older and began to drive, I liked fast gas-guzzling cars and crashed a few until I became energy conscious. Like my father, I chose to study electrical engineering. When I had graduated with a bachelor's degree from Stanford University in 2014, my parents rewarded me with an international trip, the same as my father and grandfather had enjoyed before me.

"You might come home with a wife, but it has worked out in the past, so we'll just have to wait and see what happens," Dad said. I knew that Grandpa Bill had met Grandma Stella in Sweden, and that my dad had met my Norwegian Mom in Australia, but I wasn't ready to settle down with any woman.

It was 2014 and Japan made better cars than ever. In addition to making fuel-driven cars, Honda, Mitsubishi, Nissan, and Toyota all made electric cars. The four automakers had united in building a common charging network. They were ahead of us in the U.S. While poring over literature on the subject, I learned about a company in China that owned an electric car plant in Trollhättan, Sweden. Having heard so much about Sweden, I decided to go there first. My aunt Lisa, her husband Göran, and their two children lived in the Göteborg area, and I intended to visit them.

Aunt Lisa met me at Landvetter Airport. At first sight, I saw that she looked like her mother, my grandmother Stella, but younger. I used the ATM at the airport to get Swedish money. Sweden belonged to the European Union but still had its own currency.

"So how do you like it here in Sweden?" I asked Lisa as we walked to the parking lot.

"I've lived here for 25 years and I feel totally at home. When we're starved for sun in the wintertime, we fly to the Mediterranean or to Thailand."

Lisa and her family lived in Mölndal, a name that rang a bell. My grandfather Bill had talked about it. He had visited the town before he was married and located the place where my great-great-grandmother Anna once lived. I asked Lisa if she had seen the Olson nursery, and she said she had been there many times. "I buy most of my plants there," she added.

"What are your children doing?" I asked.

"Mattias is a doctoral candidate at Uppsala, and Emma is studying at the university here. They're both at home now so you'll get to meet them."

"This is where we live," she said, turning into their driveway. Looking around, I saw several newer single homes surrounded by thriving trees and flowers.

"It's beautiful here," I said.

"Summer arrived this week. Göran and I are sailing up the coast. You can come along or you can stay here by yourself. The kids are taking off for vacations in Europe with their friends."

Göran came outside and greeted me with a hearty "Welcome to Sweden, Henrik" and a strong handshake. He was probably in his 50s, looked Swedish and athletic.

"What brings you here?" Göran asked.

"I want to go to Trollhättan and see how far the NEV has come in making electric cars at the former Saab plant."

"I don't think they've started yet." It was disappointing to hear, but I liked to find out for myself.

"I understand the plant is owned by the Chinese," I said.

"Yes, that's correct. They bought it from Saab, but the employees in Trollhättan are Swedish. Their work consists mostly of rebuilding the plant. If they're on schedule they should start producing electric cars for the Chinese market in a couple of years."

Göran opened the car trunk and retrieved my duffel bag.

"Are you going to stay out here or are you coming in?" Lisa asked from the front steps.

"We're coming," Göran said. I slung my backpack over my shoulder and Göran carried my bag upstairs.

"You should go to Germany. BMW, Mercedes, and Volkswagen have all come out with electric cars and they are cheaper than the American Tesla," Göran said while putting the bag in my room.

"I would like to go to Germany."

"Here's the bathroom if you want to freshen up before lunch."

"I need to shave," I said, rubbing the stubble on my chin.

"Come downstairs when you're ready, and we'll have lunch."

We ate lunch on the back porch and continued our discussion while savoring shrimp sandwiches with cucumber slices and dill that we ate with a knife and fork.

"These are my favorite sandwiches. I remember them from Norway. Mom still makes them," I said, as I accepted a second one from the plate that Lisa extended to me.

"Maybe I'll make a stop in Trollhättan before I go to Germany," I said.

"Or you could go sailing with Lisa and me? We plan to sail to Strömstad. Then you could cross over to Norway and be on your own."

"Sounds like a good idea. I have fond memories of Norway, but we always stayed in Stavanger and I didn't get to see Oslo."

"We're setting sail the day after tomorrow, so you don't have much time to think about it," Göran said as he gathered up the used paper napkins and tossed them in a recycling bin that said, Papper.

"I appreciate your offer. I would love to sail with you to Strömstad."

"Actually, you have time to drive up to Trollhättan tomorrow and visit the plant," Göran said.

"Then I need to rent a car."

"You can borrow one of ours. The Volvo has GPS so you won't get lost."

"It's very kind of you, and I appreciate your offer," I said, suppressing a yawn. "Thank you for lunch, but if you'll excuse me, I'll go upstairs and take a nap, so I can stay awake this evening."

"That's fine because we need to prepare for our vacation. The kids are coming home in time for dinner so they can meet you. Mattias will vacation in Prague and Emma in Barcelona," Göran said. "Swedes travel a lot."

"So, I've heard."

During dinner, I talked with my cousins about their studies. Mattias looked like a modern Viking with a reddish-blond, short beard. Emma was a pretty girl with long blonde hair that she tossed over her shoulders. The conversation covered the various branches of the family, and how far apart we lived geographically.

"We haven't been to California yet, so we might come and visit you," Lisa said.

"I hope you will."

After dinner, we all took a walk in the neighborhood. Göran proudly showed me an area of new homes. The owners were outside, working in their yards.

It took less than two hours to drive to Trollhättan, a small town with no tall buildings. I drove straight to the NEV facility and was lucky to be able to meet its president, a man in his 40s. I think his first name was Morgan. He said they collaborated with two other Swedish companies to produce electric cars starting in 2017, one year earlier than projected. I didn't get to see any manufacturing at all, but we discussed the problem with sustaining battery power for longer distances and the necessity of having enough charging stations. Morgan said Norway was ahead of Sweden in the use of electric cars. I told him I was half-Norwegian and had spent just about every summer in Stavanger while growing up. "My uncles are working with wind energy at Statoil, and my father works in the same field in California," I said.

"And what do you want to do, Henrik?"

"Well, I have a degree in electrical engineering, but I would like to learn to make electric cars."

"You can tell me about it over lunch," Morgan said. He drove me out in the country to a restaurant located at a former estate manor surrounded by level fields with higher elevations visible in the background. Morgan said that's where the moose roamed. Over lunch, I told him I might go to Germany and look at their electric car plants.

"It's a good idea, but you should plan on coming back here in 2017 when we will be making cars."

"I might do that. Why is it taking so long to get into production?"

"We want to make certain we don't make any mistakes that will take us back to the drawing board."

"That's smart if you have the funding to proceed slowly."

"So far, we do."

I thanked Morgan for the tour and the lunch, reprogrammed the GPS, and drove back to Mölndal. Before parking the Volvo, I filled the gas tank. That's when I realized that the high price of gasoline would justify the development of electric cars.

Lisa said it would be good to have another deck hand on the sailboat, so she would be free to read and do some knitting. Göran brought out a map and showed me the sailing route. "If the wind is favorable, we'll make our first stop at Ellös. That's where they make the sailboats that your grandpa worked on for a few weeks the first time he was in Sweden in 1960."

"I would love to see the place," I said.

"We'll sail up the coast, past the city of Uddevalla, stay overnight in Smögen, and perhaps also in Grebbestad, before we reach Strömstad," he said, pointing to the map. It will take two to three days, but we'll quit early in the afternoon to make sure we have docking places.

"You'll need a hat to protect you from the sun, Henrik," Lisa said.

"I brought a baseball cap, shorts, and T-shirts."

"Do you have a rain jacket?" Göran asked. "If not, you can borrow one."

"I did bring one. Mom always packed rain gear when we went to Stavanger. We also had to be prepared for chilly days when we needed sweatshirts or sweaters."

Chapter 22

It was nice and warm as we left Göteborg behind us and sailed north. I breathed in the salty, clean air and relaxed.

"I'm surprised to see so many boats with Norwegian flags," I said to Göran, who was sitting by the wheel.

"There will be many more as we get farther north," he said. "The Norwegians come over every summer and sail in Swedish waters. They always wave to us, and we *snacker* with them when we're in port." I had to smile when I heard the word *snacker* which meant talk. It rolled easily off my tongue.

At Ellös, we toured the shipyard and admired the finished boats. Mr. Hallberg had retired in 1972. Another boat-builder owned the business. The latest model, launched in 2012, was being exported to countries around the world.

"My dad told me he slept on a boat for three weeks while he was here," Lisa said.

"I'm sure he didn't mind," I said. "Grandpa liked to make things with his hands. My dad never got the chance, but I think he wishes he had. I'm the same way. I want to see the result of a day's work."

"We don't see much of that in teaching," Göran said, with a laugh. "What would you like to manufacture, Henrik?"

"I would like to make electric cars, better electric cars."

"Tesla makes electric cars in California."

"That's right. I might try to get a job there.'

"So, you don't want to continue your education?"

"Not full-time. I know my parents will be disappointed, but I have to do it my way."

"The Whitmore boys always have," Lisa said, nodding.

After a while, a sudden rain shower and high wind chased her below deck.

"Henrik, take down the sail while I start the engine," Göran yelled. "We're going ashore."

I hurried to winch down the sail as Göran steered toward a nearby island.

"Take the wheel and do what I say," he commanded. "We're aiming for the other side of the island where it's calmer. I have to check if it's safe to get close."

When we had rounded the island in pouring rain, he stationed himself in the bow and looked down in the water. "Not here," he said, "Try a little farther to port." I backed up and slowly started forward again until Göran signaled it was safe. He took a rope and hopped ashore on the bare cliff searching for a place to moor the boat.

"Stop the engine and let down the anchor," he said. Once we had secured the boat, the rainstorm passed. Göran and I went below and changed into dry clothes. Lisa had coffee and a snack ready. She called it *fika*. We sat and talked until the sun was out a short time later. Together, we explored the small island. The crystals in the granite glistened in the sun. I saw fish in the water and asked Göran if he fished.

"Sometimes, I do. You can fish if you like. You might catch a mackerel or two, but we have stocked the fridge with food for the first two days."

We decided to continue and enjoyed a beautiful sail in the archipelago until we arrived in Smögen, a tourist area crowded with people. Göran had called ahead and reserved a docking spot. We took a walk and looked at all the outdoor restaurants and stores. Most of the tourists spoke Swedish or Norwegian, but I heard other languages as well.

"I'll be glad to treat you to dinner at one of the restaurants, so you don't have to cook," I said.

"I don't think we can find seating this evening," Lisa said. "But we'll take you up on your offer in Strömstad."

"How about a beer then?" They accepted and we stood by the bar and drank it.

"Life can't get much better than this," I said, as I looked around and admired all the young women in skimpy shorts and tops.

"I'm not going to shave until I get back home," Göran said, rubbing his whiskers.

"Then I'll follow your example," I said.

I bumped elbows with a girl in the crowd, and quickly said, "*Undskyld*." (Norwegian for I'm sorry.) She turned to me, and asked, "*Norske gut?*" (Norwegian boy?)

"You are half right."

"What do you mean?"

"My mom is Norwegian and my dad American."

"What are you doing in Sweden?"

"I'm visiting an aunt who lives here, and she and her husband took me sailing. I'm Henrik."

"I'm Linda," she said. She put up a hand for a high-five, and I responded.

"Do you want a beer or a soda?" I asked.

"*Öl* (beer), *tack*."

Lisa and Göran said they were going back to the boat.

"I'll meet you at the boat," I said. "This is Linda and I'm treating her to a beer."

"*Hej* Linda. See you later then, Henrik," Göran said with a wink to me.

"I think you should have something to eat, too," I told Linda. "What do you want?"

"Maybe a *varm korv*" (hotdog).

"I've been waiting for a chance to have a *pölse* (Norwegian for sausage) in a bun. Mustard or catsup?"

"Mustard, please." I found an empty table and we sat down with our hotdogs and a bottle of beer each.

"Aren't you with someone?" I asked in Norwegian and she answered me in Swedish.

"Yes, but I'm free to mingle. Where do you live, Henrik?" She took a small bite from her hotdog.

"San Francisco. And you?"

"A town called Trollhättan."

"Trollhättan! I just came from there."

"Really, I didn't think you had heard of it."

"The name means the troll's hat. We have trolls in Norway too." We laughed at the thought and had a good time together finishing our hotdogs and beers until I felt obligated to return to the boat.

"I'll be back in Trollhättan as soon as they start making electric cars," I said.

"You really surprise me, Henrik."

"May I have your phone number just in case you aren't married by then?" I asked with a grin.

"If I can have yours."

"Sure, but I don't know if I can get my phone charged on the boat, so it might be dead soon."

"Where're you going next?"

"We're sailing to Strömstad, and then I'll go to Norway from there," I said.

"I'm sure you can get your phone charged in Norway," Linda said, "if you have the right adapter."

"I do. I'm sorry but I have to go now. My relatives are waiting for me."

"Thanks for the *öl och korv*."

I took one last look at Linda to memorize her pretty face, and said, "You're welcome." I didn't think I would ever see her again. When I looked around, she had disappeared in the crowd.

Back at the boat, I apologized to Lisa and Göran for having parted company.

"It's okay," Lisa said. "You're young and you should have some fun."

"Linda's hometown is Trollhättan, so I enjoyed chatting with her."

"What a coincidence."

"How about supper? I'm hungry," Göran said.

We sat on the open deck and ate cold meatballs, smoked fish, and potato salad until dusk at about 11 o'clock, when we went to bed. I was tired from the jetlag, the sun, and the wind, and slept soundly. Lisa and Göran slept in a double bed in the bow of the boat, while I slept in the stern.

After breakfast the next morning, we started the engine, hoisted the sails and were on our way to Grebbestad.

"If the tailwind continues, we'll reach Strömstad this afternoon," Göran said.

"How will I get to Oslo from Strömstad?" I asked.

"You could rent a car or possibly take the train, but I don't know what the train communications are like. Interstate E-6 crosses into Norway and ends up in Oslo. But since you're not going back to Strömstad, there will be an extra charge for the return of the rental car."

"I'll decide when we come to Strömstad."

We docked some distance from the city and took a ferry ride into Strömstad. I stood in line to make a dinner reservation, and when it was my turn, I said, "Iversen, table for three," in Norwegian. My last name was Whitmore and not Iversen, but I didn't have to spell out Iversen.

I stood and talked to Lisa and Göran about Stavanger when a Norwegian man approached me saying, "I couldn't help overhearing that your name is Iversen and that you mentioned Stavanger. I used to work for Statoil and knew a man by the name Bjarne Iversen."

"That's my uncle," I said." Small world. I'm Henrik."

Well, that resulted in a hearty handshake and introductions all around. The man's name was Martin. Like most Norwegians, he was tall, and slim with light hair. He and his wife Elin lived in Oslo but used to live in Stavanger. We talked about Bjarne and Statoil's work on wind energy at sea.

"Do you happen to know the best way to get to Oslo?" I asked Martin.

"We're driving," he said. "It's the best way if you have a car."

"I don't have a car. I came here from Göteborg by sailboat and I'm not returning to Göteborg. I want to go to Oslo."

"Let's meet after dinner and talk about it," Martin said.

When I heard, "Iversen, your table is ready," my relatives and I entered the restaurant. We studied the menu and decided on flounder. "The fish is very good here," Göran said. As we walked out, Martin and Elin caught up with us.

"Do you want to come with us to the boat and have a glass of wine?" Göran asked them.

They accepted and we had a pleasant evening together. When they left, Marty offered me a ride to Oslo. "We're going home tomorrow morning and it's only the two of us in the car," he said, and I accepted.

I met them outside the restaurant with my duffel bag in one hand and the backpack over my shoulder. "Hey, you have an electric car," I said.

"Yes, electric cars are common in Norway. This is a hybrid, so it runs on gasoline on the highway, but it's very economical. I get free parking in Norway because I drive electric, and I can charge the batteries for free at work. I don't get as many privileges as people with all-electric cars," he said.

"You can sit in the front, Henrik," Elin said. "I'm smaller." I protested, but she insisted. I was happy as a kid. The car was quiet and it made talking easy. Once we were out on E-6, the gasoline engine kicked in and we could drive faster.

"This is terrific," I said. We talked about the high price of purchasing an electric car, but the Norwegian government subsidized that as well. I commented on how different the landscape was from the coastland. I saw quite a bit of farmland.

Chapter 23

Martin and Elin drove around Oslo to show me the sights: The Royal Palace, the Akershus Fortress, the Viking Ship Museum, the Norwegian Museum, the Kon-Tiki Museum, and the Fram Polar Exploration Museum. I wanted to see those museums on the inside, but I would have to go on my own because Martin and Elin had toured them several times. I treated them to dinner as a way of thanking them for the ride, and we said good-bye outside my hotel.

I couldn't possibly see all the museums and decided on the Kon-Tiki Museum first. Grandpa Bill had told me that Thor Heyerdahl had built a balsa raft and sailed it from Peru to Polynesia. I admired him for his effort and success. I found the Fram Museum to be equally interesting since it featured the Norwegian Roald Amundsen's feat in being the first to reach the South Pole. He arrived 34 days ahead of the British explorer Robert Falcon Scott.

When I picked up my phone, I saw the number to Linda and decided to call her.

"*Hej* Linda, it's Henrik."

"*Hej*, where're you?"

"I'm in Oslo, and I'm thinking about flying to Stavanger."

"You're really getting around." I pictured Linda eating hotdogs in Smögen and regretted that I had missed the opportunity to kiss her.

"What are you doing now?" I asked.

"I'm still in Smögen. I got a summer job as a waitress."

"Good for you. Then you're making a lot of money in tips."

"Sometimes."

"It was nice meeting you."

"Same here. I have to go now. Have a good trip."

"Thanks."

Next, I called Bjarne's number to see if anyone was home. No answer there, so I called the number to my grandparents, Iver and Marita.

"Hi *Morfar,* this is Henrik. How're you and *Mormor*?"

"Not bad, just getting slower."

"Are Bjarne and Olaf in town or are they on vacation?"

"They're in town. They should be at work now. Where're you, Henrik?"

"I'm in Oslo and I might fly to Stavanger."

"Go ahead. We'll be glad to see you. It's been a long time. I can pick you up at the airport if you tell me when you're coming."

"Thanks, I'll call you back as soon as I have booked a flight."

"Do that. You can stay with us."

Sitting on the plane and looking down at the mountains below, I felt excited about going to Stavanger. How could I not when I was only an hour away by plane. I hadn't seen my grandparents for a few years and hoped to get together with my uncles, Bjarne and Olaf, and their children, my cousins. I used to play with Bjarne's boys when we visited Stavanger in the summertime.

Landing at Sola Airport, I was met by *Morfar*, who had lost most of his hair since I saw him last.

"You've become a man Henrik," Morfar said.

"I'm 22."

"Yes, I know you're about the same age as Bjarne's boys, Thord and Johan.

"What are they doing now?"

"They have summer jobs. We have invited Bjarne, Siv, and the boys to our house tonight. You can see Olaf and his family later."

"*Morsomt*" (Cool). At my grandparents' home, I looked around the familiar surroundings with the view of the bay. *Morfar's* accordion stood by the piano. I kissed *Mormor* on the cheek and asked if I could help her with anything.

"We've ordered in food," she said. *Morfar* showed me to my room. "It's the room I used to sleep in," I said. I shaved and changed clothes before dinner because I remembered it was customary to dress up when Norwegians had company.

When I heard voices outside, I went to greet Bjarne and his family. They arrived in an electric car.

"Do you have room for everybody in that car?" I asked.

"No problem. We've enough legroom and as you can see we're all tall." Thord and Johan stood shoulder to shoulder to me. I bumped fists with the boys and greeted Bjarne and Siv with handshakes and enthusiasm.

"I've seen many electric cars since I got here," I said. "I'm impressed."

"We already have 10,000 electric cars on the roads in Norway. We don't have to pay import taxes, and vat taxes are exempt. We pay no fees on toll roads or ferries, and we have access to the bus lanes," Bjarne said.

"The government predicts 50,000 electric cars in Norway by next year," Thord said. "Per capita it will be the most of any country."

"Why don't you make the cars in Norway?" I asked.

"We tried, but the car was too small to be successful," Johan said. "Sweden is working on it."

"I know, I visited the plant in Trollhättan, but they're not ready to start production yet. Electric cars don't have many moving parts and still it takes time to develop them."

When the food van arrived, we all went inside and continued our discussion. Siv helped *Mormor* with the transfer of the food to the table. The meal consisted of *smörgåstårta*, a large sandwich creation that looked like a cake but was made of bread and various fillings. It was decorated with mayo, shrimp, cucumber, dill, and who-knows-what. Obviously, my grandparents remembered my fondness of shrimp.

When Mormor said "*varsågod*," we sat down at the table.

The women wanted me to tell them everything that was new about my family. I began by talking about my visit with Aunt Lisa and Göran and their kids.

"We don't live that far from each other, but we haven't seen them for several years," Siv said.

"It takes a long time to drive around the coast," Bjarne added.

I told them I had seen many Norwegians sailing along Sweden's west coast. "Of course, it's not far if they live in the Oslo area."

"We miss our Amanda. How is she and your dad?" *Mormor* asked.

"They're fine. They decided to go on a cruise to Alaska this summer. Michael is with them."

"Are you two working at Statoil this summer?" I asked Thord and Johan, looking at them.

"No, I'm getting some experience in shipping," Thord said.

"And I'm working with marketing at a fish company," Johan said. "It's just a summer job."

"Shipping and fishing are Norway's biggest industries, next to oil, of course," I said, as I turned to Bjarne. "How's the offshore wind energy coming along?"

"We're still working on it."

"It's the same for Dad. He's impatient about getting a field in the bay."

"It seems to me that California would be wise to invest in solar energy," *Morfar* said. "You have so much sun all year round."

"I know, and it's coming, but that, too, is incredibly slow. It's getting cheaper now, but the high cost is prohibitive. Electric energy from coal is so much cheaper."

"But it pollutes," Johan said.

"I agree with you. It's ridiculous to ship coal to the desert. The sun could power all the air conditioning they are using. Dad thinks I should study solar energy."

"Sounds like a good idea. Where are you going next on your trip around the world, Henrik?" Thord asked.

"I'm going to Germany to take a look at their electric car plants."

"BMW probably has the largest plant. Have you been to Japan?"

"No, I've researched the four electric car plants there, but I'm not going to Japan."

When we were finished with the meal, *Mormor* invited us to the living room. I offered to help clearing away the dishes, but the women chased me away. *Morfar* said he had something to show me in the yard.

"It's a robot, and it mows my lawn," he said, pointing to it. I had to take a closer look.

"I have never seen one before."

"Here in Norway, it's hard to get a human to do yard work. The robot is doing a fine job for me. If it rains, he goes back in his little house. I think it's amazing," *Morfar* chuckled.

"It sure is," I said. "I can see that he's doing a good job." The big lawn was beautifully trimmed.

"Programming robots has become a popular occupation here in Europe. The universities offer degrees in robotics. Both Thord and Johan study robotics, but they like to do other things as well."

"We have robots in our American factories. They're cheaper in the long run than workers, and they can do the repetitious work better than humans."

"It looks like more and more workers will be replaced by robots," *Morfar* said, as we walked back to the house.

Morfar had taken a few days off from work, and the next day, he and *Mormor* took me to see Old Stavanger. Not surprisingly, the old town was tastefully preserved. I told *Morfar* that my ancestor John Whitmore became interested in restoring old Victorian homes in Boston after he had seen *Gamla Stan* (Old Town) in Stockholm.

For the first time, I saw big cruise ships anchored in Stavanger's harbor. Tourists spilled out on the streets and swamped the souvenir shops. Lots of little handmade trolls awaited eager buyers.

"We have a deep harbor in the middle of the city. In Bergen, the ships have to anchor far outside the city, so they like it better here," Morfar said. I always thought Stavanger was beautiful with its many red-painted buildings reflecting in the water.

The next day, Olaf and Camilla invited us to dinner, and I looked forward to seeing them and their girls. They lived close enough for us to walk there.

"Welcome, Henrik," Olaf said, shaking my hand. "Have you found a future wife yet in your travels?"

"I met a girl from Trollhättan in Smögen, but so far I only have her phone number."

"It's a start," Olaf said. Camilla and the girls came outside to meet us.

"Sonia and Stine, please greet your cousin Henrik from San Francisco," Camilla said.

They both said "hello" and curtsied in their pretty dresses. I felt older than my years.

"I have a little brother who is 17. You've met him," I said.

"Yes, we remember our cousin Michael," Sonia said.

"You haven't seen our new house, Henrik." Olaf invited me inside.

Like all my Norwegian relatives, Olaf and Camilla lived in a roomy house with hardwood floors in all the rooms, even the kitchen. The bathrooms and the entry had heated floor tiles. We walked out on the huge patio in the back, where the table was set for dinner.

Olaf grilled Norwegian salmon, and as expected, it was delicious. We enjoyed good wine and had a delightful evening. Olaf and Camilla had traveled the world before they settled down, but we hadn't been to the same countries. They had visited China, Thailand, India, Africa, New Zealand, as well as most of the countries in Europe. Olaf had been to Australia, but Camilla hadn't.

"I heard the stories about the roaches in Sydney, so I didn't want to go there," she said. We all laughed about that because my dad had told me he killed a roach that scared Mom.

When I was alone in my room that evening, I called Linda in Trollhättan again, and we talked for about 15 minutes. She had an evening off from the restaurant.

"What are you doing the rest of the year?" I asked.

"I'm going to the *högskola* in Trollhättan. It's the same as college."

She asked how long I would be in Stavanger, and I said, "My stay here is up. I'm leaving for Germany tomorrow."

"Happy travels," she said. I hoped that our paths would cross again.

Chapter 24

Olaf recommended that I fly to Leipzig, Germany, where BMW assembles their successful electric i3 model. While waiting in Copenhagen for my next flight to Berlin, I looked at the varied merchandise offered by the airport stores and used an ATM to get euros for Germany.

From the Berlin airport, I took a train to the city center and went to the Brandenburg Gate which symbolizes freedom after the Berlin Wall opened in 1990. From Berlin, it took two hours to travel by train to Leipzig, a city of about half a million people. When I arrived, I asked a cab driver to take me to the BMW plant. I saw remnants of the communist years in the form of ugly high rises and some dilapidated areas. Other than that, Leipzig looked like any other modern European city.

At the plant, I had to check my backpack and duffel bag at the entrance. The guide was an attractive average-height girl dressed in slacks and a shirt with a nametag that said Heidi. She told my group that BMW had made and tested electric cars for more than 40 years, beginning in 1972. The Munich Olympic Games featured the car with much success as it had no exhaust. Since then, the company had steadily improved the performance of the batteries, and in 2014 the range had reached 114 miles. The i3 model had a two-cylinder gas extension that would kick in if the batteries failed.

After the tour of the plant, I asked Heidi if it was possible to meet someone in management. I said I was on a European trip to study electric cars.

"Who do you represent?" Heidi asked, looking up at me.

"Stanford University in San Francisco." Thanks to the fine reputation of Stanford, I got a meeting with one of the vice presidents. He gave me a chart showing the projection of i3 deliveries from 2013 through 2015 listing global deliveries of 41,500 vehicles, with the largest number going to the United States, and the next largest to Germany, followed by Norway, U.K., France, Switzerland, Netherlands, and Denmark. More than half went to Europe and a small number to Japan and Canada.

On my way out, I thanked Heidi for her help and asked her where I could find a hotel. She gave me a brochure, which didn't tell me much since I didn't know the location of the hotels.

"I'm sorry to bother you again Miss Heidi, but could you tell me how I can get to the nearest hotel or motel?"

"Do you have a car, sir?"

"No, I don't have a car. I came here in a cab from the train station."

"And where are you going next?"

"I don't know. Where are you from?"

"Switzerland."

"Are you by any chance free tonight, Heidi? I would like to learn more about Switzerland." It was just an excuse to see her again.

"I'll get off work in a few minutes, and then we can talk some more."

"*Wunderbar,*" one of the few German words I knew.

Wheeling my carry-on, I walked with her to the bus station and boarded a crowded bus. She got a seat, but I stood holding on to the luggage rack. When we got off the bus, she pointed to a hotel and said she'd continue on another bus.

"May I treat you to a drink before you go? You've gone to a lot of trouble, and I want to show my appreciation," I said.

She looked at her watch, and said, "Maybe a coffee then?"

There was a coffee house nearby and we went there. I ordered the kind of coffee she wanted and chose the same for myself. "How about a muffin to go with your coffee?" I asked.

"Yes, please."

I paid with my euros, and Heidi got a table for us while I waited for the order. Finally, we could talk in private.

"Where in Switzerland are you from?"

"I'm from Geneva."

"How come you're working here then?"

"I went to the University of Leipzig and then I got a job as a guide at the plant."

"Do you think you'll stay here?

"No, I'm saving money so I can move to California. I have relatives there, and also on the east coast. Since you're asking me so many questions, may I ask you one, sir?"

"Please call me Henrik. Ask away."

"Okay, Henrik. Are you in the electric car business?"

"No, but I would like to be. I've graduated from the Stanford University. Now that I have seen the electric car plant here, I think I'll apply for a job at the Tesla plant as soon as I get home."

"When are you leaving?"

"I'll take the train back to Berlin tomorrow afternoon. Would you join me for breakfast at this coffee house in the morning? I don't know anyone here, and I would really appreciate your company."

I could see that she hesitated, so I said, "I'll be glad to show you around in California." As I expected, her face lit up.

"We can have breakfast here at 7 in the morning if you're awake?" she said.

"I'll be here. Thanks for your help, Miss Heidi. Now I can escort you to your bus."

Happily, I checked into the hotel. When we met in the morning, I started out with an honest compliment.

"It's early, but you look great, Heidi. What would you like for breakfast?"

"I don't eat much for breakfast, just coffee and a roll, please." I was hungry and ordered a full breakfast with eggs and German sausage.

"I have time for sightseeing today. What do you recommend I do?"

"What are you interested in Henrik?"

"I would like to learn about the history of Leipzig."

"Then you should go to the Museum of History. If you take the bus to the City Center, you'll find it. Do you speak German?"

"I'm afraid not. I just learned some technical terms in college."

"At the museum they have ear phones that will tell you the history in English."

While we talked, I studied her looks and mannerism. Her brown hair bounced when she moved. She had dark blue eyes and dimples in her cheeks. Again, I accompanied her to the bus that would take her to another day's work. "I'm glad you're coming to California," I said.

"First, I have to get my papers; and not until then can I resign from my job, but I'll come as soon as I can. We could keep in touch via email," she suggested.

"Good idea," I said. We exchanged email addresses and then said *Auf Wiedersehen* before I caught a bus in the other direction.

At the history museum, I looked at the exhibits while listening to the description in English. The University of Leipzig dated back to

1409. The first printing press was established in 1479. I listened absentmindedly to a long string of events until I came to the Battle of Breitenfeld in 1631 during the Thirty-Year War when the protestant Swedish Army fought the Imperial Army of Austria represented by the Roman Empire. Sweden's King Gustav II Adolph won a decisive victory at Breitenfeld but did not survive the Battle of Leipzig. He died on November 6, 1632. During his reign, Sweden had become considerably larger. His name made me think of the *Vasa* ship in Stockholm that the same king had ordered to go into battle in the 30-year war, only *Vasa* didn't make it out to sea. My parents had told me about it and one day I hoped to see the relic myself.

On the train to Berlin, I researched the Renault plant in Bologna, France, just seven kilometers from Paris. Renault had formed an Alliance with Nissan, and the company had sold 6,000 electric cars in Europe during the first six months of 2013. Compared to 2012, the electric car market had increased by 50 percent and for hybrid cars by 60 percent.

BBC reported that ISIS had taken control of Mosel. A Malaysian passenger liner had crashed in Ukraine killing all 298 passengers and crew. It wasn't good news for someone who would be flying a long distance.

Chapter 25

I slept away some of the many hours on the plane to San Francisco. I was anxious to start a new life supporting myself. My parents met me at the airport.

"Tell us all about your trip," Dad said.

"Did you meet any pretty girls?" Mom asked.

"Actually, I met two pretty girls, Linda in Sweden and Heidi in Germany, but Heidi is from Switzerland."

"Where did you meet her?"

"She was a guide at the BMW plant. She has relatives in Monterey and Kingsburg and is planning to come to California."

"What about Linda?"

"I met her only briefly. I don't even know her last name."

"What are your plans now, Henrik?" Dad asked, bringing the conversation back to reality.

"I want to get a job."

"So, you don't want to continue your education?" Mom asked.

"I might do it part-time, but first I want to get a job and support myself. You've spent a lot of money on my trip to Europe."

"Some of it came from your inheritance from your great-grandparents, Henry and Sharon."

"I know. I wish they were alive, so I could tell them about my adventures. How was Alaska?"

"Chilly and beautiful just about sums it up," Dad said.

Being too tired to do anything else, I just had to get some sleep before I could think straight. I didn't wake up until the next morning.

While having breakfast with my parents, I asked Dad how the wind farm in the bay was coming along.

"I don't know if it will ever materialize," he said. "I've been waiting for years. Now I'm planning to put solar panels on our house, and learn more about that kind of energy."

"*Morfar* said we should utilize the sun more here in California."

"He's right. It would be a good field for Michael to get into."

Michael. Why not me?

We had moved from the tall and narrow house in the downtown area to a big house with a pool in the suburbs. Solar panels would decrease some of our carbon imprint. I sat down at my laptop and wrote an email to Heidi telling her I had arrived safely in San Francisco. Then I uploaded pictures from my camera and some from my cell phone and showed them to my parents and Michael. Most of the pictures were from Stavanger, and they drew many excited comments from Mom.

We talked about electric cars and agreed the price had to come down to make them viable. "Norway gives so many incentives to buy electric cars that the price there isn't prohibitive. Electric cars make 40 percent less of a carbon imprint than conventional cars, and people in Europe are much more aware of climate change than we are here. I believe Tesla can make a difference," I said.

The next day, I put on a suit and tie to apply for a job at Tesla's R&D, which was close to where we lived. The man behind the counter looked at my short resumé and said I was too young and inexperienced, and that I needed more education to work in R&D. It didn't help that I had been to Europe touring an electric car plant. I could apply for a blue-collar job though. My choices weren't great. If I went back to school, my dad would be my professor, and the blue-collar job would be on an assembly line.

Dad said my grandpa in Boston was serious about sailing on the proposed Titanic Princess. He wanted to bring all three of his grandsons, which meant my brother Michael, me, and our cousin Matthew in Boston. I called Grandpa Bill and told him about my trip. After speaking enthusiastically about his plans to sail on the Titanic Princess, he asked what I wanted to do with my life. When I said I wasn't sure, he asked, "Would you like to go into business for yourself?"

"Perhaps, but I don't know what kind of business."

"How about solar energy? If I were young like you, I think it's something I would pursue."

I told him my dad was putting solar panels on our house. "Look into it, and see what you think, Henrik," Grandpa said with conviction.

I promised to do just that. "See you on the Titanic Princess, if not before," I said.

"Does he really mean we're all going on that trip?" Michael asked me.

"I think he means it."

"It's going to cost a lot of money, isn't it?"

"Yes, but Grandpa can probably afford it."

"If it sails in 2016, I'll be 19 years old," Michael said.

"Yes, but it might not be finished by then."

"If you go, Henrik, I want to go, too, but it would be more fun if cousin Matthew came along."

"I know. I can imagine how much fun you two would have together."

"What time of the year do you think it will sail?"

"Probably in April because that's when the first Titanic sailed, but I don't know."

When the solar panels arrived, and workers were busy installing them on the roof, I followed their progress with great interest and read all the material the company supplied. I understood electricity and the solar panels fascinated me.

"Are there any openings for installers at your plant?" I asked the foreman. He gave me a card with the company's name and contact information. Dad said that the solar panels would heat the pool and the water in the house. He planned to buy more panels later that would heat and cool the house.

I couldn't think of a better job than promoting that kind of energy. Without hesitation, I went to the solar panel company and applied for a job. I could start the next day either as a salesman trainee or as an assembler in the manufacturing department. I chose assembly. Grandpa had said I should look into the business. Now, I had a chance to learn more about it.

When I told Dad about my new job, he said, "I envy you, Henrik, I wish I could do the same, start with something new and exciting."

I received an email from Heidi saying she had received an offer from her company to work for three years at its new plant in South Carolina once it was up and running. It was the only way she could get a visa. She ended the email by saying, "That's probably what I'll do."

My short answer said only, "Good luck with your move to South Carolina."

Time would tell if we would meet again, but I didn't think so.

With great enthusiasm, I began my new 8-to-5 job at the solar plant. My colleagues were mostly young, college-educated men and women. We held meetings, discussing applications and solutions. I was part of the team and anxious to use my knowledge of electricity in my work. Best of all, I considered solar energy to be an emerging field with great expansion possibilities, especially in California and other states blessed with an abundance of sunshine. Like wind energy and electric cars, the initial purchase price was high, but I expected it to come down.

The plant employed young people from other countries who wanted experience so they could apply their knowledge to similar jobs in their own countries. They had three-year contracts just like Heidi had been offered. I became acquainted with Aldice from Copenhagen, Denmark, my type of woman, blonde and blue-eyed. Aldice carried her chest high as she walked around the plant on long legs.

"You're new here," she said to me while we combined our efforts in fitting a part to a panel.

"Yes, I am. My name is Henrik, and I know your name is Aldice and that you're from Copenhagen. I was there this summer, but just at the airport. My mother is Norwegian and I speak the language." Aldice said a phrase in Danish that I didn't catch, so she continued in English.

"The two languages are similar, but it still takes a little practice to converse," she said.

"Are you interested in sailing, Aldice?"

"Yes, we sail at home in Denmark."

"Would you like to go sailing with me? My family has a boat."

"I would love to."

"That's great. I haven't had much time to sail this summer because I toured Europe."

"Where did you go in Europe?"

"Sweden, Norway, and Germany."

I could tell that she was impressed.

Chapter 26

On Friday afternoon, I asked Aldice if she was free to go sailing with me on Sunday. She was ready, and we made plans for me to pick her up where she lived. As I drove to the marina with Aldice, I asked if she had been back to Denmark since she moved here.

"Yes, I was back there on my two-week vacation this year," she said.

"I suppose that wasn't long enough for you."

"No, but at least I got to see my family."

"So, are you staying one more year?"

"Yes, three years is how long I'm allowed to stay on my visa."

"What are you planning to do with your solar panel experience in Denmark?"

"I thought I could use what I'm learning here to expand the industry in Denmark."

"I'm sure you can," I said. As she got out of the car, I let my eyes take in her long and slender body dressed in shorts and a top that barely covered her bosom. I had stocked the boat the day before with drinks and snacks and readied it for our sail. I preferred to sail a small boat that I could manage on my own. Aldice donned a life vest and sunglasses and asked what she could do to help.

"Can you pull up the fenders?"

"Sure."

"What else can you do?"

"I can start the engine and steer the boat. But I don't know anything about the sea chart here in the bay."

"You can be my first mate." She saluted me with a big grin. In the strong sunshine, I could see that she had freckles on her nose.

"Start the engine and back up, mate," I told her.

"Ay, ay, skipper." She did a good job. I hoisted the sail, and we were off. We sat beside each other in the stern as I navigated between other boats. When we got out on the open water, the wind was in our favor and we made good speed. I planned to sail to a small port and dock.

"Do you ever get seasick?" I asked.

"No, not any more, unless there is a storm."

"We're not going to run into a storm today."

"No, I don't think so either. The weather is beautiful."

"I have cold water in the fridge below if you get thirsty. If you like, we can take a break later and go swimming."

"I would like that. Will we come close to Silicon Valley?"

"No, Silicon Valley lies along the southern shore of the bay."

I pointed out the cities that we could see from the boat and told her about the companies that had plants and offices around the bay, and my father's ambition to establish a wind farm along the coast. We talked about the wind farms in Denmark and elsewhere in Europe. She was concerned about climate change caused by fossil energy.

"At one time, I wanted to make a career in the electric car industry," I told her, "but now I'm more interested in solar energy."

"When you live in California, you should be. The possibilities are endless here."

"I agree with you one hundred percent," I said, as I aimed for port.

"Please take the wheel and I'll lower the sail," I said.

She started the engine when I said so. "Thanks mate," I said as I took my place at the wheel again.

"Do you want to go swimming before we eat?" I asked.

"Yes, I would love to."

As soon as I had dropped anchor, she wriggled out of her shorts revealing her bikini. I was already dressed in my swim shorts and needed only to shed my shirt.

We lowered ourselves into the water from the stern and began to play tag. She was quick, but when I caught her, I held on to her as long as I could. When she swam away from me, I just let her get a little ahead of me before I caught up with her and brought her back. She climbed up the steps to the boat ahead of me. I swung myself up and we both collapsed on the floor of the boat. I stroked her wet hair out of her eyes and held her head in my hands while zeroing in on her salty lips until she said she was thirsty. "Water coming up," I said, as I went down to the galley to fetch the picnic food and two bottles of water. I handed her one bottle that she immediately opened and gulped down.

"I have more water," I said. "You can drink as much as you want." I raised the table and placed salty snacks and sandwiches on top.

"Did you make these sandwiches, Henrik?" she asked.

"Yes," I said, but I didn't tell her that the maid had prepared the filling.

"They are delicious." We both ate with good appetite. I was already making plans to date Aldice again. When I told her, I might sail on the Titanic Princess, she said she hadn't heard of it, and I had to tell her. She said a new Titanic would mean going back to old world technology, and she was more interested in new inventions. She had a point, but I thought we could learn something from the mistakes of the past.

When I had worked at the solar plant for one year and changed places with other workers, substituted for installers, and learned every aspect of assembling the panels, I was ready to accept an offer to work in the office. I missed my friends at the plant but was anxious to learn about costs and profitability. I kept my girlfriend Aldice.

It didn't take me long to advance in the office. By investing in the company, I could have become one of its vice presidents, but I had other plans. I talked to my dad about starting my own solar panel business. Although it was a competitive market, I felt I could make it. My plan included asking some of my coworkers to join me in my venture. Naturally, I wanted to be the largest shareholder, and for that I needed capital. Dad listened to my plans.

"I have preliminary numbers," I told him. "My only concern, besides financing, is that I would be a competitor to my current employer."

"Call your grandpa, Henrik. He knows more about business than I do," Dad said.

Grandpa had encouraged me to get into the solar panel business and now I could tell him I had followed his advice. The first question that Grandpa Bill posed was, "Have you signed any no-compete papers?"

"No, I haven't signed any papers."

"Then you're free to break out on your own, but it would probably be best to start your company in another town."

"I'll look for a place."

"You do that, and don't say anything to your employer until you're ready. You'll need a business-savvy partner, because you'll probably devote most of your time to technical matters and marketing."

"Yes, could you be that business person, Grandpa?"

"Maybe. Do you have skilled coworkers who're willing to join you?"

"Yes. I think so, although I haven't asked them yet. Could you fly out here and help me get started, Grandpa?"

"I could do that, but first you should find a suitable place."

"I also need capital."

"If I think it's a sound investment, I'll provide the capital, Henrik. But I'll research the solar business to make sure you're not taking on something that will fail." I could depend on Grandpa to give me sound advice.

I didn't say anything to Aldice about my plans. She'd be going back to Denmark in a few months, and I would have no time for women anyhow. I invited four of my most trusted and competent colleagues for an outing on my sailboat where we could talk in private and asked them if they were interested in working for me if I started a new company. I offered them profit sharing and the possibility of becoming partners. They all said they were interested but needed more information.

I used my vacation to scour a wide area for a suitable place for my business. I needed a shop and an office. It had to be accessible to big trucks and have a loading dock, or room to build one. It needed a solid roof for the solar panels that I planned to install. The commute had to be reasonable for my most important partners.

On the outskirts of the city, I found a place with a "For Sale" sign. I called the number listed and a person came and opened the back door with a hidden key. He said the place was in receivership. It was messy inside but had potential. I visited the bank that owned the property and learned the price. Then I called Boston.

"Grandpa, can you come out here? I found a place and it's cheap."

"Alright. I'll come as soon as I can. Meanwhile, you can go to Sacramento and inquire about possible state government incentives.

Then call me again."

"Okay, Grandpa. I have only a week left of my vacation. When are you coming?"

"I don't know yet. I have to book a flight."

I needed someone to go with me to Sacramento, someone older and wiser than me, so I asked Dad. He would be my partner, and as a professor and expert on wind energy, he would have more influence than a kid like me. First, I showed Dad the property and asked what he thought of it.

"I think you've found a good location," Dad said. "But before we buy the property, it has to be inspected. Dad had talked to Grandpa and received instructions. We took photographs and picked up the papers for the property at the bank. I didn't know there were so many hurdles, but with Dad and Grandpa at my side, I felt secure. In a way, I was living Dad's dream to be an entrepreneur.

Our visit to the State House in Sacramento went well. If we had called for an appointment, we might have been able to meet with the governor. California is environment friendly. We could apply for state money in one form or the other and needed to fill out an application, but first we had to incorporate the business. Grandpa had told Dad that a corporation would be an entity that would protect the owners.

I picked up Grandpa at the airport and drove him out to the property. He looked at the grounds first. "We need to go to the courthouse and ask what kind of businesses have been located here in the past. There can't be any problems with toxic waste."

"Dad and I have already been there. There's no problem with contamination. The building has been used for storing lumber."

From my last visit, I knew where the key to the back door was and I had the permission to use it. I unlocked the door and we walked inside. It felt warm and dusty.

"Is this enough room for your plant?" Grandpa asked.

"Yes, it's as large as the plant where I'm working now."

"I suppose you need some sort of an assembly line."

"No, solar panels are made more or less by hand. We just need a few tables to assemble them." I showed him the office that needed a good renovation.

"You should get an estimate on how much it will cost to renovate this place," Grandpa said.

"Yes, I'm assuming it will run into thousands of dollars with furniture and all."

"It will be a small part of your investment."

"The building has a corrugated roof, but as soon as I can afford it, I plan to cover it with solar panels."

Chapter 27

"Well Henrik, it seems to me the price is low enough for you to make the purchase," Grandpa said. "What will you call your business?"

"I thought I would call it Whitmore Solar, Inc., or something like that."

"It's best not to use your family name, Henrik."

"What do you suggest, Grandpa?"

"From looking at the area, I'm inclined to call it Valley Solar, or something like that."

"Good idea. How long can you stay?"

"As long as it takes to make the purchase. We have to negotiate the price, of course."

"Of course." Grandpa would be the negotiator. We drove to my parents' house and continued the discussion. The maid had cooked dinner and served it. Mom didn't come home until later and was glad she didn't have to listen to all the business talk.

Before Grandpa flew back to Boston, he had negotiated a great purchase price, invested in my company, and guaranteed a loan from the bank. We had a preliminary meeting of officers and sent in the application for the incorporation of my company. Grandpa told me how he had started his shipyard with a loan from his father and had made it into a profitable business. I hoped to do the same.

"I might be too busy to sail with you on the new Titanic," I said.

"Well, the ship isn't finished yet and no sailing date has been set, so you might be established by the time it sails."

"Thanks for all your help, Grandpa. Hug Grandma from me."

"Of course, I'm always glad to hug your grandma." I smiled because I knew about their love story that just seemed to go on and on.

Dad said I should quit my job and work full time to get my business established. "You must have college buddies who work with solar energy. Look them up and solicit their help," he said.

When I thought about it, several guys had planned to go into the solar panel business.

I used my private cell phone as I began to call the guys in my graduating class of 2014. Much had happened since then. I had traveled and lived a carefree life until now. As it turned out, three of my college buddies were interested in joining me. Adam had been to the Philippines to see how solar panels were made there. He knew where I could buy the "cooker" that would heat the modules, probably the most expensive equipment I needed. Adam and I, and two more guys from college got together on the sailboat to discuss the business. I took them out to the plant to meet with the men from my former job who would come to work for me. Day laborers had cleaned out the junk, and electricity and water had been connected. On a rickety table in my future office, I rolled out the blueprint I had made. With a few adjustments, everyone approved of my plan.

Dad had called an office design company, and a female representative came out while we were there. I told her how I wanted the office to look, and she promised an estimate in a few days. Of course, I needed at least one other comparable estimate. Dad had some free hours at the university and did much of the calling for me. I still lived at home, but that too would have to change. When I told my parents, I needed to live closer to my workplace, my mom objected. She said I could save money by living at home. She also wanted to make sure I ate properly and got my clothes washed and ironed.

"You should live at home until you have a wife to look after you," she said.

"That might be a very long time," I mumbled. I aimed at having my business operating from the first of the year 2016, and we were only a couple days late. The company sign was up outside the building that had been painted red. The solar panels on the roof produced electricity, and my former colleagues operated the assembling tables. When someone was absent, I gladly took his place. My accountant, a woman named Janice, answered the phone while designing a data system suitable for our company. I bought a delivery truck and applied the company sign to its doors. To attract customers, I had to undersell my competitors, at least in the beginning. Adam and I produced a television commercial that was expensive but paid off when the phones began to ring. I visited all potential customers myself and presented our portfolio. Most of the customers were homeowners who wanted to save energy on keeping their pools warm.

Only a fraction of all solar panels carried a "Made in America" stamp, and they cost more than the imported ones. Still, many Californians preferred the American-made panels. When we mentioned the advantage of the state sponsored rebates and tax deductions, it didn't take long to fill the order book. We delivered the solar panels as soon as they were ready and installed them. In the spring, we couldn't keep up with the orders. I thought about employing more people, but Grandpa advised against it.

"It's more economical to offer the employees overtime. You cannot be sure how long the high demand will last. The competition from China is fierce." I had to listen to Grandpa. He complimented me by saying, "Good job," Henrik. I knew you could do it."

It was the proudest moment in my life so far. But the business climate could change fast, and I didn't take anything for granted. My company could sink as fast as the Titanic.

"How is the new Titanic coming along, Grandpa? I asked.

"I don't know. Haven't seen anything online about it lately."

"Guess we'll have to wait and see."

Janice asked if I didn't want a salary now that the business was doing well. "Yes, Janice, you can put me on salary. Make it the same as Adam's." It was another satisfying moment. In the spring, I hired a gardener to put in a lawn and flowerbeds in front of the office. The result pleased me as I parked my car outside and walked through the doors to my domain.

I had everything I could wish for except a girlfriend. Aldice had moved back to Copenhagen. But there was no shortage of women in California, native born or foreign. Adam and I ran into two of them while jogging in the university area. We went back to the same place almost every evening just to meet them. One of them, Malena, was from Iceland, and she attracted me like a magnet. European women seemed to interest me more than others. Malena looked even more Nordic than my mom and grandmother. Her blonde hair was almost white and definitely not colored. She had bangs reaching to her eyes. Her light eyes were bluer than the sky and deeper than the oceans. I drowned in them. She told me about the geothermal energy in her country that powered a steel mill. Wow! I had to know if she was here on a three-year visa because there was no use spending time with her if she had to go back.

"I have a green card, a real one," she said with a bright smile. "I'm a permanent resident and entitled to citizenship." It was a good start.

"Are you working for a living, Malena?"

"I work in R&D at the electric car plant."

"Wow, you must be highly educated."

"College only, but I had experience working in the geothermal field in Iceland."

She must be older and smarter than me, I thought. When I told her about my business, she said she wanted to see how I made solar panels. It gave me an excuse to take her to my plant and spend a day with her. After that, I didn't want to move away from our common neighborhood. I dated Malena on weekends and worked hard at the plant during the week.

Grandpa and Grandma came from Boston for a visit, and since Grandma was from Sweden, Mom from Norway, and Malena from Iceland, we had a three-woman Nordic assembly at our home. Grandpa came with me to the plant and complimented me on my progress.

"I couldn't have done it without you and my colleagues," I said. "Adam has been especially helpful, but he doesn't have money to invest in my company."

"He could work for "sweat money," which means that you'd deduct a certain amount from his salary every month and apply that to shares."

"Good idea. I'll talk to him about it."

As we drove back home, Grandpa commented on my choice of girlfriend. "Malena seems to be an exceptional girl, and you didn't have to go to Iceland to find her."

"I know, but I still want to go to Iceland and study the geothermal energy they use to power a steel mill. Do you think it's profitable?"

"I don't know, Henrik, but you could find out. It's clean energy. I remember when steel mills polluted the air so we couldn't see driving anywhere close to the mills. I wonder how many people got sick and died from the toxic air and water. Thank God, that has changed. But all it takes is a new administration that removes the regulations."

"We're a lot smarter now," I said.

"I hope you're right, Henrik."

Malena was a modern woman with no reservation about us living together. I moved in with her and she made me happy. My happiness lasted until Malena told me she was returning to Iceland to join her father in the steel mill.

"I'm not coming back," she said, "and I know you wouldn't like living in Iceland."

I was shocked. Everything happened so fast. Malena cancelled her apartment and the next day the movers came and packed up all her furniture and belongings to be shipped to Iceland. I got my stuff together and moved it out before they took that as well. Malena completely disregarded my feelings. She was as cold as the island she came from.

"Good thing we aren't married," she said, and I agreed. The apartment was hers. I had only paid half the rent and helped with our common expenses. There was nothing to settle.

I took my suitcases and checked in at a hotel. In the evenings, I sat in the bar and drank beer until Grandpa came from Boston to give me a lecture.

"I invested in your company and I can't see you ruining it by drinking and neglecting what you have accomplished," he said.

When I didn't answer him, he said, "For now, you're moving in with your parents, so they can keep an eye on you. You must be at work every morning at 8 o'clock, clean-shaven, and looking like the boss you are. There're plenty of other women in the world and they aren't all like Malena. You were smart not to marry her."

"You're right, Grandpa. Easy come, easy go. Next time, I'll be more careful."

"I would like for you to look into buying a house of your own. Your company balance sheet tells me you can afford it."

I realized that my feelings were hurt. I hadn't meant as much to Malena as I thought. I could understand that she wanted to take advantage of the opportunity to be a partner in the steel mill, but I couldn't understand how she could dismiss me that easily. Not even a goodbye kiss or an apology. When Grandpa came and shook me up, my bitterness turned to anger. Damn it, I would buy a house and select the furniture. No more lodging with a woman. My home would be mine and no one was throwing me out of my own house!

Mom suggested I write down what I had experienced in my travels. It would get me to think about something else than my sudden breakup with Malena. She was right. Once I got started, I ended up writing about my life from the time I graduated from college until now and this is it. I still haven't found a wife, but perhaps I will find the right woman when I sail on the Titanic Princess.

Henrik Whitmore

PART II

Chapter 28

Roberto Cosentino, 1888-1920

Boston, July 1925

My beloved Julia,

I know that you don't want to talk about my demise, so I'm writing you this letter. I have bought a family cemetery plot. It will make it easier for you when my time comes. Don't forget that I have life insurance that will secure our son's future. I realize that you are capable of supporting him, but this is what I would like you to do:

Half of it should go to Joshua when he is 21. Take the other part of the life insurance to pay off as much of the mortgage as you like. Then buy shares in the newspaper enterprise that you work for. It will pay you handsomely in the future.

You are too young to remain a widow all your life. If you find a good man to love, I want you to be happy. I know that your future will be secure because you are a good journalist. I admire you, Julia. I love and appreciate you more than ever. I'm sorry I will not be around to help you raise our precious son, but I know you will do a good job. I'm enclosing the papers I mentioned. I'm not saying goodbye because I will see you again. I will talk to Anthony and ask him to notify Mother in Genoa when I'm gone. I have loved sharing my last years with you, my beloved Julia. Love and kisses to our son for me.

In life and death, Your Roberto

Please give the attached letter to Josh when he is older.

Dear son Joshua,

I am your dad, Roberto Cosentino, a Titanic survivor, born in 1888 in Genoa, Italy, where my father was a cabinetmaker. We lived close to the harbor, and I watched the passenger ships coming in with disembarking Americans and Englishmen. Many of them came every year to escape the cold winters up north.

I swam like a fish, and I wasn't more than 14 years old when I got a job as a lifeguard. Being around tourists all the time, I quickly picked up English phrases. I ran errands for the visitors and earned good tips. My older brother taught me to sail a small sailboat, and I began to offer sailing lessons to tourists. I loved being on the water. The rich Americans recognized me as the brown skinned, black haired Italian kid who spoke English. I almost felt like I was their pet.

When I was in my 20s, I became acquainted with Miss Lydia Addison.

"Could you teach me to sail, Roberto?" she asked.

"Yes, of course, Miss Addison," I stammered.

"Good, I'll pay you," she said. It was a huge fringe benefit to have the beautiful Miss in my boat.

By the time she had learned to sail, I was her secret beau, but we both knew it would end when Lydia and her parents moved to the French Riviera. Lydia surprised me when she gave me money for a second-class ticket on the Titanic. We would meet on the ship and sail together to New York. It was a dream-come-true for me, that is, until it turned into a nightmare on that fateful early morning of April 15 outside Newfoundland's coast.

Mrs. Addison's lady's maid, Anna, was injured helping third-class passengers escape, and when Anna, her sister Christina, Lydia, and I finally reached the boat deck, all the lifeboats were in the water. When I couldn't persuade Lydia to jump off the ship with me, I took the leap alone and sank deep down before kicking my way to the surface. Gulp-

ing for air, I saw the forward funnel crushing down on deck. The ship tilted forward and passengers hurled overboard. People bumped like corks in their lifejackets all around me. Others clung desperately to debris from the ship. I suspected that Lydia had plunged into the sea when the funnel came down, and I desperately called her name and looked for her in the water but could not find her. Then I saw Anna and swam to her. She was unconscious but had a heartbeat. My lifeguard experience came to good use as I swam with her to one of the lifeboats that had room for us. Once I had Anna in the boat, I looked back and saw the Titanic already low in the water and leaning forward. The lights were still on. If no ship would come to our rescue, we were all doomed. Having worked on Anna until her heartbeat improved, I began to row. The lifeboat was filled with women and children but had only one crew member. When I saw there was a mast on the bottom of the boat, I located the sail, attached it to the mast, and we made much better time. All the boats headed in the same direction toward a distant light that we assumed came from a ship. When the light disappeared from our sight, we feared we would freeze to death. My clothes were wet, and I didn't think I would survive. Finally, after many hours, a ship once again became visible. The Carpathia *took us on board and headed back to New York. Without the kindness of Captain Rostron, his crew and passengers, all of us would have perished.*

Onboard the Carpathia, *I saw Lydia Addison's name attached to Anna's bed. At that time, I didn't know if Mr. and Mrs. Addison and Lydia had survived, but when they were not on the* Carpathia, *and no other ship had come to the rescue, I feared the worst.*

When Anna woke up from her coma in a New York hospital, it was clear to me that she had lost her memory. If she could continue to be Lydia, I could be her beau. As I had hoped, the Addison lawyer took both of us to the Addison Mansion. When Anna began to show signs of regaining her memory, I left the mansion leaving a note for Anna.

I had a hard time starting over with empty pockets. A fellow passenger on the Titanic helped me find a job as a house painter. Eventually, I supported myself as an interior painter for the Addison Company. My brother Anthony joined me in Boston and gave me a sense of having a family. He was a better painter than I, so I let him have my job. I had begun to write stories for the Italian-language newspaper La Gazetta *and smaller pieces for* Boston Globe *and hoped to become a reporter. I had met and fallen in love with your mother, Julia Nicolo, then a young woman determined to attend college. I promised to write to her, but when I contracted tuberculosis and had to be isolated in a sanatorium, I didn't tell her. As I was released from the sanatorium in 1916, I decided to return home to Genoa to recuperate.*

It was good to be with my family again. I helped my uncle on his fishing boat and breathed in the clean fresh air that was good for my lungs. My papa had made me a beautiful desk, and while we moved it into the house, he suffered a heart attack and later died of a massive coronary.

The war that was supposed to end all wars had begun in Europe in 1914. When Italy declared war on Austria in 1915, my brother Sal, a farmer, was among the first to be called up to serve at the Austrian front. Sometime after I had arrived, I was in danger of being drafted into the Army, so I signed up with the Navy and shipped out on board the hospital ship l'Italia. I did several tours to Gallipoli, where we rescued Allied troops.

While on duty, I had opportunities to rescue drowning people, as was the case when Titanic's sister ship, Britannic, sank. Medals and promotions came my way. I learned the Morse Code in my spare time. Food was scarce among the civilians. While home on leave, I helped my mother the best I could with money and food. Many children died of measles. My older sister lost a child to the disease.

While in uniform, I wrote several articles about the war and mailed them to Boston either to the Globe *or the* Gazetta. *When the war ended in 1918, I decided to return to Boston. I had received a letter from Julia, a reporter for the* Globe. *She wrote that the paper wanted more articles from me about the war. I crated my desk and hired on as the wireless operator on a freighter headed for New York.*

Having arrived in Boston, I visited the Globe *and met with Julia. To my great relief she was still single and happy to see me. Her parents put on a large wedding for us. Julia continued to work part time at the Globe while I worked for the Gazetta. Two years later, she gave birth to you, Josh. I was very happy to have a son. Your mom soon went back to work, and your grandmother helped us take care of you. We moved from the apartment into our own home and looked forward to a secure and happy future.*

Everything went well for us until I once again became ill with tuberculosis. For your sake, I went to a sanatorium to recover because the illness is contagious. It was hard to be away from you, Josh. When your mom came to see me, she said you asked for me all the time. We had been such good pals, you and me, going fishing and swimming together. You will be older when you read this, and I hope you will understand how much I loved you. I wish you a good and healthy life.

Your loving dad,

Roberto Cosentino

Chapter 29

Joshua Cosentino

Boston, December 1986

I am Joshua R. Cosentino, born in 1920, the son of Roberto Cosentino and Julia Nicolo Cosentino. I lost my father when I was 5 years old. Everyone said, "Sorry, you lost your dad," or "Sorry for your loss." It led me to believe that Dad was just lost. I looked for him everywhere and asked Grandma why my dad couldn't find his way home.

"Oh, my dear child," she said, wiping her eyes with her apron. I knew we were Italians and that Dad was born in Italy. "Maybe he went to be with his mom in Italy," I said. All I got from Grandma was more tears and hugs.

Uncle Tony came and took me fishing at the same spot where Dad and I used to fish. When I asked him about my dad, he sat me on his lap and said that Dad had become very ill and died and gone to heaven.

"Don't we always get well when we are sick?" I asked.

"No, everybody does not get well when they are sick."

I knew what it meant to die because I once had a hamster that died and we buried him in the yard. But just when I was going to tell Uncle Tony about my hamster, I had a fish on my hook. Uncle Tony had to help me haul it in because it was huge.

"Here, Dad, can you see how big it is?" I said, holding it up as high as I could for Dad to see it from heaven.

"I'm sure your dad can see that you caught a big one," Uncle Tony said. We laughed together and had a good time. Uncle Tony looked and talked so much like my dad that I was happy again as we carried the fish home to Mom. It didn't occur to me that the fish had to die so we could eat it.

After I started school, the memory of my dad began to fade, but I had a picture of him and looked at it often. My mom worked hard at the newspaper office and tried to be home to pick me up at school. I showed her my school papers, and she said I did good work.

Occasionally, she took me along to her office cubicle, where I sat on the floor and played with cubes that had letters and numbers on them. I put them together to spell my name. Mom said the cubes had been used for headlines. They were black on one side, and my hands got black from touching them.

What I really wanted to do was to learn to type. Mom placed an old typewriter in front of me on the floor and showed me how to press one letter at the time and it would show up on a paper that she inserted. After that, I wanted to spend as much time as possible in her office. At one time, she took me to Dad's newspaper office, the Gazetta, and showed me where he had worked. There, I got to see the pressroom and how the newspapers came out already folded. I told Mom that I wanted to be a reporter. She said that would be fine, but I had to go to college first and learn to write good English.

I knew my dad had been on the Titanic and that he was a hero for having saved a woman's life. My mom showed me the medals Dad had received for saving lives during World War I in Europe. I was proud of my dad. Mom also showed me pictures of the Titanic that she said was the biggest ship built at the time, but that it sank after hitting an iceberg. I asked if it was still dangerous to sail on ships like that, but she said that passenger ships were now safe.

As I grew up and began to shave, the mirror told me that I looked like my dad. I held up his portrait beside the mirror and saw the resemblance. In 1938, I began my studies at Boston College and majored in journalism. My mom had attended the same college and Dad had taught English to foreigners there. I still lived at home.

In 1939, the Second World War began in Europe. My college friends and I listened to the news and had many discussions about why one war always led to another. The United States declared itself neutral. The day I turned 21, I could cash in Dad's life insurance. I wished to travel, but it was 1941 and the war still raged in Europe. The money stayed in my account. After the Japanese bombed Pearl Harbor, America joined the war on the Allied side, and I was in danger of being drafted. I thought of Dad who had fought in World War I in Italy and Uncle Tony who had fought as an American soldier in the trenches of France. My mom said I was her only child and she was scared of losing me.

In World War I, Italy fought on the same side as the United States, but now its leader, Benito Mussolini, joined Germany in trying to take over Europe. News about the war covered the pages of every newspaper. Young men my age volunteered to serve or answered the draft. Since I was still in college, I could get a deferment. Mom was scared I would go and sign up for service like many other young men did without realizing what it meant. But she didn't have to worry because I would not fight against Italy and made sure that I got a deferment.

Mom remembered World War I and all the shortages of food and gasoline. We experienced rationing in the 1940s as well, but the shortages were not nearly as severe here as they were in Europe. At least we could get some gasoline, but it was not a good time to get a car of my own. Mom said I had to wait until the war was over. I could borrow her car when she wasn't using it. I went to dances with my college buddies and had a very good time because we were practically the only men present. Almost all the men our age served overseas or at home bases. Still, the girls seemed to prefer the few military men who were in uniforms.

When I graduated from college in 1942, Mom had arranged for me to be a war correspondent in England, which kept me out of the draft. But sailing to England in the mined waters had its risks. I served as war correspondent in London until the war was over. During that time, I learned a lot about war strategy, life and death. Many of our planes didn't return from their bombing missions. I had to report on the missing men and presumed dead. Dances, drinking, and romancing lightened the severity of the war. When young people don't know if they are going to live the next day, they take liberties and chances. Some couples married in a hurry, and the brides became widows the next day.

In 1940, London had been bombed incessantly. Later, German bombers still got through our air defense, and we had to run to bomb shelters. On one such occasion, I found myself sitting on the floor in a shelter beside a pretty girl. Vanessa was English, and we began to talk. She said she was one of the secretaries on General Eisenhower's staff and was on her way home when the sirens warned of the raid.

"Are you an American?" she asked. I introduced myself just before the "all clear" sounded and we all scrambled to get above ground and I lost her in the shuffle.

At least I knew where she worked. The next afternoon at 5 o'clock, I positioned myself outside the large headquarters of General Eisenhower and waited for the employees to come through the doors. It was like looking for a needle in a haystack. Vanessa spotted me first and I tipped my hat to her.

"Hello," she said. "What are you doing here, Josh?"

"Waiting for you, Vanessa. Would you have a drink with me so we can talk some more?"

She looked at her watch. "I was headed for the tube, but I guess I can spare a little time," she said.

"Good." I took her arm and steered her in the direction of a pub. Many others had the same idea and the pub was crowded. I didn't mind standing close to Vanessa, but perhaps it was too close. The top of her head reached to my eyes, and I could feel the fragrance of her shampoo.

"I don't think we'll get service here," she said. "Let's go outside and you can walk me to the tube instead." She wore a trench coat, same as I. When it began to rain, she unfolded her umbrella. I took it for her and held it above her head.

Chapter 30

"Where do you live?" I asked.

"Between here and Manchester."

"Are there any pubs in your area?"

"Yes, of course."

"Do you mind if I ride with you then?"

"No, I don't mind, but the tube is crowded at this time of the day. We might not get seats."

She was right about that. It felt good to get off at Vanessa's stop and walk on streets that were not crowded with people. She took me to a quiet pub, where I hung up our coats and promptly got a secluded table. Vanessa looked a little tired, but her blue eyes brightened after she had consumed a pint of ale. We talked about the war, my job and hers.

"How long are you here for, Josh?"

"For the duration of the war."

"Where are you from?"

"Boston. I write for a paper in Boston."

She looked at her watch and said, "My parents are expecting me. We usually have dinner at this time."

"I'm sorry to take up your time. May I walk you home?" When she agreed, I asked her if she would have dinner with me on Saturday night.

"I don't normally go into London on weekends," she said.

"I could meet you here."

"That would be fine." We agreed on a time. She said she knew of a place where we could eat and dance.

"This is where I live," she said, stopping outside a two-story home. "You can pick me up here." I memorized the house number and kissed her on the cheek. In wartime, people meet under the most unusual circumstances, and I didn't think my dates with Vanessa would amount to more than a fling.

One day, I received a letter from Mom saying her publisher had proposed to her and they planned to marry. It was a big surprise to me, but I looked at it as a second chance for Mom. She had been a widow for a long time, and now that I had moved away from home, she must be lonely. The publisher had lost his wife. They were both in their 50s. I wrote to Mom and wished her the best. At the end of my letter, I mentioned that I had met an English girl.

I liked Vanessa's family although they were not at all like my Italian relatives. The English people were more reserved and didn't all talk at the same time. They were formal. We always had tea together in the afternoon. In time, I learned to like tea.

They talked about the sinking of the Lusitania during World War I, which led me to talk about the Titanic and my father who was a Titanic survivor. I told them he had been in Italy during World War I and served on a hospital ship. "My dad wouldn't have liked that Mussolini sided with Hitler," I said. Vanessa's father said England had lost a lot of soldiers in World War I.

"And England is losing many young men as we speak," I said.

"How come you're not a soldier, Josh?" he asked.

"I'm serving my country as a war correspondent," I said. "My family is in the newspaper business and I'm a journalist."

The food shortages in England were getting more severe as the war went on. We ate a lot of spam. Tea became scarce. I asked Mom to send me tea and coffee and she did. I gave the tea to Vanessa's family and kept the coffee for myself.

Vanessa and I fell in love. I asked her if it mattered to her that I was Italian. She said it made no difference to her because she thought of me as American. She said her family was originally from the Netherlands. I accompanied her to their Episcopal church.

While listening to Prime Minister Churchill, I learned that the Allied forces were making progress, and the Axis countries would be defeated. Finally, there was hope for peace. General Patton's forces made inroads in Germany but with great sacrifices. Our allies, the Russians, conquered Berlin. Hitler committed suicide.

In May of 1945, the war in Europe was over, and I would be going home. Vanessa and I were married in the Episcopal church, and I brought my war bride with me to Boston. Mom had moved into her new home with the publisher but kept her house for me. I assumed my role as editor and eventually became the publisher. We acquired more newspapers, and the corporation promoted me to chief executive officer.

Vanessa gave me two wonderful children, a boy and a girl. I raised both Ronald and Rachel for careers in the family newspaper business. As a family, we flew to London many times to visit Vanessa's parents. We went across the channel to France and Germany and saw the devastation caused by our extensive bombing.

Later, we lived through the Vietnam War and all the unrest it caused. It seemed like every generation had a war to fight. Our young president John F. Kennedy launched space exploration. The first astronauts walked on the moon. What used to be science fiction happened in our time.

In 1962, fifty years had passed since the sinking of the Titanic, and the world remembered it with new books and a movie. Molly

Brown, the woman from Denver, who encouraged other women in their lifeboat to row, became famous. She was married to a gold miner but traveled alone. Her husband had built her a mansion in Denver, while he lived up in the Rockies. We read about the manager of the White Star Line, Bruce Ismay, who had saved himself by stepping into a boat and suffered from guilt the rest of his life. It seemed there had been a race to get to New York in record time. The inquiry into the Titanic accident criticized Captain Lord of the *Californian* for not coming to the rescue of the passengers and crew on the Titanic.

Vanessa and I took Mom to see the first movie about the Titanic in 1962. Mom cried when she saw the people in the lifeboats. The *Globe* republished the story of Dad pushing the cot with the comatose Anna, saying that she was Miss Lydia Addison. Our connection to the Titanic was strong.

My mom died in 1975. She had enjoyed a remarkable career and was one of the few women of her time to amass a fortune. I was her only heir. When our children had left the nest, my wife worked at one of our smaller papers, heading the food section.

After my retirement in 1985, we traveled and marveled at the progress that Europe had made since the war. Our European tour included Belfast, Ireland, the birthplace of the Titanic. In Italy, we visited Genoa where Dad was born and met with our cousins. I recognized Dad's description of the city. From there, we went to Tuscany where Mom's father had his roots. We went to Rome and Venice. Dad had been to Venice while serving on the hospital ship. On another trip, we flew to India and saw the Taj Mahal. Over the years, we went to most of the famous landmarks in the world, the Pyramids in Egypt, the Great Barrier Reefs in Australia, the Great Wall in China, and the Inca ruins in Peru. In the United States, we visited Niagara Falls and the Grand Canyon.

In 1986, Dr. Ballard discovered the wreck of the Titanic on the ocean floor. Looking at the pictures of the wreck gave me chills. I saw suitcases and gloves that had survived and recalled my dad's suitcase that was lost but later found.

The advances in technology have changed the world. We have established a station in space, and shuttles go back and forth with supplies and astronauts. Fax machines spit out news releases and correspondence. Computers are making an inroad. I hope I will be around to see what new inventions the next generation will benefit from.

I have enjoyed reflecting on my life.

Joshua Cosentino

Chapter 31

Ronald J. Cosentino

Boston, December 2000

I am Ronald J. Cosentino, born in 1947, the eldest child of Joshua and Vanessa Cosentino. I have a sister, Rachel, two years my junior. My dad inherited a large part of a newspaper enterprise and raised me to continue in the business. As a child, I listened to my parents talking about the news in the U.S. and the world. I was only 6 years old when the Korean conflict ended, but the Vietnam War that began in 1954 still raged when I reached military age. My grandfather and father had both worked as war correspondents when they were young, and my father expected me to do the same. Being in Saigon when it fell into enemy hands in 1975, I reported on the panic that ensued when we evacuated American soldiers and our allies in South Vietnam. American ships in the area picked up the locals who fought for their lives in small boats.

As I was ready to board a plane back to the U.S., I heard a familiar child's voice.

"Wait for me Ron," it said. I turned around and saw my little friend Binh, a young Vietnamese boy, who had helped me to gather news and warned me of enemy fire. I scooped him up and told the officer stationed below the steps to the plane that the boy was with me. Binh was dirty and smelled bad, but I couldn't leave him behind. He had no family. As far as I knew, he had lived on the streets of Saigon for several years, scavenging for food, or stealing it until he came under my protection.

"What's your last name, Binh?" I asked when we were seated on the plane.

He thought about it a long time. Then he said Pham. He probably picked a name from someone he knew.

"How old are you?"

"I'm not sure, but I could be 10," he said with a grin.

He had four new well-developed teeth in his upper jaw, so he could be right.

"When is your birthday?"

"Birthday?"

"When were you born? In which month and on what date?"

"How'd I know?"

"Your parents would've told you."

"I don't have any parents."

"Everybody has parents."

"Not me."

"All right. How about if I give you my birthday, only the year will be different. Then we can celebrate on the same day with birthday cake."

"Sounds good to me."

"Life will be different when you come to the States," I told him. "You can't steal and cuss, and you have to keep yourself clean."

"How am I going to do that?"

"You'll see. You'll also have to go to school and learn to write English, do math, study history, and geography, and all that good stuff."

His eyes became twice as large as usual. He wasn't malnourished because I and other American soldiers had given him food, but he ate everything with his fingers.

"You'll have to learn to eat with a knife and fork."

"I have a knife," he said.

"I know you have a knife, but in the States, you won't have to use it to defend yourself. You can't threaten anyone with it either."

After all that talk, Binh fell asleep and slept all the way to Los Angeles.

I had to stay in California until Binh was cleared to come with me to Boston. He shadowed me everywhere as I pleaded his case.

"He's an orphan," I said, "and he was my informer in Saigon. I can't leave him behind."

"Are you willing to take him into foster care?" I promised I would arrange for his foster care. If not with me, with someone else.

A hot shower, a haircut, and American clothes that fit him made him look clean and descent, but it would take a while before I had cleaned up his foul language. It was not his fault that he spoke like a sailor. He didn't know that many of the words he had learned from American soldiers were swearwords. We went through them one by one. Still, they would slip out until he corrected himself.

"You have to give me other words instead, Ron," he said. It was a struggle, but his language gradually improved.

Back home in Boston, I introduced Binh to my parents. I had taught him to shake hands, say hello, and look people in the eye. He wouldn't sleep in his soft bed unless we moved it into my room. I pulled up his covers and said good night. I still had nightmares of the war, and when I thrashed in bed and talked in my sleep, Binh, said, "It's okay Ron. You're not in the war anymore. You're safe." He didn't touch me because he knew I would have hit him in my sleep. In the morning, he was asleep on the floor by my bed. His table manners were deplorable. Mom worked with him, showing him how to use our silverware and a napkin.

Dad wanted me to go back to work, but I wasn't ready. Both Binh and I suffered from post-war traumatic stress disorder, but I believe Binh got over it before I did. Mom suggested that I take some time off and visit her relatives in England.

"I can't leave Binh," I said. "He still depends on me."

"We'll enroll him in school, and he'll get new friends," Mom said.

I waited until Binh had gone to school a couple weeks and had adjusted to his new environment. Then I told him I had to leave.

"My parents will take good care of you. Promise me that you'll be a good boy and do what they tell you. You can't steal pens or anything else from your classmates, and you can't take things in the stores without paying. My parents will give you a little money every week."

"I promise," he said. He was a smart boy. His teacher said he learned fast, but sometimes he forgot to give back a pen or a crayon that he had borrowed. He already had a best friend, another Vietnamese boy, who had arrived with the boat people. My parents would be responsible for Binh, at least for now. I promised to write to him.

"But then you have to learn to read what I write," I said. He promised that, too. He cried when I left.

I had visited England several times with my mother and sometimes with both of my parents. I knew how to use the public transportation and took the tube to the town where my grandparents lived. They were expecting me.

"Welcome, Ronnie," Granny said, answering the doorbell. Her hair was grayer and she wore glasses that sat low on her nose.

"Just in time for afternoon tea," she said.

I put down the suitcase and delivered my message from my parents first.

"Mom and Dad sent hugs and kisses, and here they are," I said, as I bent down and hugged and kissed Granny before stepping farther into the hallway. Gramps emerged from the living room, with a pipe in his hand. "Good to see you, my boy," he roared in his deep voice as we shook hands. We used to be the same height, but now his posture made him look shorter. He worked for a building contractor, and I could picture him lifting heavy loads.

"Come on in, Ronnie, and make yourself comfortable. I'll take your suitcase upstairs." Before I could stop him, he was on his way up the stairs carrying my suitcase.

"You'll have your usual room, Ronnie," Granny said. "We're glad you came to keep us company for a while. As soon as you've washed up, we're having tea in the dining room."

I entered the small, familiar lavatory in the hallway, where there was hardly room to turn around, and looked at my face in the small mirror. I had inherited features from both my father and my English mother. My stubble and eyebrows darkened my fair skin. I combed my dark hair, but the shave would have to wait. Afternoon tea in England was more important. I could smell Granny's freshly-made scones that would still be warm. The butter would melt on top before I put the jam on. My mouth already watered.

Granny served tea from her brown porcelain teapot, the one I remembered from years back. The coziness of it all made me relax. No one was in a hurry to go to work or anywhere else. The phone didn't ring. We talked and talked. I told the story about Binh.

"You've done a good deed for that boy," Gramps said.

"I hope he'll live a happy life," I said. I showed them a picture of him that I had in my wallet. He stood on the doorstep with his schoolbag ready to go to school.

"He looks like a fine boy," Granny said.

We talked about the war. "It seems like it was all for nothing," Gramps said. "Vietnam will be unified again under the communist regime."

"I would rather not talk about it," I said. "I need to forget."

We took walks and I noticed the changes in the neighborhood. I saw many new homes and businesses. We attended the church where my parents had been married. Everything was peaceful. My nightmares were not as bad. I read books that made me want to write books myself. Having bought a pack of postcards, I sent one every day to Binh. I printed the text in bold caps and hoped he'd be able to read the words. I got a postcard from him that he clearly had written himself and it made me proud. Mom wrote that Binh was doing fine. It put my concerns for him to rest. I could go on with my life. Having received an inheritance from my grandmother Julia, I intended to spend it and began by booking an airline ticket to Italy.

Chapter 32

First, I flew to Genoa and walked in Grandpa Roberto's footsteps. I recognized the beautiful waterfront and everything else he had described in his writings. He died when my father was a little boy. Thinking that we might still have relatives in town, I looked in the phonebook for my family name, but couldn't find it. I recalled that Roberto had many sisters, and they had probably married and changed names. Why didn't I ask my father for names and addresses?

Having explored the city, its old churches and museums, I took a cruise to Venice. On the ship, I danced with several women. Most of them were American and Northern European. I decided to stay in Italy until I had learned to communicate. My nanny and gardener had taught me a few Italian phrases that I loved to use, but I didn't understand the language. We passed Sicily and rounded the 'heel of the boot' to the south. I sent postcards to Binh along the way. After I disembarked in Venice, I stayed there a week before I headed to Rome. I had the itch to write again and thought I could do it there.

Having arrived in Rome, I rented a small apartment and bought an Olivetti typewriter and typing paper. While sightseeing during the day, I thought about what to write. When I dropped in at a casual eating place, I met some interesting people—American men who had settled down with Italian women and American women who were cohabitating with Italian men. I noticed a substantial homosexual community of mixed nationalities, but mostly Americans, who preferred partners of their own sex. They drank grappa or cava before, with, and after their meals. I'm sure that some of them also used drugs. What they did for a living was more difficult to discern. During these late nights, I picked up many Italian phrases. I loved Italian food. My parents used to have an Italian cook and I recognized all the entries on the menus in the restaurants.

Wanting to learn more, I went to a "library" that was actually a store filled with used books for sale. I bought a language course on cassettes that came with a textbook. The attractive young woman who sold it to me asked me where I was from. When I told her, she said her father had lived in America for several years before returning to Rome.

"Where did he live?" I asked just to make conversation.

"In Boston."

"That's where I'm from." We spoke English. She didn't know where in Boston he had lived, but it was still something that linked us together. I decided to return to the store and make more purchases.

Every morning, I listened to the cassettes and followed along in the text. Eventually, some of it stuck in my brain. I loved the lingo. Almost every word ended in a vowel. It sounded like opera without the music.

I typed out stories and mailed them to my father. If he liked any of them, he could print them in one of his newspapers. My first stories described the cruise and my visit to the Vatican. It was all clean family reading. If I were to write about the people I had met, it would have to be a novel. I could start it and see if I could finish it. Rolling a new sheet into my typewriter, I wrote, "My Life in Rome," on the first page. I planned to write a chapter each day about what I saw and heard. For more inspiration, I went back to the bookstore. But behind the counter stood a man, not the attractive woman. I browsed the shelves, looking for titles in English. Finally, I asked the clerk.

"*Scusami.*" He went behind the curtain into another room. Then out came the woman I had met earlier appeared.

"Hello," she said in English. "You're back. How can I help you, sir?"

"Do you have any books in English?"

"Yes, they are over here. Not very many, but we have Ernest Hemmingway and a few English classics." I enjoyed looking at her as she walked ahead of me and stretched to take down some of the books.

"I'm Ron Cosentino," I said.

"Oh, you have an Italian family name, but you don't look Italian."

"My mother is English, and people say I look like her, but my grandfather was from Genoa."

"My name is Barbara Marino," she said, stretching out her hand. I took it and squeezed it.

"Pleasure to see you again, Signora Marino." I looked at the books and said that I definitely would like to buy a Hemmingway book. "Are they also available in Italian?" I asked.

"Certainly."

"Then I would like to buy one of each."

"Over here, sir." She walked ahead of me to the Italian section for English authors.

I bought *The Old Man and the Sea* in both languages and planned to compare the texts.

"You've been most kind and helpful, Barbara. May I buy you a cup of coffee to show my appreciation?"

"It would have to be after hours. I work until 4 o'clock."

"Then I'll meet you here at that time."

I wondered if she was unattached. Having located a café with red-checkered tablecloths, I returned to the library.

"Hello again, Signora Marino. Are you ready to go?"

"Yes." Barbara wore a pretty dress. She had let her hair down and it hung freely on her shoulders. I cupped her elbow and escorted her to the café.

"Is this place okay, Signora Marino?"

"Yes, but please call me Barbara."

"If you call me Ron."

I told her I had come from England where I had tea and scones with my grandparents in the afternoon. "I like the custom. Do you prefer tea, Barbara?"

"Actually, I do prefer tea, but sometimes I drink coffee."

"Then we'll both have tea."

I ordered tea and scones that were called Scone fritto in Italian.

"How long are you staying in Rome?" Barbara asked.

"I don't know. I have started a book. Maybe until it's finished."

"Oh, you're an author."

"I'm a journalist, but this will be my first book, if it ever gets finished."

"I write children's stories."

"Oh, really. Have you had any published?"

"Yes, I have. I'm also an illustrator."

"Wonderful," I said. She was creative and I liked that. "Where did you learn to speak English?"

"At the American School in Bern, Switzerland. When I graduated, I said my goal in life was to be an author. I have accomplished that goal, but I can't live on it yet. That's why I work at the book store."

I enjoyed our tea and conversation and I tried to stretch it out as long as possible, but she said she had to go.

"May I escort you to where you're going?"

"I'm taking the bus."

"All right. Then perhaps I can walk you to the bus?"

"Certainly."

"May I call on you again, Barbara?"

"You'll find me at the store most of the time."

"Thanks. Hope to see you again." I waved to her as she entered the bus. She seemed to be a descent girl, and I hadn't had a girlfriend for a long time. I could use my imagination to make her the heroine of my book. I went home and typed several pages describing Barbara as a hot brunette with luring brown eyes, a chest that invited touches, swaying hips, and shapely legs. But a man also had to eat. I loved Italian food and had a favorite restaurant where I wouldn't risk running into any of the American expats. Italians ate dinner late, usually not before 9 o'clock at night.

I couldn't make a go of the novel because I didn't have enough material yet. Thinking that it wasn't right to exploit Barbara, I crumbled up the last sheet I had typed and threw it in the wastebasket. On the other hand, I had enough memories from the war to write several books if I stopped suppressing the sights that swirled in my head. Writing them down might put them to rest. I rolled a blank sheet into my typewriter and typed, "My Life in Vietnam."

I worked furiously for hours. Once I had started, I couldn't stop until my stomach growled for food. After I had been to a restaurant to eat, I bought groceries. I would make my own tea and eat sandwiches, fruit, and raw carrots at home. I would get more writing done that way. I recalled that some 58,000 members of the U.S. forces had died in the Vietnam War. It was a small number compared to the more than 200,000 South Vietnamese soldiers who had died.

The nightmares returned, but they reminded me of what had happened. I didn't have to search my mind for words. I wrote about Binh and Saigon, the missions that I had gone on while riding with the soldiers—about Agent Orange, death and destruction but also about the local women who satisfied our lust in return for bread and a better future. I hoped I would get it all out of my system by writing about it. My beard grew long. If I had run into Barbara, she wouldn't have recognized me.

Chapter 33

I ran out of typing paper and bought more. The finished pages piled up, and I didn't take the time to reread them. My landlady must have wondered about all the clicking noise from my Olivetti, but she didn't say anything. My back and neck stiffened up. I stretched my body to get rid of the kinks in my back. When that didn't work, I jogged in the hilly neighborhood while thinking about what to write next. The roses bloomed, welled over fences, and climbed up walls. At night, I thought about what I had written. I lost track of the time until I realized that winter approached. What should I do with my manuscript? Perhaps I ought to explore the possibility of publication before I invested more time and work on writing. I made photocopies of what I had written so far and sent them to another former Vietnam-War correspondent, Joe Brown, at my newspaper office. Perhaps he could tell me whether it was worth publishing. Having sent it off, I took a break and cleaned up. My shower stall was a simple attachment to the outside back wall of my apartment. The surrounding walls reached only to my shoulders. It was cold but refreshing.

I went to the bookstore to see if Barbara was still there. She was.

"I didn't think you were still in town," she said.

"I'm sorry, but I've been busy writing. If you'd have tea with me, I'll tell you about it."

She was a good listener. I had been shut in with my writing and needed to talk to someone. I told Barbara about my subject and that

I had been a correspondent in Vietnam.

"I think I have found my calling," I said.

"Do you like it here in Rome?" she asked.

"It gives me enough solitude to write," I said.

"How is your language class going?"

"Haven't had time to listen to the tapes lately, but I'll start again while I'm waiting to hear from the editor in Boston."

"Perhaps I could help you."

"Would you really? That would be wonderful."

"The language recorded on the tape is old-fashioned and not used anymore."

"Is that right?" I was surprised but it made sense. The course was written a long time ago. I cleaned up my apartment and invited Barbara to come and tutor me.

Instead of long, tiring sentences that were difficult to remember, she taught me short conversational ones. Then I took her out to dinner. We continued my lessons until I got a letter from the editor, who had read my manuscript.

"This is damn good, Ron," he wrote, "but it needs editing. You have been in a hurry writing."

I hadn't taken the time to polish my sentences. Having read his comments, I called him from a telephone office. Letters took too long. I asked him if he could do the editing for me if I paid him.

"Yes," he said. "It will be nonfiction and probably a best seller. There's very little literature about the Vietnam War. It seems like we're ashamed of it."

"I agree."

"Your father is wondering when you're coming back. Your sister Rachel is taking your place in the family dynasty."

"She's probably better suited for corporate life than I am."

"She has met a newspaper man and is going steady."

"Oh, I didn't know that. Say hello to everyone. Please return the edited pages, so I can retype them. If you need to reach me you can send a telegram." I gave Joe Brown my address and hung up.

Feeling elated, I just had to tell Barbara the good news. It was just a matter of time before we ended up in bed, and that night it happened. She was as starved for love and affection as I was.

The day my manuscript came back from the editor, I returned to my Olivetti to retype it. Again, my dark beard grew long. One day, Barbara knocked on my door.

"I just wanted to check to see if you're alright," she said.

"I'm alright, just busy. I'm so sorry I haven't contacted you. As soon as I'm done with the retyping, we can see each other again."

"It's okay, because I'm also writing." She had created a longing in me by just standing outside my door, so I couldn't let her leave.

"Now that you are here, please come in. I can make some tea, but you've to excuse the mess. There are papers everywhere."

We sat on my bed and drank tea. What happened next was inevitable.

"You give me creative energy, Barb," I said. "My nightmares are not as bad as before."

"Glad to hear it. What are you going to do when your book is finished?"

"I might go to Boston to see if I can get it published, but I'll come back here. I think this is where I belong. My sister can take over my responsibilities at the company. It will be the first time a female is at the helm, but that's okay with me. Women are climbing the corporate ladders. I don't have to feel guilty about relinquishing my duties as the only son."

"How is Binh doing?" I had told her about him.

"I have neglected Binh, but I just received a postcard from him the other day. His writing is much improved, but he is waiting for me to return. I was like a father to him over in Nam."

"How long will it take for you to retype your book?"

"It won't take long, but then the last part has to be edited in Boston. My guess is that it will be ready in the spring."

"Would you like to meet my family, Ron?"

"Yes, of course. What's your father doing for a living?"

"He manufactures yogurt and his business is quite profitable."

As we began to tell each other stories about our families, it felt like our relationship turned into a commitment. Barbara suggested that I spend Christmas with her and her family, and I thought it was only fair, so I said, "I'd love to."

I finished the retyping and began to write the finishing chapters. Would I have more books in me after this one? Perhaps I could write about the Titanic and my grandfather's heroic rescue of Anna. I sent my retyped pages along with the rest of the manuscript to Boston before Christmas and another package with Christmas gifts to my family. I thought for a long time about what to give Binh, and finally decided to buy a souvenir crucifix from the Vatican.

Christmas at Barbara's home reminded me of the Christmases I had heard about in the Nicolo family a long time ago. Barbara was one of five children, and most of them were married with children of their own. Barbara was the last single sibling. I felt the pressure, but I was not a good candidate as Barbara's husband, only a fledging author with no income other than from my family trust.

While I waited for the last chapters, I picked up where I had left off on "My Life in Rome," and wrote more about Barbara except I changed her name. The story began to sound like a wonderful future for me in Rome.

Spring had sprung and it was warm. The cherry trees bloomed. The Italians called them *sakura*. On that positive note, I wrote post-cards home to Boston and my grandparents in London. I said good-bye to Barbara and gave her the key to my apartment so she could use it while I was in Boston.

Binh jumped into my arms as soon as I got inside the door, and I caught him. He had grown, looked and acted completely civilized.

"I sleep in your room," he said, "but you can have it back now."

"How is school?" I asked.

"It's okay, I guess."

"What subjects do you like best?"

"Drawing and painting. I'll show you." He ran to his room and came back with his sketch book. He had covered page after page with art in vibrant colors.

"These are good, Binh. You have talent. If you continue to practice you might become an illustrator."

"What's an illustrator Ron?"

"They do the artwork for children's books, for one thing. You know that children's books wouldn't be very interesting without pictures."

"Yes, that's true."

I was thinking he could draw pictures of what he had seen in Vietnam and I could use them for my book, but he didn't need to be reminded of all that.

My parents and I had long discussions about the family business. Dad wanted to retire. Rachel was engaged to a Dutch man. If I didn't claim my post as head of the company, there might be a Dutch name at the helm.

I told Dad I would like to return to Rome and continue writing. "If I can make a go of it, I'll be glad to relinquish my role in the company."

"Well, you take your time, son, and we'll see what happens. I'm not retiring yet, but we'll need children to take over in the future. I have no grandchildren yet to bequest to when I die."

"You are not dying for a long time, Dad."

I met with Joe Brown as soon as he had read my last chapters.

"I think you should contact a publisher in New York," he said. "It's best that you go there yourself."

"Alright, but if it becomes a book, I'll use a pseudonym and not my own name."

"Do you have any pictures from Vietnam?"

"I have lots of pictures."

"Bring them with you to New York."

I went to my room, found the pictures in a shoebox, and sat down to look at them. Each one brought back both bad and good memories. I stuffed the photos in a large envelope and put it in my briefcase.

Chapter 34

I had four publishing houses on my list, and at the first one, I didn't get past the front desk.

"Sorry, we're not accepting unsolicited manuscripts at this time."

I could check that one off my list. At the next one, I got to see a man in the manuscript division. He looked at my business card before he spoke.

"You're a newspaperman, Mr. Cosentino."

"Yes, my family has been in the newspaper business for three generations. I was a war correspondent in Saigon, and I have a non-fiction manuscript, "My Life in Vietnam.""

"It's good that you have written it down while your memories are fresh, but unfortunately I don't think it's a timely subject. We lost that war and people resent it, but in a few years, it will be history. Keep the manuscript until then. Do you have something else, Mr. Cosentino?" I was shocked at how fast he had dismissed my most important work.

"Well, eh, I have lived in Rome and I've started a manuscript that I call "My Life in Rome," but it's not finished."

"Go ahead and finish it, Mr. Cosentino. It might be of interest to us, but we have a big "slush pile" of manuscripts, so write to us first. Submit a synopsis with a letter telling us why we should publish it."

Could it be true that people weren't interested in reading about the war in Vietnam? We wrote about it in the newspapers for years and people bought the papers. I wasn't giving up until I had visited the other two addresses on my list. It was lunchtime, and I bought a hot dog from a vendor on the street and then headed to yet another publishing house.

It was another rejection.

The fourth and last one was my only hope. It was getting late in the afternoon. There was no one at the front desk to stop me. In the hallway, I ran into a man who looked important.

"Sir, I'm a newspaperman from Boston."

"We don't give interviews to reporters."

"I'm not asking for one. My name is Ronald Cosentino, and I was a correspondent in Saigon. I have written about my life in Vietnam."

He interrupted me. "That's interesting. Follow me, Mr. Cosentino."

"Tell me what your manuscript is about in as few sentences as possible."

With no time to waste, I began telling him about Binh.

"That's a human-interest story among all the devastation. Tell me more."

I spoke for five more minutes before he said, "We've been looking for something like that. Do you have any pictures to go with your story, Mr. Cosentino?"

"Yes, sir." I dove into my briefcase and handed him the envelope. He browsed through the images, and asked, "Do you have the manuscript with you and is it finished?"

"Yes, and it's edited by someone else except for the last chapters." I had my hand on the heavy manuscript in the briefcase and put it on my lap.

"May I see it?"

"Of course. It's the original, but I've made copies." He read the first page and looked up at me.

"You obviously know how to write since you're a reporter, but I always want to see if the beginning is captivating enough. I believe yours is."

"Do you think people will be interested in reading it?"

"About 60,000 Americans died in that war. Many of their relatives will read a book like this to try to justify their sacrifices. I'll take it home with me today to take a closer look. Will you be here tomorrow?"

"Yes, I'm staying overnight."

"My name is Williams. Come back in the morning and ask for me."

I thanked him and left with hopes of having found a publisher for my book. In the evening, I walked the city streets and imagined what it would be like living in New York as a successful author. The reporter in me always hunted for stories, but I tried to ignore any ideas that I came across. Instead, I wrote a letter to Barbara telling her about my day.

My meeting with Mr. Williams the next morning went well.

"I liked what I read last night. Of course, someone else will have to read it and decide. If we are interested in publishing your work, you'll need to make yourself available here in New York for discussing editorial changes or additions. Can you do that?"

"For how long?"

"That's to be determined."

"Well, I was going to return to Rome, but it can wait."

"Do you live in Rome?" He sounded surprised.

"Yes, I took time off to write this book in Italy and to recover from my post-war traumatic stress disorder. But my home is in Boston."

"We'll contact you in Boston. You have to be available if we are to pursue publication."

"I understand, sir." We shook hands and I thanked him for his interest.

I fully intended to return to Rome to finish my manuscript, "My Life in Rome," but I didn't know when that would be. I had brought the manuscript with me and could work on it in Boston for the time being. When I received a telephone call to my hotel room from Mr. Williams, I was ready for whatever he had to tell me. I listened intently as he spoke.

"Mr. Cosentino. I have good news. We have decided to go ahead with your manuscript, but we will make some editorial changes as we always do. You'll be working with Miss Benson. I have set up an appointment for you to meet with her. She has read your entire manuscript."

I took the train to New York and went to Miss Benson's office expecting a mature female, and was delightfully surprised to meet a young, attractive woman. When she stood up to greet me, I saw I had the advantage in height, but she definitely had the advantage in looks. Dressed conservatively in a suit, she wore a white blouse with the top buttons open showing her olive skin. Her black shiny hair hung straight to her ears except for bangs in the front. She looked at me with dark, slightly slanted eyes and smiled prettily.

Chapter 35

"First of all, Mr. Cosentino, I suggest that we use our first names. Mine is Anita. May I call you Ron?"

"Certainly."

"It's easier to communicate that way. I have read your manuscript, Ron, and most of it is fine. However, there are sentences that need clarification. This is very common. I also have some suggestions about moving paragraphs. Does that sound reasonable to you?"

"Whatever you say, Anita." I was ready to cave before this beautiful creature.

"Then we have to discuss the photographs. Can you identify them?"

"Some people I can identify. The rest are mainly for illustrations."

"Good. I have edited some of the text and suggested changes. I'll give you copies of the pages that I've edited so you can either approve or disapprove of them. Then we can meet again tomorrow morning at 9 o'clock. Is that okay with you?"

"Yes, Anita, that will be fine."

While reading her suggested changes, I knew she had misunderstood certain things. She had no war experience and couldn't possibly know what it was like. As carefully as I could, I wrote my clarifications on the reverse side of the sheet or in the margin. It was something we'd have to discuss.

As I leaned into her and pointed to the places in question, I got close enough to smell her loveliness. Our hands touched. I noticed her manicured nails and her rings, none of which appeared to be an engagement or wedding ring.

It took days to work out our differences, but I didn't mind. When we came to the pictures, we needed more time to write the captions. I had to think about what the images portrayed, and sometimes it took a while for me to remember.

When we were finally done, I asked if she would have dinner with me.

"Normally, I don't agree to dinner dates with my clients, but I guess it would be alright."

We met at the restaurant. Sitting with me at the table, she asked me questions about my family and life in Boston because she said she had to write a bio about me.

"What are you doing when you're not here in New York, Ron?"

"After the war, I lived in Rome for almost a year. That's where I wrote the book about Vietnam. Before the war, I was a news editor in Boston."

"Did you like Rome?"

"It's amazing how different it is outside the Vatican, for one thing."

"Do you have any family connection with Italy?"

"Yes." I went on to tell her about my grandfather Roberto and the Titanic story.

"That's fascinating. Have you ever thought about writing a book about that?"

"Only briefly."

Anita told me something I didn't know. "For the 50th anniversary of the sinking, a book was published, titled *A Night to Remember*. The author had interviewed survivors, and the book was tremendously successful. I think it stirred up the interest for more of that epic story."

"I'll think about it," I said.

"Have you written anything else?"

"Other than newspaper articles, I've started a book about my life in Rome."

"I think that would be interesting."

"I'm working on it."

"Do you have pictures for that one, too?"

"I have some, but I might have to go back for more."

The server came with our meals and interrupted our conversation. I thought about what my next question would be.

"Will I get royalties when my book is published?"

"It's not my job to write your contract, but I know that royalties depend on how many copies are sold. You'll likely get a certain advance when you sell your book to us. A literary agent could negotiate things like that for you."

"How do I get an agent?"

"I can give you some names. Then you can decide which one you want to work with."

"I didn't know I needed an agent."

"Not necessarily, but it would be useful. Then when the book is published, you have to be prepared to go on a book tour and promote your book. Our company will pay for that."

"It doesn't sound like I can go back to my regular work for a long time."

"Being an author is a full-time job whether you're successful or not."

After our dinner, I put Anita in a taxicab. Besides having had the pleasure of taking my beautiful editor to dinner, I had learned some useful things.

I met with the two New York literary agents and selected a Korean war veteran, who had attended college after his service. He told me he would negotiate my advance and royalty. We would keep in touch on the phone. For now, I could return to Boston.

I wrote a letter to Barbara and told her I had to stay in Boston for the foreseeable future. I had never told her that I loved her and had no promises to keep. The only thing I had left behind in my apartment was my typewriter and she could keep it. Lastly, I wished her success in her own writing. When I tried to get back to "My Life in Rome," I had lost interest in it. It might make a good novella but not a book.

My sister Rachel announced that she would marry her Dutch man, a newspaperman who was anxious to take on a major role at one of our newspapers. Rachel held the title of corporate secretary and she'd likely continue in that capacity. Knowing that I was going on a book tour, I couldn't very well take on a steady job at our company. I substituted as copy editor for a while, but what I really wanted to do was write and not to read and edit what other people had written.

I went to the library and borrowed as many books as I could about the Titanic, including Walter Lloyd's *A Night to Remember*. I read that one first and decided that if Mr. Lloyd could interview survivors, I could do the same. Some of them must still be living. I would just pick different ones to talk to, preferably third-class immigrant passengers, and find out how they had fared after the terrible tragedy. Whether I would write my next book as nonfiction, creative nonfiction, or historical fiction, I didn't know. I began by researching the *Globe* from the time after the sinking.

While in New York, I researched the *New York Times* that had much information about survivors. Perhaps, I could follow up on their stories. I imagined that many suffered from nightmares, something I would understand. Once I found out where the survivors had settled down, I could search the local press at the state historical societies. It meant traveling, but my cash advance would more than cover the expenses. Anita reminded me that I had to be available for a book tour. Perhaps I could do research at the same time. I began to write at my old newspaper office.

Binh kept asking me when the book about Saigon would come out. He was anxious to read it, he said.

"Is your reading that good?" I asked.

"Yes, I read books all the time."

"But are they books for adults?"

"Some are, and others are for teens. I know that I'm supposed to read books for children, but they are boring. I have lived a different life than my classmates."

"I know you have."

"What are you doing now, Ron?"

"I'm researching people who survived the Titanic to see where they came from and where they settled down."

"Could you research my family to see where I come from, who my parents are, and what happened to them?"

"It would be much harder, Binh. You have changed your date of birth. You don't know your parents' names."

"But there must be people in Saigon who know those things."

"Those people might be in America now, or they could be dead, Binh."

"But still there should be someone somewhere who would know."

"Aren't you happy here Binh? Why do you want to dig in the past?"

"I am happy here, it's just that sometimes I wonder who I really am."

"I can understand that. When my book comes out, the people who read it might recognize you and come forward with information."

"I hope so, Ron. I'm glad you wrote about me."

"Now, go outside and play."

Chapter 36

Anita called and said she was sending me the first proofs. "Read it carefully and make necessary corrections. You know how to do it. Then mail the packet back to me. Normally, we do three galley proofs."

"Would the process go faster if I came to New York?" I asked.

"It would go faster because shipping takes time."

"Then I'll come down on the train tomorrow."

"See you then."

It was an excuse to see Anita again. I missed her. As I entered her office, she seemed glad to see me. I took the packet of galleys and went to my hotel to read them. As expected, the typesetters had made mistakes. I was finished just before 5 o'clock and placed a call to Anita.

"I'm done and I don't have anything else to do tonight. Is there a chance that you would go out with me?"

"Where to?"

"If you like, we could go see a Broadway show. Have you seen *Guys and Dolls* yet?"

"No, I haven't, but I would need to go home first and change."

"Would that be too much of an imposition? I don't know where you live."

"I live close to work, so it won't take long."

"If you give me your address, I'll pick you up in a cab."

At first, I didn't recognize her. "Ron, here I am," she said, waving to me as the cab waited by the curb. She wore a red sleeveless dress, high heels, and carried a small purse. I got out of the cab and offered her my hand.

"You look beautiful tonight," I said. "I already have the tickets to *Guys and Dolls.*"

"That's wonderful."

We both enjoyed the musical about the con man, the gambler, and the uptight Evangelist missionary woman. The gambler falls in love with the missionary and the scene changes from Times Square to the dance clubs of Havana, and back to the sewers of New York. When our cab stopped outside Anita's apartment house, I told her I would drop off the manuscript at her desk in the morning.

"Tomorrow is my day off," she said. It was an unexpected opening for me to ask her for another date. "Do you have any special plans?"

"I do not."

"Do you want to spend the day with me? I'm free tomorrow."

"If you take me to Chinatown, I will," she said. She explained that she had lived in New York for a whole year and had yet to see Chinatown.

We agreed that I would pick her up the next morning after I had delivered my manuscript to the publisher's office. Anita let loose and we had fun together, darting in and out of stores and teahouses. I had brought my camera and snapped pictures of her standing on the sidewalk. The Chinatown in Manhattan, population 100,000, was actually the smallest of three in New York. We saw the greengrocers and fishmongers on Mulberry Street, the jewelers on Canal Street, and the vendors selling perfumes, watches, and handbags at "knock-off" prices. For those who were interested, the negotiations continued in private. Anita looked at handbags, but said she wasn't good at bargaining. I thought about doing the bargaining for her but feared the merchant dealt with illegal goods. We ate scallion pancakes and wonton soup at one of 300 restaurants. Anita confided in me that she had a bit of Chinese blood in her veins.

"Oh, that's the reason for your beautiful slanted eyes," I said. "Do you feel a connection to Chinatown?"

"I was curious about it, but now I think I'm satisfied."

"It was the same for me in Italy."

"Do you think you'll continue as a book editor, Anita?"

"No, I'm waiting for something better. The rent is high and my pay is low."

"Maybe you could come and be an editor at one of our newspapers in Boston?"

"Do you really think so?" She looked up at me with heightened interest.

"I should have some influence in hiring."

"I might take you up on that, Ron." She invited me for tea in her apartment and I accepted. I respected her too much to make any advances. I didn't even kiss her on the cheek.

Having undergone three rounds of editing, the manuscript was ready for the print setters that would make final proofs. Anita and I celebrated by going to a fine restaurant. I lingered in the city and spent more time with Anita until I had a sample book in my hand with one of my pictures from Vietnam on the cover and a fictitious author's name. I felt like the book was my baby. "We have given birth to this baby, you and I," I told Anita.

"I've heard other authors say the same, but it's your baby, Ron, not mine."

I returned home, where a letter was waiting for me from Barbara.

She wrote:

Dear Ron,

I have met someone else. You don't have to come to Rome on my account. If you don't have any objections, I'll cancel your apartment because I am moving at the end of the month. Hope that the publication of your book is going well. I just had another children's book published. Barbara

In a way, I was relieved. No longer did I have to feel guilty about abandoning my former girlfriend and wrote back.

Dear Barbara,

I wish you a good life. I have also met someone else. My book, "My Life in Vietnam," will be published shortly. You can cancel my apartment and keep my typewriter. It doesn't look like I'll be returning to Italy. Ron"

The bicentennial celebrations in 1976 awakened Americans' awareness of their heritage. Before that, everything had been about the present time. No longer did we have to hide our ethnic roots. It was all right to be Italian or Irish, two folk groups that had experienced much discrimination. How the blacks came to America as slaves was now open to discussion. Alex Haley's book, *Roots*, probably had something to with it.

The talk about the Great War with its restrictions of foreign languages and anything German abated. World War II with its detaining of innocent Japanese people, who were citizens of our country, came out in the open. The movies depicted how important we Americans were when we finally joined the war on the Allied side. Japan was growing in importance as an economic power. The latest immigrants to our shores were Koreans and Vietnamese, refugees from war-torn countries.

My book was published in 1976, at a time when Americans wanted to feel good about themselves, so it might not have been the best timing to remind them of the Vietnam War. The publisher scheduled me for book signings at book stores and libraries, a totally new experience for me. I met many Vietnam veterans, who told me they were glad I had written the book, but few veterans could afford to buy it. Some came to my signings in shabby clothes looking unkempt. Those without jobs and money said they would borrow my book at the library using someone else's library card. The families of American soldiers killed in the war showed me pictures of dead and missing soldiers and asked me if I had met their son or husband in Saigon. I wish I had. They were more interested in talking with me than buying the book. I also received letters, and I appreciated the attention. One letter had Binh's name on it, and I gave the letter to him.

"This might be what you have been looking for," I said. "It has an American postage stamp." I saw how anxious he was when he opened it. He read it quickly.

"The letter says that my mother is alive. I want her to come over here," he said in a high-pitched voice. It was going to take some time to get that accomplished.

The publisher sent me on book tours in the eastern part of the country where many Titanic survivors had settled. I did some research but it was harder than I thought to find out where they lived, and those I found were not willing to talk to me about their experiences.

When a position as editor at one of our newspapers became available, I offered it to Anita. She said she would take the train to Boston and apply. I met her at the train station and took her to a hotel. I asked her if her family objected to her moving to Boston.

"I don't have a family," she said. "I became an orphan at the age of 12 when both my parents were killed in an automobile accident. My aunt and uncle raised me, but they are also dead." Anita had no one to keep her in New York. She was an orphan like Binh. She got the job and I found her an apartment. Feeling responsible for her move, I did my best to see that she liked it in Boston, but it might have been selfish on my part. Our friendship grew into love. I felt strongly that she was the woman I wanted to be my wife.

Binh and Anita got along well, and Binh spent as much time with her and me as with my parents. I arranged for Binh's mother to come to Boston, but she was ill when she arrived. The little woman suffered the effects of Agent Orange that we had sprayed in the jungle where she had been hiding. Binh's last name really was Pham and his age not far from his assumed one. His eyes lit up when his mother showed him a document listing his name. He could not read Vietnamese, but I arranged to have it translated. When we learned that it was his birth certificate, he jumped up and down expressing his joy.

"Now, I can become an American citizen," he said.

"I think you'll have to wait until you're 21," I told him, "but the certificate will be a good paper to have when you apply to college. Let's put it in a lockbox."

Binh's mother passed away a short time later. He felt bad about it but said he was thankful for their time together. "Now, I know who I am," he said.

I continued my research for my Titanic book for a while but abandoned it when I realized I could earn much more money as the CEO of our company than from writing books. Anita and I were married in 1980 after a long courtship, and I wanted to provide her and our future children with a stable income. Our son Sean was born in 1982, our daughter Michelle in 1985, Caroline in 1992, and Lauren in 1997 in my 50th year. Binh grew up, graduated from college, moved to New York, and became an illustrator.

We can now read our newspapers on the computer, and I wonder how long we will continue to deliver them. Emails are replacing the fax machines as a way of communicating. Our daughters study computer programming.

Chapter 37

Sean's Story

Our son Sean is no longer with us to tell his story. We raised him for a career in the newspaper business, but he rebelled and enrolled at West Point. He said he wanted to be a soldier and not a journalist who wrote about them. We felt immense pride as we attended our son's graduation but worried that he would be deployed to serve in Afghanistan. For the time being, he continued with his training to achieve his goal of becoming a ranger. It was during that time that he met his future wife, Jenna, the sister of another soldier. In 2009, when our country added thousands of troops to the war effort in Afghanistan, Sean declared that he was eager to be able to use his training in the war. He proposed to Jenna the night before he left for Afghanistan and gave her a ring. Not long after that, Jenna discovered she was pregnant. I called Sean and told him he had to come home and marry her. When that didn't happen before the birth of their child, we invited Jenna to come and live with us. Her parents were not thrilled about her situation and blamed our son. Anita and I were happy to welcome our first grandchild Justin, but we were even happier when Sean came home on leave to marry Jenna. As soon as he had bought a house for his little family, he had to take off again. We were all sad to see him leave so soon.

He carried his phone and had access to the internet. He and Jenna communicated on Skype. His first email to us said it was 128 degrees when he landed at the Kandahar Airfield in impenetrable dust and heat that felt like stepping into a furnace. Centuries ago, Kandahar had been a stop on the Silk Road between Europe and China. It sounded so romantic and I couldn't help smiling when I thought about it.

Sean was stationed in Gardez in southern Afghanistan. In one of his emails, he wrote that his unit had set up base in a medieval fort with dirt walls. Another email described the unbelievable dust the troops had to live with.

"We go on patrol in our Humvees, always watching out for possible enemies. It's hard to tell who they are because they could be hiding among the locals. We inhale the ever-present dust. It's on the pads I write on, on our clothes, on our eyelashes, in our noses. We sneeze and cough. Our throats dry up. We drink gallons and gallons of water. The roads can hardly be called roads. Most of them are one continuous track of potholes. Americans have built a good road between Kandahar and Kabul, and we traveled on one stretch of it when we went to Ghazni to visit the governor. While there, we enjoyed a few days of luxurious accommodations, but that was the only time so far."

Sean also wrote about the fighting and how it affected him, but I doubt he gave Jenna any of the gruesome details.

"We have had our first KIA (killed in action). It happened when the enemy ambushed our patrolling platoon. I had just talked to the soldier who was fatally shot. What a devastating experience. It should have been me. I was his captain, and I should have protected him. This is war. It hurts in your heart and in your guts. With all my training, nothing had prepared me for this. I cried. Perhaps it was better than trying to control my emotions. The soldiers put the dead man's helmet, boots, and gun on display at camp as a grim reminder. I saw the tears of the brave soldiers. We were not yet hardened by the war. I couldn't write about it until now."

That was the last email we received from Sean. The next time there was an ambush, it was his misfortune to be killed. The officer who delivered the shocking message said this about our son: "Captain Sean R. Cosentino showed extraordinary bravery as he risked his own life protecting his men. You can be very proud of him."

Yes, we were proud but devastated. Jenna collapsed on the floor, screaming, "no, no." Their life together had lasted only a few weeks. "It's not fair," she said, over and over again. Anita was devastated about the death of our firstborn but tried to remain strong for all of us. She and I, and our daughters accompanied Jenna to Arlington National Memorial Cemetery in Washington for the burial. We stood there with heavy hearts almost unable to comprehend what had happened.

Somehow, life went on. Anita consoled herself by taking care of Justin as much as Jenna would allow while they both mourned. I had my job that demanded my attention. Jenna didn't want to live alone in her house, and she and Justin moved in with us. Our grandson reminded us of Sean when he was a child. Justin, of course, didn't understand anything about what had happened. He distracted us with his smiles and childish play, and for his sake we put on our happy faces. Thanks to Justin, we overcame our deepest sorrow although we will always miss Sean.

Ronald J. Cosentino

Chapter 38

Caroline L. Cosentino

Boston, May 2016

I'm Caroline Lynn Cosentino, the third child and second daughter of Ron and Anita Cosentino. My brother Sean and sister Michelle were never interested in working in the family business. Then when Michelle had chosen her career as a teacher and Sean had chosen the military, Dad turned to me and expressed his hope that I would continue in his footsteps. I kept it in mind as I chose to study business.

In 2012, while I was still in college, 20 schoolchildren were gunned down by a lone gunman at Sandy Hook Elementary School in Connecticut. It drastically changed my outlook on life. If children couldn't be safe in our schools, how could we be sure that any one of us would be safe as we went about our daily chores. Michelle said she did everything she could to keep her students safe but worried it wouldn't be enough. Dad often spoke of another tragedy, the Titanic sinking, when more than a thousand passengers and crew perished on its maiden voyage. My great-grandfather was on the ship but saved himself by jumping into the water.

A few months after the Sandy Hook shooting, the Boston Marathon bombing on April 15, 2013 hit close to home. Several of the students at my college and at Dad's company took part in the race. Dad and I and many others were there to cheer them on. There was no room for us at the finish line, so we stood about 100 yards away when we heard the explosion.

"What happened?" I screamed. People pushed and shoved in all directions. The racers continued to run. It was organized chaos. "Did anyone get hurt?" No one knew. We hoped the runners were safe.

"Go home," the police said. "The best you can do is to leave this area."

We used our cell phones to try to get news about what had happened. "There has been a terrorist attack," someone said, waving his phone. "A bomb has exploded and there might be more. We have to get out of here." Dad grabbed my arm and we ran toward the parking lot. I shook uncontrollably and cried. Dad put one arm around me as we tried to find a path to his car. We were stuck in traffic for hours as everyone tried to leave at the same time. We didn't find out what had happened until we got home. Many bystanders had been injured. Later, we learned that the final count was five dead and 280 injured. One of the two bombers had been killed; the other fled but was later found and arrested.

Dad and I both knew we could have been victims. It was just luck that we were not at the finish line. We held each other as we watched the scenes over and over on television. I was thankful not to be alone but worried about those who had taken part in the race. Our cell phones rang constantly. Michelle called first. "Thank God you're safe," she said.

The television continued to broadcast the tragedy. At my college, it was all everyone talked about. My fellow students and those from the company who had participated in the race were physically okay. Some said they would never run the marathon again while others said we couldn't let fear run our lives.

Following my graduation from college in 2014, I joined my father's business as secretary-treasurer. Aunt Rachel had paved the way for me by being the corporate secretary. I had the additional responsibility of being Corporate Financial Officer, which meant a lot of accounting work, including payroll. Thankfully, the computers had relieved us of keeping the handwritten ledgers used in the past. I quickly got to know all the employees as they came to my office to turn in time cards or report changes in their tax status. Some took out more sick days than others. Not surprisingly, it was the women with children. I talked to my dad about opening a daycare facility at work, and he agreed. I found a suitable area and outfitted it for its new purpose. It was costly, but I think it paid off. Not many employers offered the same benefit, and we were able to keep the women we had trained.

The day came when I needed an assistant. Several applicants answered our ad in our papers, and I interviewed a few of them. One of them was a Certified Public Accountant, a handsome man with black hair and a close-trimmed beard. I chose him among several applicants. I watched him discretely as he took over both Accounts Receivable and Payable. One Friday afternoon, he asked if he could take me out to dinner.

"Thanks for asking, Harold, but I don't date employees," I said. "Besides, I'm seeing someone."

"Oh, you are. That's good because you are too young and pretty to be alone on a weekend."

"You don't have to worry about that," I said, as I grabbed my purse and walked out of the building. I could feel his eyes on my back. Had I brushed him off too quickly? I thought of what my weekend would be like. Craig would come to my apartment at 6 p.m. We'd go to our usual place for dinner and be home by 8 p.m., have a drink in front of the television, and watch a movie. Then we'd yawn and go to bed just like a married couple. No excitement there. Craig was a banker whom I had met in our business dealings. It wasn't much different than dating an employee. He had mentioned marriage once, but I didn't want to commit. I couldn't imagine living with him every day. As it was, we knew what to expect of each other.

I realized I wanted a change, any change. One day, I surprised Craig by saying I would be busy for a couple of weekends. He said it would suit him fine because then he could go to the ballgames. I think we both realized that we needed a break from each other.

Mom and my sisters joined me on a shopping trip, and we had fun trying on clothes and comparing looks. I thought about how Mom always invited Craig to come with me to the dinners and birthday parties at their house, but it sounded like she had given up on asking me if we were ever going to get married. When asked, I usually referred to Michelle as being older than me and not married. It was her turn, I said. She didn't even have a steady boyfriend like I had. Steady, yes, but perhaps too steady with no change whatsoever.

As it turned out, Craig used his free weekend differently than I had expected. One day in the middle of the afternoon he called and asked if I wanted to have coffee with him downtown. I said yes because I planned to use the opportunity to break up with him, but as it turned out, I didn't have to since he broke up with me first.

"I have met someone else," he said.

"That's great."

"And here I have been worried about hurting you."

"No, you are not hurting me at all. It saved me from breaking up with you," I said, as I left without drinking my coffee.

Feeling free and light as a bird, I went back to my office to finish the work I had left undone. Harold was there. On a whim, I told him my boyfriend and I had parted ways.

"Sorry, but you don't look sad at all," he said.

"No, actually I'm relieved."

"Do you want to go out and celebrate? We don't have to call it a date."

"Yes, I'll be glad to go out and celebrate with you."

"What do you want to do?"

"I think I feel like dancing."

"I know a bar with music where we can dance."

I took extra care to get ready, blowing my long blonde hair and trying on different outfits. Happily, I slipped into my red cocktail dress and a pair of high heels.

"You look fantastic," Harold said. It was good to hear a compliment. I really enjoyed myself. Harold was a good dancer. He even sang along with the lyrics or hummed as we danced cheek to cheek. When the band stopped, he went up to the stage and said something to the bandleader, who then announced, "We have a request for *Sweet Caroline* by Neil Diamond."

Harold smiled as he spread out his arms inviting me to join him on the dance floor. His dark blue eyes looked mischievous. We swayed to the music and held each other close. Harold sang the chorus, "Swe-e-e-t Caroline." It was heavenly, but I was afraid of where it might lead. Dad wouldn't approve of me dating an employee.

We sat and talked at a table while sipping our drinks. I think I found out more about Harold that night than I ever knew about Craig. In return, I told him about my family, even Sean's tragic death. When I mentioned my dad's fascination with the Titanic, he wanted to know more. We realized how late it was when the band stopped playing.

"How did you get here?" he asked.

"I came on the bus, but I'll call a cab," I said, as I fingered my cell phone.

"I'll flag one down for you." He waited by my side and said goodbye as I sat down in the cab.

"Thanks for tonight. See you at work," he said.

"I enjoyed it. See you at the office."

"*Sweet Caroline*" played in my head all weekend. I wasn't supposed to date an employee, but what would happen if Harold and I fell in love? We tried to avoid each other at the office, but it was not always possible as we had to discuss our work.

"This is going to be hard," Harold said.

"Yes, I know."

I had never felt this way for Craig. The next day, I had big news for Mom and my sisters as we had lunch together.

"You broke up with Craig!" Mom exclaimed.

"Actually, he broke up with me, but I was going to do it the first chance I got."

"It's about time you two made a decision one way or the other," Michelle said.

"Don't tell Dad, but I went out with a new employee last night and had the best time." Mom and my sisters showed their surprise by putting down their forks.

"Don't look at me like I've done something wrong. We were just going out to celebrate my breakup. We're not dating."

"From the sparkle in your eyes, I think it was more than a casual evening," Mom said.

"Well, we did enjoy our evening together," I admitted.

"You should know that your dad dated me while I was an employee."

We all laughed at the thought. I had already planned to use that argument for dating Harold, but it was too late because Harold had begun to date a former college flame.

The first time I heard that a replica of the Titanic was going to be built was in 2013. An Australian billionaire said he was going to make it happen. He would place it in passenger traffic but first there would be a maiden voyage. Dad said people were already booking tickets. He talked about it so often that we began to believe it. I mentioned it to Harold, and he said he hoped the ship would stay afloat. A lot of people were skeptical.

I don't know what the future has in store for me, but for now I'm focusing on sailing on the Titanic Princess when it's ready for its maiden voyage in a couple years. It will be my first trip abroad. Perhaps I'll meet someone new.

Caroline L. Cosentino

PART III

Chapter 39

The Maiden Voyage from Jiangsu, China, to Dubai

May 10, 2018

Bill, Stella and their grandsons Henrik and Michael, all members of the Whitmore clan, held first-class tickets to sail on the Titanic Princess on its maiden voyage from Jiangsu, China, to Dubai. The 27-year-old bachelor Henrik owned a business. His younger brother Michael had recently graduated from college. Bill, having reached the age of 80, would not pass up the opportunity to sail on the new ship. His wife, Stella, looked forward to the voyage, especially since their son, David, would serve as the chief officer.

Unknown to the Whitmore family, Ronald and Anita Cosentino stood on the pier ready to board the ship along with their daughters Caroline and Lauren. Ronald had recently retired as head of the Cosentino newspaper business and could well afford to travel first-class with his family. Miss Caroline, 26, took after her English grandmother with her light skin and blonde locks. The shorter Miss Lauren, 22, had inherited her mother's black hair and slightly slanted eyes. Both girls were striking beauties. Pleasant surprises awaited the two families. The first one materialized in the shape of Binh Pham, now in his 50s.

"Hi Ron, good to see you."

"Binh! Surprised to see you here."

"I'm in third class, but I hope to see you on board."

"You shouldn't have to travel in third, Binh. I'll try to upgrade you."

"Second class will be fine if you can do it, Ron."

"You'll have to go to third class first and then move from there. Good to see you, man."

At boarding, an officer greeted Ron with a cheerful, "Welcome on board, Mr. Cosentino."

"Would it be possible to upgrade a passenger from third class to second?" Ron asked. "His name is Binh Pham." Ron spelled Binh's name.

"The ship is fully booked, sir, but if someone has cancelled in the last minute there might be an upgrade available. I'll make a note of it, sir, and we'll contact you on your cell phone. We have your number."

The Whitmore and Cosentino families sat on opposite sides of the table at their first meal on the ship. Stella admired the plates with the wide, blue rim encircling the Blue Star Line logo in the center. She and Anita wore hats.

Bill began the introductions. "I'm Bill Whitmore," he said.

"I'm Ronald Cosentino. Are you by any chance a descendant of Anna and John Whitmore?"

"I am. They were my grandparents. Could you be a descendant of Roberto Cosentino?"

"Roberto was my grandfather."

"What a coincidence." Bill adjusted his eyeglasses and introduced his wife and grandsons. Ron followed his example by introducing his wife and daughters.

"It's the second nice surprise of the day," Anita said.

Henrik bowed to the ladies and let his eyes rest a little longer on Caroline as he decided that she was his type of a woman. Michael settled his eyes on Lauren and unabashedly kept them there.

"We have to get together and reminisce," Bill said.

"I'd like that," Ron replied.

Everyone eagerly awaited the first taste of a Titanic meal. Two hours later they rose from the table. Ron's cell phone pinged announcing a text. He excused himself, saying, "I have to read this."

"It's one thing we can do now that is different from 1912," Bill said with a chuckle. Ron's text said that Binh Pham could move to second class if Mr. Cosentino would pay the difference in price.

"I certainly will," Ron texted. "Take Mr. Pham to his room and charge the difference in price to my credit card."

"Credit cards, that's another thing different from 1912," Anita said smiling.

Ron and Bill met in the first-class u-shaped men's smoking room, now a social room for both men and women. The two men walked up to a square table surrounded by four comfortable easy chairs.

"Since I'm the eldest, I suggest we do away with the formalities. We don't have to follow the customs of more than one hundred years ago," Bill said.

"I totally agree, Bill." Ron offered his hand for a shake. Bill's suit coat covered a bulging middle while Ron looked thin in both body and face. His dark hair showed gray at the temples and a receding hairline. Bill had a bald spot on top of his head and his remaining hair was totally gray.

The two men looked around the elaborately decorated room with its mahogany wood panels and inlaid mother-of-pearl patterns, the illuminated stained-glass windows, and the large fireplace.

"It's a beautiful ship, don't you think, Ron?" Bill said, as he sat down in one of the comfortable chairs. "Although it's small compared to today's cruise ships."

Ron selected a chair opposite Bill. "I agree with you Bill, but when

I saw it from the pier, long and sleek, I thought it was beautiful compared to the tall cruise ships." Ron gestured with his hand above his head.

"I agree. It's almost unbelievable that we're on a replica of the Titanic. I can imagine our ancestors walking up the gangplank," Bill said. "My grandmother, Anna, traveled in second class, but she worked as a lady's maid for a family in first class, so she was just as much up here."

"My grandfather, Roberto, also traveled in second class, but was invited to first to have lunch and tea."

"No women could enter this room. I suppose it was filled with cigar smoke and card-playing men," Bill said, with a laugh. "Do you smoke Ron?"

"No, I don't. Do you, Bill?"

"No, I gave that up years ago, but we could have a drink, if you like," he said, pointing to the small bar.

"We should probably wait until the women have joined us." Ron looked toward the door to see if they were coming. "You and I are the ones who know the most about our ancestors," he said.

"Yes, we're the link between the older and younger generation. I have a copy of my grandmother's family tree and the diary she kept on the Titanic. I remember her and my grandfather, John."

"I don't' remember my grandfather because he died long before I was born. My father was only 5 years old at the time and he can barely remember him."

"I didn't know that," Bill said. "Roberto saved my grandmother's life."

"That's true. He was trained as a lifeguard and saved many lives."

"What did your grandmother do after she was widowed?"

"Julia was a newspaper reporter and became chief editor and part-owner by marrying the publisher. We've been in the same business for years."

"Interesting. In our family, we didn't stay with architecture and real estate," Bill said.

"My eldest son, Will, became a professor, and my grandson Henrik, who is here with us, started a solar panel business and is doing well."

When Stella and Anita arrived together, their husbands stood up and offered them the two empty chairs at their table.

"What do you want to drink?" Bill asked. They all agreed on Manhattans. After the drinks had been served, the conversation became livelier.

"I found my wife in Sweden, and I consider myself very lucky," Bill said, looking at Stella and sipping his drink. "Our son, Will, found his wife in Australia, but she was actually from Norway."

"And I found my wife in New York," Ron said with a broad smile, "but my father found his in England."

They were interrupted when the young people, Henrik and Michael, Caroline and Lauren, entered the room. "It looks like my grandsons have found your daughters," Bill said.

"Take this table here next to us before someone else comes," he said to them. Henrik and Michael didn't waste any time offering two chairs to the young ladies and then sat down themselves. Henrik sported a short beard.

"You have young daughters, Ron," Bill commented.

"Yes, I know. I was almost 50 when my youngest was born. My wife, of course, is younger than me."

Stella and Anita were already calling each other by first names. Stella had the distinctive Grace Kelly look with a broad face, high cheekbones and forehead.

"Stella is a former librarian, and I'm a former editor," said Anita. "We have the love of books in common, and we both gave birth to four children."

Turning to Ron, Bill asked, "So you do have other children?"

Clearing his throat, Ron said, "Our eldest, our son Sean, was killed in Afghanistan."

Bill dropped his head. "Sorry, to hear that. He was your only son."

"Yes, and he was married and fathered a son before he died. We are happy to have an 8-year-old grandson. Our next oldest is Michelle, and she's a teacher."

"Were you in the military, like your son?" Bill asked.

"I was a war correspondent in Vietnam, stationed in Saigon."

"Ron wrote a book called, "My Life in Vietnam," Anita added.

"I remember that book," Bill said, "but I don't recall that the author's name was Cosentino."

"No, he used a pen name."

"I read the book and found it both enlightening and interesting."

"Ron brought an orphan boy home with him," Anita said. "His name is Binh Pham and he is also on board."

"My parents raised him," Ron said, "He's an illustrator."

"Stella, if I may call you that?" Ron began.

"Yes, I wish you would."

"The boys here are your grandsons. There is a whole generation missing."

Speaking with a slight accent, Stella began:

"Yes, our son Will and his Norwegian wife live in San Francisco. Will is in charge of Henrik's solar panel business until Henrik returns. Our daughter Lisa is married to a Swedish professor, and they live in Sweden. David is a naval officer and chief officer on this ship. We'll meet him tonight." Stella's lips clamped as she continued. "We lost our youngest the day he was born. He had a birth defect. It might have had something to do with the pollution of the 70s, and the DDT that was used at the time."

"I'm sorry to hear that," Ron said, bowing his head.

"We had an unfortunate death in the family earlier than that," Bill said. "My younger brother Norman flew bombing raids over Vietnam, crashed, and was killed."

"Both of our families have been affected by wars," Ron commented.

"Our son David graduated from the Naval Academy. He has served as captain on other ships, but on this ship, he's second in command." Now, you can see why we didn't want to miss this voyage." The pride in Bill's voice was unmistakable.

"Amazing," Anita exclaimed. "It's an honor to sail with you."

"David brought his son, Matthew, so we have three grandsons on board," Bill added.

Michael didn't hear that piece of news because he looked up and saw that the ship was moving.

"May I be excused? I want to go up on deck," he said.

They were all up on deck watching as the ship blew its whistle and slowly left the harbor guided by towboats. The temperature was 68 degrees and sunny. The Blue Star Line had wisely planned to start the voyage before the monsoon season began in June. A big crowd had gathered to see the departure. Hundreds of reporters from all over the world aimed their cameras at the ship. Ron's phone pinged. Having taken the message, he hastily told Anita that he would go and meet Binh in second class.

"It was nice to chat with you all. See you tonight," he said.

Chapter 40

Binh opened the door for Ron with a big grin on his face, and the two men hugged.

"Thanks for getting me this fine abode. A Chinese man will be my roommate, but he's not here now. Please come in." Binh gestured to Ron to sit down on the sofa bed upholstered in a green-patterned material. Binh remained standing leaning against the two bunk beds. A carpet in brown and gold colors covered the floor. Wisdom marked Binh's face, but he was small in stature.

"How have you been, buddy?" Ron asked.

"I went to Saigon before I came here. It was renamed Ho Chi Minh City in 1975, but most people including the city officials still call it Saigon. It's now a modern city of 10 million people with no signs of the war we experienced. People seemed to be happy. I met a former friend of mine. We used to pilfer food together to survive. He's now a police officer and a communist. He said he didn't like America for abandoning them. I have pictures to show you, but it can wait until Anita can see them at the same time. I'm so thankful for what you and Anita did for me and also your parents. Without you I might be a communist."

"If so, you'd have been a fine communist, Binh. How's your family?"

"My wife and I broke up, got divorced. I seldom see my son. I used to pay for him, but now he's grown." Binh walked back and forth in the small cabin while talking.

"How's your work?"

"Not bad, I've taken up photography to supplement my income, but everything is expensive in New York. I saved every cent to be able to fly to Saigon and then to come here and go on this voyage."

"You could have saved some money by boarding in Singapore."

"I know, but since I was on this side of the world, I wanted to see Hong Kong and Shanghai."

"Have you thought about moving back to Boston?"

"I have, but then I would never see my son."

"I understand."

"I don't think I could have met up with you if I had been in third class."

"Oh, they can't be that strict now, but I was glad to help you with the upgrade."

"It means the world to me to be able to see you again, Ron. We went through some tough times together in Saigon, you and I."

"We sure did." They talked about it for a while before Ron looked at his watch, saying, "I'm sorry, but I have to go back to Anita. Do you have a cell phone, Binh?"

"Yes, I hope it's working." While pressing buttons and seeing the screen light up, he gave Ron his number. "Let's keep in touch on the ship," he said.

Anita was in their parlor suite as Ron entered. "Have you seen Caroline and Lauren?" he asked.

"No, I haven't. I've been resting. The girls are probably enjoying themselves with Bill's grandsons."

"I talked with Binh. He just came from Saigon. Sounds like the city is unrecognizable."

"I'm sure it has changed for the better. I'm glad you could upgrade Binh."

"So am I. Perhaps, we can bring him to the Veranda Café for tea."

"Let's do that tomorrow. I have to get ready for dinner."

The girls came back to the suite and began to tell their parents how much fun they were having with the Whitmore boys.

"You can hardly call Henrik a boy," Ron said, "He's a successful businessman."

"Alright, then we'll call them the Whitmore brothers," Caroline said. "They'll escort us to dinner tonight."

"I'm impressed," Anita said, "But now you should take a look at your clothes and decide which dress you want to wear tonight."

"Do you really have to wear a different dress every evening?" Ron asked.

"Yes, but we're not wearing any hats like Mom is."

"Hats are coming into fashion again, and so are long gloves," Anita said.

"I'm going for a walk on the promenade deck while you women change," Ron said. He met Bill up on deck and they talked while walking back and forth.

"I understand this ship has a welded hull rather than the riveted one on the first Titanic," Bill said.

"Yes, the welded hull should be much safer. The ship also has stabilizers so we won't feel the rolling of the sea as much."

"Perhaps I should get a shave in the barbershop," Bill said rubbing his chin.

"We could both do that now." The two men went to the barbershop, leaned back and got ready for the hot-towel treatment.

"It's too bad that the stubble will grow back in a few hours. The women's hairdos are good for at least another day," Ron said. "Anita has gone to much trouble to find dresses for herself and Lauren that look old fashioned but beautiful. It's easier for us men. The black tails look almost the same now as in 1912, only the shirts are less restrictive around the neck."

"Women used to wear corsets that clinched their waist. That must have been torture," Bill said with a laugh.

When Ron returned to the suite, Anita and the girls were already in their gowns, and a hairdresser stood ready to brush and pin their hair in 1912 style.

"I'll go to the dressing room and change," Ron said.

The hairdresser departed as the Whitmore brothers came for the girls. Henrik and the fresh-faced Michael linked arms with Caroline and Lauren, while Ron tucked his wife's hand under his arm. "Let's go and see what a 1912 dinner is like," he said.

Bill led the way as they walked down the grand staircase while cameras clicked and rolled to record the occasion. At the bottom of the stairs, a thick white carpet awaited.

The owner of the Star Line, Mr. Cleaver, stood at the entrance to the dining room and welcomed them. Bill and his family were already mingling with other passengers when there was a hush in the room. The captain had arrived.

"Welcome ladies and gentleman. We'll have drinks before dinner. I'm happy to introduce Chief Officer David Whitmore and his son Matthew. I believe they have relatives in this room," the captain said. Matthew wore his Naval Academy dress uniform.

Michael smiled and waved to Matthew. Bill came forward saying to the captain, "I'm David's father, Bill Whitmore, and I'm here with his mother and our two grandsons, Henrik and Michael."

Michael went to one side to greet his cousin Matthew. "Why didn't you tell me you were coming?" he said.

"I thought it would be more fun to surprise you."

David looked splendid in his white uniform as he bowed deeply to his mother and kissed her on the cheek. Bill and David shook hands, hugged, and tugged at each other's sleeves. It was an emotional moment. The family took their places with Stella beside David and all the other family members. Bill told David about the members of the Cosentino family that were seated at the adjoining table.

"What a story! Descendants of two Titanic survivors meeting on the ship," David said.

"Let's enjoy the meal," the captain said from the head table. "We have the same menu as in 1912."

The menu was printed with both the White Star Line Logo and the Blue Star Line Logo.

Hors D'oeuvre Variés, Oysters, Consomme Olga, Cream of Barley, Salmon, Mousseline Sauce, Cucumber, Filet Mignons Lili, Sauté of Chicken Lyonnaise, Vegetable Marrow Farcie, Lamb, Mint Sauce, Roast Duckling, Apple Sauce, Sirloin of Beef Chateau Potatoes, Green Peas, Creamed Carrots, Boiled Rice, Parmentier & Boiled New Potatoes, Punch Romaine, Roast Squab & Cress, Red Burgundy, Cold Asparagus, Vinaigrette, Pāté De Foie Gras, Celery, Waldorf Pudding, Peaches in Chartreuse Jelly, Chocolate & Vanilla Eclairs, French Ice Cream.

After what seemed like hours, they finally rose from the table. "I've never seen so much food in my life," Henrik said.

"You didn't have to eat it all," Michael said. Matthew joined them and suggested they go for a walk on the deck.

"We want to escort the ladies back to their room first," Henrik said, "Then we'll meet you on promenade deck."

When Matthew met up with his cousins on promenade deck, he said to Michael, "I wouldn't mind dating Miss Lauren."

"You stay away from her," Michael warned him. "She's mine."

"We'll have to see about that. I'm studying at the Naval Academy in Annapolis," he said, and I'm wearing my dress uniform. What are you doing Michael?"

"I just graduated from college, and this voyage is my graduation gift from my parents. I'm two years older than you."

"I want to put you guys on notice," Henrik said. "Stay away from Miss Caroline. She's mine."

They found their grandparents in the social room. The Cosentino family sat at a separate table. Matthew spotted them and at once went up to them and carried on a spirited conversation with the girls until Ron asked him to sit down.

"He's working himself into position for Lauren," Michael said to Henrik.

"There are other girls on the ship," Henrik said.

Michael looked around and said, "The picking is meager here tonight. I'll challenge Matthew to a card game and see who wins Miss Lauren."

Somehow, Michael managed to have Henrik and Matthew join him for a card game at a separate table. "The winner gets the date for tonight," he said.

"Does that include me?" Henrik asked.

"Well, you can date Miss Caroline if you win."

"I'll date her regardless. The game is between you two young bucks."

Matthew dealt the cards. "Winner takes all," he said.

"I thought we were friends," Michael protested.

At the end of the game, Matthew had won and Michael looked defeated.

"Thank you, gentlemen, I'll go and claim my prize," Matthew said.

He rose and resolutely walked over to the Cosentino table and bowed in front of Miss Lauren.

"Do you want to go dancing with me, Miss Lauren?"

"Is there dancing somewhere?"

"I don't know but come with me and we'll find out." With a pretty smile that lit up her face, Lauren reached for the crook of his arm.

"Dancing," Michael said with a gleeful smirk. "I don't hear any music."

"I hear it now. Matthew must have gotten it started," Henrik said. "Let's all go."

As on cue, everyone rose and strolled to the ballroom. They sat and listened to the music for a while until the orchestra began to play a waltz. Matthew at once bowed to Miss Lauren and they glided out on the dance floor. Michael looked around at the young women and hurriedly strolled over to a potential partner, bowed and danced with her in wide circles claiming most of the floor. Henrik took Caroline for a whirl, and other dancers joined them. Bill said his knees were too stiff, but Ron and Anita danced.

"What do you think about Matthew and Michael's competition for our daughter, Ron?"

"It's fun to watch. Lauren has a choice."

At the end of the evening, Matthew accompanied Lauren to her door and called her his Titanic Princess before clicking his heels together and saluting her.

Chapter 41

The passengers in first class were overwhelmingly white, but there were several Chinese upper-class people among them. Binh didn't stand out among the tea drinkers that gathered at the Veranda Café with its white furniture and black-and-white tiled floor.

"I brought some pictures from Saigon if you want to see them," he said to Anita.

"Oh yes, I do."

She studied them and said to Ron, "These look very different from the ones you took during the war. I'm glad the city has been re-built. You have to see these," she said, handing them to her husband.

Ron looked at them one by one and turned to Binh saying, "I'm sure that one of our papers could publish an article using some of these pictures, Binh. You should write it and submit it. We'll pay you."

"I don't know if I can, Ron."

"Sure, you can."

"If you think so, I'll try."

"I could write an introduction that would be an attention grabber. "Saigon native returns to his childhood city after 40 years in America." With you as the author, it would be a good byline."

"I suppose so."

"The Asian people are known for being curious about their past. Many children who were adopted by Americans want to go back and see where they come from. We might be able to do a series of stories like that."

"I would like to read about what other Asians have experienced in America," Binh said.

"Then it's settled. Start writing as soon as you can."

They ordered tea and cucumber dill sandwiches. For dessert they enjoyed the famous Titanic sponge cake filled with berry jam and topped with a dab of whipping cream.

"That was delicious," Binh said. "My Chinese roommate, a well-to-do businessman, exports athletic goods to America. He told me that many Americans come to his country asking to have their inventions or sales products manufactured in China. "They can't afford to make them in America. The salaries are too high."

"I believe that," Ron said.

"In the department stores, I can't find anything made in America," Anita said. "I have done a lot of shopping lately, and everything we bought is made in Asia."

"We're a clever race," Binh said with a grin. "We know how to market ourselves."

"I believe we're making a stop in Singapore. If we're allowed to disembark, we could check out the stores there," Ron said.

"You'd be the one looking like a foreigner, Ron," Binh said with a mischievous grin.

"I'm willing to take the risk. You'll be there to protect me."

"With my life."

While Ron and Binh were ashore in Singapore, Anita had the surprise of her life. As she stood by the railing looking at passengers boarding and disembarking, her daughter Michelle boarded.

"Michelle, what are you doing here?" Anita yelled to her.

"I couldn't join you earlier, but here I am," she shouted back. "I'm sharing a cabin in second class with my friend Vicky. She boarded in Jiangsu."

"Wait there, and I'll be down to meet you," Anita shouted back.

In the rush of boarding, Anita and Michelle found a place to hug and talk. Taller than her mother, Michelle looked more like her father with fair skin.

"I'm so glad you are here, Michelle. You won't believe it, but there are passengers here from the Whitmore family."

"Wow, I can't wait to meet them."

"One of the men is the same age as Caroline. I believe they are sightseeing in Singapore right now."

"I'm going to my cabin to change clothes. I'll call you when I'm ready, Mom."

"Binh is in second class," Anita said.

"Binh is on the ship?"

"Yes, he's exploring Singapore with your dad."

"I want to meet Binh!"

When Ron returned, Anita surprised him greatly saying, "Michelle is here. She's in second class. You have to get her a pass so she can join us for dinner."

"What? Slow down. How can Michelle be here?"

When Anita had told him, he said, "That's wonderful. I don't know if I can get her a pass, but I'll certainly try."

"She is 33 years old and still single. She needs to find a husband," Anita said matter-of-factly.

Michael and Matthew had buried their hatchets and played squash together. After the match, they went swimming and found

Lauren sitting in one of the deck chairs.

"What're you doing here all alone, Princess?" Matthew asked.

"I had to get away from you and Michael."

"We're not fighting anymore," Matthew said. He was sweaty and his hair was hanging down in tangles. Michael didn't look as attractive as before either. "Let's swim," he said, diving into the pool. Matthew and Lauren joined him. At once, Michael drew Lauren under water, but Matthew rescued her.

"If you're going to continue fighting, I'm leaving," Lauren said as she gulped for air.

"No, don't leave," the boys said at the same time.

In second class, Michelle met Binh in the narrow corridor. He was with his roommate, the Chinese gentleman.

"Hello, Michelle, this is a surprise," Binh said. "I didn't know you were on board."

"I just boarded. Good to see you, Binh."

"This is my roommate, Mr. Kim."

"How're you, Mr. Kim."

"I'm enjoying my trip so far. Pleasure to meet you, Miss Michelle. Are you related to Binh's friends?"

"Yes, I grew up with Binh around."

"Hope to see you again, Miss Michelle. We're going to afternoon tea. Won't you join us?"

"I'll ask my roommate, and if she says it's okay, we might." Her friend, Vicky, was expecting Michelle. "It's about time you got here," she said.

"I'm sorry, but I ran into my mom and Binh. You remember Binh?"

"Yes, how come he's on board?"

"He's a paying passenger the same as we are. He shares a cabin with a Chinese gentleman here in the same corridor. He invited us to join them for afternoon tea. Are you up to it?"

"I am, if you are."

"I should unpack, but I can do that later. I'm just going to freshen up and check my makeup. It was hot outside."

As soon as Binh and Mr. Kim saw Michelle and her friend walking into the tearoom, they stood up and gestured to two empty chairs by their table.

"Ladies, so glad you could join us," Mr. Kim said.

"This is my friend Vicky Johnson," Michelle said. The men bowed deeply. "We're honored to have you ladies join us," Mr. Kim said. Binh hurried to hold out a chair for Vicky, while Mr. Kim was already seating Michelle. Vicky was older, how much older was difficult to tell. She carried her medium stature with a straight back and high bosom. Short curly hair framed her round and pretty face. Michelle knew Vicky colored her hair because it had started to show gray. They were both teachers and taught at the same school.

"Yesterday, I had tea with your family at the Veranda Café in first class," Binh said to Michelle.

"So, you could get up there?"

"Yes, your father invited me."

"This tearoom is not as beautiful as the Veranda Café, but the tea and scones are just as good, " Binh said.

"It would be an honor to accompany you ladies to dinner tonight if you'd agree," Mr. Kim said, looking at Michelle.

"Thank you, Mr. Kim, we'll accept, won't we Vicky?"

"Of course."

"Thank you, mademoiselles. Now, Binh and I will accompany you both to your room and come for you later."

No one paid attention to Henrik and Caroline sightseeing in Singapore.

"On the ship, I feel like I'm watched like a teenager," Caroline said.

"I feel the same way. I would like to be alone with you."

He stopped and took Caroline into a store with high racks of clothes that shielded them from the public and kissed her.

"That's much better," he said. "I adore you, Caroline," he said, and he was ready to kiss her again when a clerk separated the racks. "May I help you, sir?" he said.

"Yes, I'm looking for something for my wife," Henrik said. When he noticed they were in the women's lingerie department, he turned to Caroline and said, "Pick out something for yourself, darling." Caroline reddened but quickly said, "Not today, honey."

"That was weird," Henrik said when they were out on the sidewalk again. "May I see you in Dubai when the voyage is over?"

"I don't know if that will be possible."

"I'll make it possible," Henrik said, getting closer to her as they walked. When someone bumped into them, they separated and walked side by side for a while.

"Are you in the newspaper business, Caroline?" Henrik asked.

"Yes, I am, but because I want to be."

"Have you ever been to California?"

"I've been to L.A., but not to San Francisco."

"Have you ever been married?"

"No, not even engaged, Caroline said. What about you?"

"I've managed to remain single so far. Where do you live?"

"In Boston."

"I have relatives there."

Chapter 42

As soon as Vicky and Michelle were alone in their cabin, Vicky said, "Wouldn't you rather have dinner with your family?"

"No, not tonight."

Michelle was busy unpacking and held up a purple sheath dress for Vicky to see.

"Do you think Mr. Kim will like me in this one?"

"I'm sure he'll like you in whatever you're wearing. And meanwhile I have to put up with Binh."

"Actually, he's quite interesting. My dad holds him in high regard. I think he'll look good in evening clothes."

Michelle's phone pinged. "Hi Michelle, welcome aboard." It was her dad. "I'm sorry I can't get you a seat at our table tonight, but you have one for tomorrow night."

"It's okay, Dad, because I already have a date with a Chinese gentleman."

"Mr. Kim?"

"Yes, Dad. Have you met him?"

"I have, but don't you want me to upgrade your ticket to first class? I don't know if I can, but I could try."

"No, Dad, I think I'll be happy here, and I don't want to leave

Vicky."

"Alright then. Enjoy your day. See you tomorrow."

It was late when Michelle and Vicky returned to their cabin with a promise of seeing the gentlemen on the sun deck in the morning. "I flew all day yesterday, and I'm dead tired," Michelle said, "but dinner was fun, don't you think, Vicky?"

"Better than I expected. I thought Binh was married, but he didn't bring his wife."

"He was divorced several years ago. Lives in New York."

"Well, with the Titanic Princess sailing from China we could expect Asians to flood the ship."

"They haven't exactly flooded the ship."

"Good night, Michelle. It's definitely more fun now that you are on board."

When the bugle sounded for breakfast, Michelle and Vicky were ready. "We'll have to change clothes several times," Vicky said. "Now, a breakfast outfit and then a sundress, and that's just the beginning of the day."

At breakfast, they met two gentlemen from Chicago, who asked them to join them at their table. Michelle looked around the room and didn't see Kim and Binh, so she accepted. "You don't mind, do you Vicky?"

"Heavens no, they are gorgeous," she whispered.

When they left the room, Vicky accepted a dinner invitation by Harry Thomas from Chicago. Michelle couldn't commit since she would dine with her family.

"That worked out well," Vicky said, as they said goodbye to the gentlemen from Chicago. "Sun deck next."

Mr. Kim cast a discrete look at Michelle in her skimpy dress with bare shoulders. He wore sunglasses, a Hawaiian shirt, and shorts.

Binh wore a white shirt and shorts with a sunhat on his head and flip-flops on his feet. The time passed fast, and soon it was time to return to the cabin and dress for lunch.

"I'll be gaining weight if we're going to eat this often," Vicky said. She was always mindful of her weight. At the luncheon, she and Michelle were seated with people from California. Afterward, Vicky said, "It's interesting to get to meet new people from different parts of the country."

"I think so too, it's great to mingle. We have to take a walk up on deck after all this food, don't you think, Vicky?"

Michelle's cell phone buzzed. This time it was her mom.

"How're you doing, honey?"

"I'm having a great time," she said, and went on to relate how busy she and Vicky were.

"Dad will come and pick you up at 7 tonight. Is that alright?"

"Yes, Mom, I'll be ready."

Michelle put on her emerald green gown and long gloves. Vicky took a picture of her and said she would post it on Facebook.

"Then I'll take one of you and do the same." The slim Michelle wore her gown well. Vicky's silvery gown accentuated her curves. "Mr. Thomas will be pleased with the way you look, Vicky," Michelle said. Harry Thomas had already come for Vicky when Ron arrived to pick up his daughter.

"Your dress is beautiful," he said to Michelle. "How was your dinner last night?"

"I enjoyed it, and today we had lunch with two gentlemen from California. Mr. Thomas from Chicago is escorting Vicky to dinner."

"First class looks great," Michelle said, as they entered. "Can't wait to see your parlor suite."

"It's comfortable. Here we are."

"I'm stunned by your beauty, ladies," Ron said with a bow as he saw his wife and daughters all dressed in gowns. "May I escort all four of you to dinner?" Caroline was in blue, Lauren in pink, and Anita in pale yellow. The colors blended beautifully with Michelle's emerald green. On top of the Grand Staircase, they stopped to chat with the Whitmore family, and Ron introduced Michelle to them. Chief Officer David Whitmore welcomed her aboard with a deep bow and admiration in his eyes. First Officer Jurgen Fischer acted as host at the Cosentino table and paid special attention to Michelle. It was one of his duties to tend to single ladies, but he enjoyed it, and so did she. He danced with her after dinner, another favor of the Blue Star Line.

"I enjoy dancing with you Miss Cosentino," he said. "You're a very good dancer. May I call you Michelle?"

"Yes, Jurgen."

He pulled her closer, and then asked, "Would you like a private tour of the ship?"

"Would you give me the tour?"

"Yes, I would be glad to."

"Then I'll accept. I would love to take a closer look at the ship."

"Wear comfortable shoes. How about tomorrow morning, after breakfast?

"That would be fine. I'm in second class."

"Oh, I thought you were in first class with your family."

"No, I didn't sign up until later. I boarded the ship in Singapore. My father arranged for me to get a pass so I could join them for dinner."

"Are you a journalist, too? I have to watch out for those."

"No, I wanted to be different. I'm a teacher because I enjoy working with children, even if it's for less money."

"That's commendable."

"How come you went to sea, Jurgen?"

"It was an occupation that was available to a poor boy like me."

"Where do you come from?"

"From Germantown, Pennsylvania. Have you heard of it?"

"Yes, I have. Isn't it hard to have a family life when you're at sea all the time?"

"I'm still single, but it is possible to have a family life at sea. How do you know the Whitmore family?"

"We're strangely connected to them through the history of the first Titanic because a Cosentino man saved the life of a woman who married a Whitmore."

"That's amazing." The music stopped and Jurgen thanked Michelle for the dance.

"I see that my parents are leaving, so I want to say goodnight to them, if you'd excuse me, Jurgen."

"Of course, I'll take you to them."

Jurgen left her with a cheerful, "See you, tomorrow at 10 o'clock."

As soon as Michelle had said goodnight to her parents, David Whitmore saw his chance and approached Michelle. David was probably 15 years her senior, and strikingly handsome in his uniform.

"Will you walk with me for a while, Miss Cosentino?"

"Yes, sir." He offered her the support of his arm.

"Are you enjoying the voyage, Miss Cosentino?"

"Yes, sir, I am."

"Please call me David. If you need anything, please let me know. I hear you are traveling in second class. I could move you up to first if there is a room."

"Thank you, but I'm sharing a cabin with a friend, and I prefer to stay with her. My dad also offered to move me up."

"Well, you can still come upstairs for our dinners, and I would love to dance with you if you don't mind."

"I wouldn't mind that at all, David."

"Would you like to see the bridge?"

"Yes, of course." David steered her in that direction. Michelle reminded herself that he was the chief officer, next in command to the captain.

The computer screens glowed in the dark. "How do we get to Dubai?" Michelle asked.

"I will ask the officer here to show you," he said. The two officers saluted each other. The second officer bowed to Michelle and gestured to the screen, "We have left Singapore, which lies just 85 miles north of the equator," he said, using a pointer. "We are now going slightly northwest to pass the Strait of Malacca. This is the busiest passageway for ships in the world. It's where the Pacific Ocean meets with the Indian Ocean. At times, we will see both Malaysia to the north and Indonesia to the south. This is the same route that Chinese mariners used when they sailed west and Arabian and Indian mariners as they sailed east. One thousand years later, not even Magellan found the straight and sailed too far south."

"This is so interesting," Michelle said. The officer continued:

"We will head to the southernmost tip of India and then turn northeast to the Oman Sea, passing south of Karachi in Pakistan, go through the 350-mile-long Strait of Hormuz, and enter the Arabian Sea, also called the Persian Sea, because Persia (Iran) is to the north and Arabia to the south. On the southern shore of the large body of water lies Dubai, which is one of the cities in the United Arab Emirates," the officer said, pointing to Dubai.

"Thank you, sir, for showing me the route. Now I can tell my students."

"My pleasure, miss."

Michelle turned to David and asked, "Is there a risk for hurricanes?"

"Not at this time of the year."

"Thank you for telling me."

"My pleasure, you're a lovely lady, Michelle, and I would love seeing you tomorrow."

"I have a date in the morning, but perhaps tomorrow night."

"Alright, may I escort you to your cabin?"

"Yes, of course."

Outside, her cabin door, David bent down and kissed her on the cheek. "Don't forget tomorrow evening," he said.

"No, I won't forget."

Michelle couldn't wait to tell Vicky that she had two high-ranking officers vying for her company.

Chapter 43

Vicky had quite a story to tell about Harry Thomas. "He is a descendant of a Titanic survivor. This is a great cruise so far," she said.

"I thought there would be many descendants of survivors on the ship," Michelle said.

She was full of anticipation as she dressed in slacks and sneakers. Jurgen arrived at 10 o'clock precisely. They walked close together in small spaces. "Shall we start on top and go down?" he asked.

"Sounds like a good idea."

"Then we'll go to the bridge first."

Michelle didn't let on that she had already seen it, but it was at night, and now she wanted to see it in daylight.

"Are you on the bridge sometimes, Jurgen?"

"Yes, of course, I have to take my turn on the bridge."

Michelle drew in her breath as she saw the view. "This is fantastic. The view and everything. Now, I can see how tall the ship is."

"It's calm and beautiful today, but it will get warm," Jurgen said. Michelle went up to the big wheel and touched it.

"We don't use the wheel," Jurgen said. "It's just there for show."

"How do you steer the boat then?"

"The ship has digital navigation and radar system. The steering is automatic most of the time, but an officer is always in the chair here as you can see."

"I suppose you try to date female passengers on every cruise?"

"No, I don't. Only when someone strikes my fancy, and you did, Michelle. This is a brand-new ship, and it's quite an honor to be part of the crew."

"You weren't afraid that a ship named Titanic would be a bad omen?"

"Not in the least. Do you want to go up in a funnel for a better view?"

"Are the funnels used for lookouts?" Michelle sounded surprised.

"One of them is. Only one funnel is needed for the exhaust on this ship. The others are mostly for show."

"Then I would like to go up with you."

"We have an elevator. Please step in." With very little room in the elevator, they stood close together and Jurgen put his arm around Michelle. There were other people at the top of the funnel, all admiring the view.

"You have heard of the lifeboats, of course?"

"Yes, I heard they are large."

"They are, and they are not open boats that expose the passengers to the elements. You can see some of them from here. They would be very safe in case of an emergency, and we have enough lifeboats for everyone on board."

"I hope we don't have to use the boats," Michelle said, shrugging off the thought.

"You don't have to worry about anything. This ship is very safe," he said looking at her.

As the elevator door opened for them, Jurgen said, "You've already seen first class, but have you seen the Veranda Café?"

"No, I haven't."

"Well, let's go there then." Michelle gasped as she saw the bright room with green vines climbing the walls between the windows. "Oh, it's beautiful," she exclaimed. "I suppose afternoon tea will be served here."

"And morning tea. It's pretty much open all the time."

"I would like to see the swimming pool and the Turkish bath and the exercise rooms."

"Then I'll take you there next." They saw the Whitmore brothers playing squash and Michelle's younger sisters in the pool.

"Here's the entrance to the Turkish bath. It would be too hot to go in there. Do you want to go below to third class?"

"Absolutely, I'm curious about those accommodations. Is it true that the steerage passengers couldn't get out when the Titanic sank?"

"I think there were some cases when they couldn't find their way out, but it wouldn't happen on this ship. We have to walk down some stairs now. The portholes are getting smaller. We're closer to the waterline. Does that scare you?"

"Not when I'm with you, Jurgen."

"Here's the common room. People of many different nationalities mingled in this room on the original Titanic."

Michelle would have liked to stay longer, but Jurgen escorted her out of the room.

"We can't go into the cabins. There are family cabins with four bunks in each. Third class also has a large room for single men that is quite inexpensive even on this ship. I could go in there to inspect, but I couldn't bring a woman."

"We had a Vietnamese refugee in our family after the Vietnam

War, and he had booked passage in third class, but he's now in second class. Are there many Asiatic people in third class?"

"I don't really know. It's the job of the second officer to tour the entire ship. I can take you to the kitchen if you like. The bakery is fantastic."

"Is it true that the first Titanic carried live chickens?"

"Yes, I think so. Refrigeration was not what it is today."

"Just checking to see if you need anything?" Jurgen said to the chef.

"We're fine, sir."

"It smells so good in here," Michelle said.

"Bread is baked every day."

"I'm getting hungry just from the smell."

"Do you want to have tea with me in the Officers' Mess?"

"Is that allowed?"

"Yes, for special people. But first I want to take you to the lower deck, and to get there we have to use the ladders. Are you up to it?"

"Yes, I am."

"Then I'll go first."

He was two steps ahead of her when she lost her balance and he caught her in his arms.

"Oops, that was close."

"I don't think there are any cameras here," he said, before kissing her. Michelle felt like she was Rose running around with Jack in the Titanic movie.

"Do you hear the engines?" Jurgen asked. Their faces were close.

"Yes, what kind are they?"

"Diesel."

As they ascended the ladder, they stopped once again to kiss. Michelle guessed that Jurgen had taken her down the ladder to have a private moment with her. If nothing else happened, that was the high point of her cruise, Michelle thought. And it was at the bottom of the boat!

They walked up steps and rode an elevator to get to the officers' tearoom.

"Is there a camera in here?" Michelle asked as they rode the elevator.

"I'm afraid so. In case the elevator gets stuck."

In the tearoom, Jurgen turned to Michelle and asked, "What would you like to have?"

"Tea and scones, please." They waited a while for the scones, but it was worth the wait.

"These are heavenly," Michelle said, as she bit into a freshly baked scone. "How can you stay so slim living on a ship like this?" she asked while meeting Jurgen's gaze.

"It's the exercise I get from walking the decks and dancing with the lonely ladies," he said, with a laugh. "But don't get me wrong," he added. "Dancing with you, Michelle, is pure pleasure."

"Do you also take other lonely ladies on tours of your ship?"

"You probably won't believe me, but you are the first."

"Then there is one more place I want to see. I've heard of the poop deck. What is that?"

"It's the top deck in the stern. Third-class passengers have access to it. From there you can watch the sea behind the ship. We can go there now," he said, standing up and leading her by the arm.

"There is no direct way to get there, but we have time," he said.

"I heard that many passengers jumped from the stern," Michelle said.

"That's true, and it's a long way to the water."

Standing on the poop deck, Michelle exclaimed, "This is amazing. I can't believe I'm here."

The hot sea breeze blew her brown hair across her face and she tucked it behind her ears.

"The propellers are huge, but you can't see them. We can only see how the water churns behind us," Jurgen said.

"It's already steaming hot, and it's still morning."

"Yes, I'll take you back to your cabin, but I want to see you again."

Chapter 44

"Do you have to work when we come to Dubai, Jurgen?"

"No, I'll be on leave living it up like a drunken sailor. I'm just kidding. Are you leaving the ship in Dubai, Michelle?"

"Yes, I'm flying home from there."

"I would be glad to show you Dubai. I've been there before with another ship, but first I want to dance with you every night while we're still on board."

Michelle felt excited as she dressed in a rose-colored gown for dinner and dancing. She knew she would have at least two dancing partners. During dinner, she felt David's eyes on her from the Whitmore table. Jurgen winked at her from the head of their table.

"You look a little flustered, Michelle," her dad said.

"Yes, I think it's warm in here."

"Not really, something else bothering you?"

"Is my dress alright?"

"It looks beautiful on you."

When they heard the music from the ballroom, Jurgen was quick on his feet and asked her for the first dance. Michelle saw David dancing with his mother. When the dance was over, he came toward her.

"May I have this dance with you, Miss Michelle?" he asked. Jurgen stepped aside for his superior officer but did not look happy.

David was shorter than Jurgen, but broad-shouldered and solid. He held her with strong arms and danced well.

"Do you enjoy being the chief officer?" Michelle asked.

"I have been the captain on other ships but being the chief officer on Titanic Princess is an honor." Lowering his voice, he said, "How come a pretty lady like you isn't married?" He was leaning into her face. Michelle blushed and missed a step.

"I'm a teacher and don't get to meet many single gentlemen, but tonight I have also promised to dance with First Officer Fischer."

"I will stand back then, but please give me another chance. It was a pleasure to dance with you, Miss Michelle." He bowed to her and left her with her sisters. When the music started up again, Jurgen approached her and they glided out on the dance floor.

"I see that I have competition," he said.

"I'm flattered, of course."

"I think David is a little old for you."

"How old is he?"

"I think he's 48 and divorced with a grown son."

"He wants to dance with me again."

"That's too bad." The next time, Michelle danced with David she asked, "May I ask you for a favor?"

"Yes, anything."

"May I bring my roommate to dinner tomorrow night. She's a teacher like me and single."

"For you I make an exception, of course. Please bring her. What's her name?"

"Victoria Johnson. She belongs to a famous family." She left it up to David to guess. "We have been best friends for a long time."

"All right. I'll order an extra place setting at your table for Miss Johnson. I'll see both of you tomorrow night."

While David was busy entertaining his parents, Jurgen escorted Michelle to her cabin and kissed her on the lips outside the door. It made Michelle want more, so she kissed him back. She was happy with her day.

"*Auf Wiedersehen*," he said.

"Vicky, are you here?" Michelle asked as soon as she came inside the door.

"Yes, I'm here."

"You won't believe it, but Chief Officer David Whitmore invited you to have dinner with us tomorrow night."

"Why? I haven't even met him."

"I asked him, and he agreed."

"Oh my. What will I wear?"

"It doesn't matter, because no one up there has seen your dresses. He is very handsome. I think you'll like him. I prefer First Officer Jurgen Fischer. He has kissed me several times." Michelle blushed at the thought.

"I can't believe I'll be dining in first class. Harry Thomas will be disappointed."

"I think he will understand."

The next day, Michelle told Jurgen about her ploy. "I hope that David will like Vicky. I think they will be perfect together."

"I hope so, because then he'll leave you alone."

"Vicky and I will come to dinner together. I think she'll feel more comfortable that way."

"Okay, I will entertain both of you at dinner because David will be at the Whitmore table as usual."

"That is until the dancing starts in the ballroom. Then I'll introduce Vicky to him."

Vicky was nervous as she was seated at the Cosentino table. She glanced over to the Whitmore table and saw the man who had arranged for her seating. "Oh, my goodness, he's gorgeous," she whispered to Michelle. "How old is he?"

"48."

"Good, then I'm not too old for him."

"No, you are not. He's a good dancer too."

"He probably likes you better."

"But I like Jurgen better, so I want you to charm David."

"I'll do my best."

After dinner, David came over to their table and Michelle introduced Vicky to him.

"Charmed," David said, as he bowed to her. "May I have the first dance?"

Off they went to the ballroom. Jurgen looked at Michelle and smiled. "So far, so good," he said. "May I have this dance with you?"

"Yes, you may," she said smiling invitingly.

When Vicky and Michelle were alone that night, Vicky said she liked David a lot. "He invited me to the officers' tea room tomorrow. Do you think I should go?"

"Why not? I've already been there with Jurgen. Your students are not going to report you. I think he's serious about finding a new wife. Do you like him?"

"Are you kidding? I could fall in love with him."

Before they were seated for dinner the next night, David stood between the tables and spoke. "Ladies and Gentlemen. I've noticed that most of the men are seated at my table and most of the women at the first officer's table. I suggest that we mix up the seating, and I'll begin by asking Miss Johnson to come to my table," he said. With those words, he walked over to Vicky and escorted her to sit to his left.

"Michael and Matthew, you can go over to the Cosentino table and keep Miss Lauren company." The boys happily complied. "Henrik, I have seen you with Miss Caroline. You may place her beside you at our table." Henrik went for Caroline and brought her to his side. "Now, that's much better. We have three women at each table. Enjoy your meal."

Titanic Princess rode the waves at a steady pace. No one suffered from seasickness until the day the ship encountered heavy seas south of India. Michelle was sick in her cabin and called Jurgen. They had exchanged cell phone numbers the day before.

"Jurgen, I'm seasick."

"So sorry to hear you're not feeling well. Do you want me to bring you a bowl of soup?"

"Thanks for the offer, but I don't think I can eat anything. Is this storm going to last a long time?"

"No, it will soon be over. I'm looking at the radar right now."

"I'm glad to hear it."

"Have you been vomiting?"

"No, but I feel nauseated."

"Is Vicky sick, too?"

"I don't think so. I think she's with David."

"Stay in bed and try to sleep. Dream about me."

"I feel better already. I suppose you don't get seasick, Jurgen."

"No, not at all. I'll call and check on you in a couple of hours."

"Thanks. Hope I can be on my feet later."

"I hope so too, sweetie."

Jurgen was right. The storm abated, and Michelle crawled out of her bunk.

For the rest of the voyage, Jurgen and Michelle met as often as they could, and so did David and Vicky. One evening when Jurgen and Michelle walked on the officers' promenade deck, they met David and Vicky. The two officers saluted each other. After a few minutes, they met again. David stopped and spoke, "Why don't we split up the deck and take half each?" he said. Jurgen agreed, and he and Michelle sat down on a bench looking at the moon. Henrik and Caroline continued to hide in dark corners on the Promenade Deck.

Chapter 45

Dubai

When the Titanic passengers and crew disembarked in Dubai, they were met by what seemed like hundreds of reporters sticking their microphones in front of them as the TV cameras rolled to record the event. The questions kept coming.

"What did you think of the voyage?"

"What prompted you to sail on Titanic Princess?"

"Was it up to your expectations?"

"Was it worth the money?"

A Chinese female reporter was seen to interview Binh.

The Whitmore and Cosentino families slowly made their way to the limos that would take them to their hotel. The reporters followed them and once again accosted them outside the hotel.

"Do you have any Titanic survivors in your family?"

Bill and Ron took five minutes each to answer that they indeed had Titanic survivors in their family. "You met here on the ship! That's an amazing story." More reporters stopped them inside the lobby, but Bill and Ron waved them away. Large television screens broadcast interviews beginning with the owner of the Blue Star Line and his gigantic undertaking to build a replica of the Titanic.

"Are you happy about the Maiden Voyage, sir?"

"Yes, I'm very happy." The large Australian man continued to talk for about five minutes. The TV reporter then announced there would be a special feature that evening about Binh Pham, who had been a 10-year-old orphan when he was rescued at the end of the Vietnam War and taken to Boston. "Mr. Pham recently visited Saigon and now he has traveled on Titanic Princess and once again met his rescuer, Mr. Ronald Cosentino," the reporter said.

"I don't think Binh has to write his story. He has already told it and it will reach the whole wide world," Ron said. Another reporter approached Ron.

"Are you the Mr. Cosentino who rescued Binh Pham from Vietnam?"

"Yes, I am."

"Then I want to talk with you. May I have a few minutes of your time, sir?"

"I need to take my family to our rooms first. Please, turn off your camera."

"If you promise to talk to us later?"

"Wait for me here in the lobby," Ron said.

Jurgen and Michelle were stopped and asked if they knew of any shipboard romance on Titanic Princess.

"You bet," Jurgen said, "but I'm not going to tell you. I'm an officer, and I do not talk to reporters." Hoping for some private time with Michelle in Dubai, he dressed in civilian clothes and invited her to dinner at a restaurant and then for a nightcap in his room.

"I want to see you in the States. I've never felt this strongly about any woman before," he told her, as he poured the champagne.

"I'm flattered," Michelle said, and accepted her glass.

"Here's to you and me," Jurgen said raising his glass. Quietly, she wondered what he meant.

"I'm serious about you. I'll bombard you with emails until we meet again. Come and sit here beside me."

"Are you coming to Boston then?" She took a sip from her drink and sat down beside him.

"Titanic Princess will be in New York in about a month. Could you meet me there if I can't come to Boston?"

"Maybe."

"I don't want to hear a maybe, I want to hear a yes." His face came closer to hers. She could smell the champagne on his breath.

"Yes, if it's still summer and I'm not teaching."

"That's better. I'm falling in love with you, and I can't wait to see you again. You've changed my life." He put their drinks on the table and took her in his arms before kissing her. Without thinking, Michelle put her arms around his neck.

"You might have changed mine," she said, when she could breathe again.

"You can sail with me wherever I go."

"Sounds so romantic. Is that a proposal?" She looked into his eyes and saw that he was serious.

"First, I have to find out if you want me for a husband. I'm 36 years old and financially secure. Could you picture living with me in a house with a white picket fence?"

He saw a glimmer of interest in Michelle's eyes and continued. "We could have children. You said you like children. I can't let you go without telling you this." His tender voice and soft eyes begged for her approval.

"I would like to have children, but I'm 33. Living on a ship would be a big change in my life, and I don't think it would be easy with children."

"I understand, but I'm not on duty all year long. I get long leaves. Tell me you'll think about it, darling. You would make me very happy. I love and adore you, Michelle." His long fingers encircled her face.

"I'll think about it. For now, I'm happy just to be here with you."

"This has been a wonderful journey, and I'll miss you every day until I can see you again. Will you miss me?"

"Yes, I'll miss you, Jurgen." She only had to think about losing him to be convinced that she was falling in love.

"I enjoy my time with you and I hope it's not over for us," she said.

"That's much better." He punctuated each word with a kiss.

"I can't wait to see you again," he said.

She knew that she wanted to see him again. There was no reason to hold back. All her misgivings were gone, and she melted in his arms.

Being in a hotel room, they didn't get to see much of Dubai, but they had a good view of the world's tallest building. In the morning, Jurgen went to a jewelry store and bought Michelle an engagement ring.

Michelle met with her parents and told them she was engaged. She showed the ring as evidence.

"That's a big surprise," her dad said. "You're marrying Jurgen?"

"Yes, as soon as possible. We've no reason to wait. We love each other."

"It's a little sudden, but of course we'll throw a wedding for you. Oh, there's no way we can arrange a wedding on short notice," Anita said, looking frantic.

"There will be no big wedding. The captain can marry us on board. You and Jurgen's family can come to New York. We have planned our future, a little house with a picket fence in the suburbs, and all that. Jurgen is not at sea all year long. He gets long leaves."

"Congratulations then. If you're sure you'll be happy?"

"I'm sure. I'm already happy, happier than I've ever been."

"You'll have to quit your teaching job."

"But eventually I can teach the ABCs to my own children."

"I hope you're right," Ron said. "We've been waiting a long time for you to find a man to share your life, Michelle, and we're happy for you. Jurgen is an honorable man. That's what the captain said, when I asked him."

"You didn't, Dad?"

"Forgive me, but it was just out of fatherly concerns."

"We'll tell your sisters when they get back later tonight," Anita said.

"Are Henrik and Caroline still together?"

"Yes, as far as we know. They are mature enough to know what they want," Anita said. "Lauren has plenty of time to decide, and I don't think it will be either Michael or Matthew."

"I wonder what Vicky and David are doing. They seemed to hit it off on the ship."

"I saw them together here in Dubai," Ron said.

"That's great. Have you seen Binh and Mr. Kim?"

"Yes. Mr. Kim hired Binh to work in his import business in New York, but now that Binh has become a celebrity, he might not have to work at all."

"This has been a fantastic cruise for all of us," Michelle said.

Michael and Matthew shared a hotel room in Dubai. They had talked to reporters, while Henrik had avoided them. He had reserved a single room so he would have a place to bring Caroline. First, he took her to an elegant dinner, just the two of them. They walked hip to hip to the hotel. In the lobby, Henrik pressed the elevator button to his floor, and Caroline pretended not to notice. He stuck his keycard in the door until it clicked and drew Caroline into the room with him.

"At last we are alone," Henrik said. "I'm so attracted to you, Caroline, that I feel I'm bursting. Will you stay with me for the rest of the night?"

"I don't know. Lauren will wonder where I am."

"I think she can guess."

Late that night, Henrik asked Caroline how she would feel about moving to San Francisco. Caroline studied her nails instead of looking at Henrik.

"It's been wonderful to be with you, Henrik, but I'm the corporate financial officer in our company, and I can't pick up and leave."

"Will you at least think about it?"

"Yes, but I don't believe it would work out."

Henrik knew she was right. They lived on opposite coasts. Caroline had a career and was close to her family. They had enjoyed a shipboard romance, and that was it.

After Caroline had left, Henrik took a shower and dressed for his flight to San Francisco. When his phone pinged with a message, he assumed it was Caroline and that she had changed her mind, so he picked it up without checking the display. To his surprise, the text was from Linda in Trollhättan. She said she was coming to San Francisco on an American tour. Henrik texted her back.

"I'll show you a good time." He had a feeling he should keep in touch with Linda and called her number. "You'll never guess where I am," he said.

"You are not in San Francisco?"

"No, I'm in Dubai. I just sailed on Titanic Princess."

"I didn't think I knew someone that daring. We have seen a lot of coverage here on TV. How was it?"

"It was great. Are you working or still going to school?"

"No to both questions. I just graduated from college."

"Congrats. Is NEV making electric cars in Trollhättan yet?"

The answer was prompt but disappointing. "No, I understand that production will begin in 2020."

"Why is it taking so long?"

"I'm not sure, but the plans have changed several times."

"I'm making solar panels now, and I really think solar power and electric cars will revolutionize how we live and drive in the future."

"I would like to see how you make solar panels."

"I'll be glad to show you. Are you still single?"

"Yes, are you?"

"I am. Love to see you again. I'm flying home today."

"Have a good flight."

"Welcome to San Francisco, Linda."

It occurred to Henrik that he needed a woman who hadn't yet started a career and that Linda might be the one. As he left his hotel room, he picked up a newspaper from the floor outside his door and looked at the headlines, "Descendants of Maiden of the Titanic and Hero of the Titanic meet on Titanic Princess." He read the first lines before putting the paper in his briefcase. In the lobby, the television blasted out Binh's story.

Michelle was alone in her room when Vicky showed up after a long absence loaded with bags from the department stores.

"You must be wondering what I've been doing," she said, unloading the bags on her bed. "I've been shopping for clothes here in Dubai because I won't be flying home with you. David has asked me to sail with him all the way to New York. Matthew is flying home to

Boston, so David and I will be alone."

"You don't say!" Michelle was aghast, but hastily added, "and I'm engaged to Jurgen."

"Really! Congratulations. That's wonderful." Vicky hugged her friend, admired her ring and said, "I want to hear all about it, but David is waiting for me. Just so you know, the captain has been flown back to the states because of illness. David will be the captain now." Her voice rose to almost a shriek.

"My goodness, that's a lot of news at the same time. Jurgen said that David has commanded ships before so he's qualified."

"Yes, and Jurgen will be promoted to chief officer. You can be very proud of him."

"I already am."

"Will you be sleeping in the captain's suite?"

"I don't know yet. David said there might be a first-class suite available for me. We're taking on new passengers here in Dubai."

"Have a wonderful journey, Vicky. This has been the cruise of my dreams," Michelle said, as she hugged her friend. Vicky hugged her back.

"Mine too. Our lives have truly changed."

"Did you see all the reporters?"

"Yes, and I'm sure there will be just as many in Southampton, and I imagine there will be twice as many reporters in New York when we get there. I'm a little scared of the icebergs up north, but David says we have radar now, and there is nothing to worry about."

"Jurgen said we will not encounter any icebergs this time of the year."

"I'm not worried. See you in Boston." And with those words Vicky waved and was out the door.

Michelle wanted to call Jurgen and congratulate him on his promotion but was afraid he was too busy to talk. Instead she sent him a text. "Congrats, Chief. Call me when you can."

Jurgen called her right back, saying, "Sorry, darling, but I can't see you before we depart. David has ordered extra security measures for boarding passengers and their luggage."

"Has there been a threat?"

"No, but we're all supposed to be on alert."

"I do hope you'll have a safe journey, honey. Nothing can happen to us now that we have found each other."

"We'll be fine. Contact me as soon as you are back in Boston, even if it's in the middle of the night where I am."

"I will. *Bon voyage*, Jurgen."

"I love you. Have a safe flight, darling."

Chapter 46

Almost all the Titanic Princess passengers remaining in Dubai gathered in the lobby to watch the movie "*Why the two sister ships, Olympic and Titanic, were switched and how?*"

Afterward, the stunned audience dispersed—except for Bill Whitmore and Ron Cosentino, who remained to discuss what they had just seen.

"If all that is true, 1,500 people died because of one man's greed," Bill said.

"My first reaction was that it cannot be true, but the evidence the movie presented is rather convincing," Ron said. "We do know that the Olympic had been badly damaged in the collision with the warship Hawke, and that it limped into Belfast for repairs, but we didn't know that the damage rendered her uninsurable."

"If the owner's plan to rescue all the passengers in the middle of the Atlantic had worked out, not too much harm would have been done, but it would still have been unethical of him to swindle the insurance company out of 12.5 million," Bill said.

"It seems like all the people involved had something to lose if they didn't go along with the conspiracy. Captain Smith must have been scared since he had been in command of the Olympic when it was damaged."

"And it was not just that one time. The Olympic had been in collisions two times before, and both times Mr. Smith was at the helm."

"Yes, but to get back to the conspiracy, the fact that the two ships were practically identical made the switch possible. The Olympic and the Titanic floated side by side and could change places during the night. The dockworkers who carried out the switch were told if they didn't keep quiet about the plot, they would end up on the bottom of the river."

"All the workers needed to do was to change the name plates on the ships and on the lifeboats. Everything else was standard White Star Line."

"Well, someone had to come in and replace the carpets on the Olympic and repaint some surfaces after nine voyages, but the film didn't say anything about those workers being threatened."

"No, I didn't hear that either. But we do know there was a fire in the coal bin, and supposedly it was that fire that was going to sink the Titanic. When it failed to do so, the ship might have scraped the iceberg on purpose. At least that's what the movie hinted."

"It's beyond comprehension although it sounds plausible that the *Californian* had been commissioned to come and rescue everyone on board. It was loaded with enough coal for the return trip despite the coal strike, and it did not carry any other cargo than blankets and woolen sweaters."

"Yes, and it left Southampton without passengers before the Titanic sailed. At least that's what the movie claimed. But things did not go as planned. The *Californian* got stuck in ice and couldn't move. Captain Smith had told passengers that a ship would come and take them off. They could see a ship in the distance, and that was probably one reason why the Titanic passengers were reluctant to go into the lifeboats."

"There must have been a third ship that didn't answer the distress call, and when it disappeared from view, everyone became scared and all the lifeboats were launched in a hurry, some only half-filled."

"The people in the boats feared they would freeze to death. If it hadn't been for the heroism of the captain on the *Carpathia*, no one would have been saved, and we would not have existed."

"That's true. And if it hadn't been for the discovery of the wreck, the conspiracy would not have come to light."

"Evidently, the upper deck windows on the Olympic were un-evenly placed while they were symmetric on the Titanic.

"There was some other corroborating evidence though. Shortly before the Titanic's departure, the owner increased the insurance value of the ship by several million and cancelled his ticket on the Titanic. The manager of the White Star Line cancelled the tickets for his wife and children, saying they were ill although they were well enough to travel the English countryside."

"Then one week after the Titanic sinking, the factual owner of the ship collected 12.5 million in insurance for what was believed to be the Titanic. If the switch had not taken place, the seriously damaged Olympic could not have lasted another 25 years, so she must have been the Titanic."

"She served as a hospital ship during the First World War. Roberto mentioned in an article that he had seen the white-painted "Olympic" taking on injured Allied soldiers in the Gallipoli Campaign," Ron said.

"It gives me goose bumps to think that two letters had fallen off the nameplate on the wreck, and underneath were the missing letters M and P."

"But the best evidence indicating the conspiracy is true is that the shipyard workers who had been sworn to secrecy eventually told their families they had been forced to make the switch. It was too much of a burden for them to carry to their graves. They didn't know that one of the ships would be deliberately sunk, and they still felt bad about the loss of all those people. The perpetrators were dead and could no longer harm them."

"The captain perished along with the ship's designer, as did the chief officer, the first officer, and many other influential people, but the manager of the White Star Line survived. He stepped into a lifeboat because, as he said, it was important that he could report to the White Star Line about what had happened, but he never revealed there was a conspiracy. Perhaps that's why he was a broken man for the rest of his life."

"Of course, the owner was safe but died within a year, so he didn't get to enjoy his extra millions in insurance money for very long."

"But his business still carries his name."

"I'm sure other researchers will refute the conspiracy theory. We'll just have to wait and see."

"Nevertheless, the movie is a shocking end to a successful maiden voyage for Titanic Princess."

"The history of Titanic will never die. It's an epic saga that will continue to fascinate people around the world."

Chapter 47

The Voyage from Dubai to Southampton

On board Titanic Princess, the ship's owner, Mr. Cleaver, its captain, David Whitmore, and its chief officer, Jurgen Fischer, welcomed all first- and second-class passengers. Many of them were Arabs dressed in white robes or business suits. All checked luggage had been x-rayed, and all passports screened. All carry-on luggage was opened and inspected. Jurgen looked at boarding passes and tried to pronounce their names as he welcomed passengers on board. Captain Whitmore and Mr. Cleaver shook the men's hands and saluted the women.

Vicky was already onboard making herself comfortable in a first-class state room. David had told her there would be a lifeboat drill before they began their voyage to Southampton. All passengers and crew had been assigned to a lifeboat and everyone was supposed to know where to go when the call came. Vicky sat down to read a book, but her thoughts wandered to the command bridge. The teacher in her wanted to know the route they were taking. She put the book down and made her way to the bridge by showing the ID that David had given her. The former second officer was now the first officer.

"Good afternoon, ma'am. I'm First Officer Hughes," he said saluting her smartly. "How can I assist you, Miss Johnson?"

"If it's not too much trouble, I wonder if you would show me the route we are taking to Southampton, sir."

"Certainly, ma'am." Mr. Hughes was a young man and obviously proud of his new rank. "As you can see here, Miss Johnson, we'll head south and round the Arabian Peninsula and then change to a northerly direction, sailing through the Red Sea and the Suez Canal. Then we'll navigate through the Nile River and one other river before we get to the Mediterranean Sea. To gain entrance to the North Atlantic, we'll follow the coasts of Spain and Portugal and go through the Strait of Gibraltar," he said, while pointing to the map on the large screen.

"I suppose the North Atlantic can be stormy."

"Yes, it can. Are you prone to seasickness, Miss Johnson?"

"I didn't get sick while sailing from China."

"That's a good sign. Lastly, we'll sail through Bay of Biscayne and the English Channel, which takes us to Southampton."

"How long will it all take?"

"It's 6,744 nautical miles and it will probably take 12 days."

"Thanks for showing me the route, Officer Hughes."

"My pleasure, Miss Johnson. Enjoy your voyage."

Vicky thought of how much her status had changed since sailing in second class from China. Then, she had been in the company of Michelle, and now she was afraid she would be lonely while David worked. His responsibility as captain would demand much of his time. As Vicky made her way back to her suite, she was surprised to see Michelle standing outside the door with a key in her hand.

"What are you doing here, Michelle? I thought you were flying home to Boston."

"I hope you don't mind, but we'll be cabin mates again. There was a problem with my flight. The airline had not confirmed my booking, and all the flights were fully booked for several days. When Jurgen heard about it, he asked me if I would like to sail with him to England. David okayed it and I jumped at the chance, so here I am. It's a good thing we have the summer off from teaching."

The two women embraced. "I was just thinking that I'd be lonely without you," Vicky said.

"Who would have thought that we'd be the girlfriends of the two highest ranking officers."

"Not me. Come on in and see our accommodations."

"This is luxurious compared to our second-class cabin," Michelle said.

"Yes, and we have more room for our dresses."

While Michelle unpacked, Vicky watched television.

The call for the lifeboat drill came at 3 p.m.

"This is your captain speaking. Put your lifejackets on and proceed at once to your assigned lifeboat for a practice drill," the loudspeaker said. The captain repeated the message several times. Vicky and Michelle looked at each other. "Do you have the card with the lifeboat number?" Vicky asked Michelle. "Yes, I have it in my purse. Should we put a coat on?"

"No, it's warm here." Vicky thought about what she would want to bring if the drill had been for real.

"How are we going to find the right lifeboat?" Michelle asked as they hurried up to the boat deck in their lifejackets.

"Someone will show us, I'm sure."

Once they were on the boat deck, officers checked their boat number and pointed them in the right direction. The crowds pushed them on. Their boat waited for them at the railing and an officer helped them board.

"I didn't hear anyone say 'women and children first,'" Vicky said.

"No, they probably aren't doing that anymore. There are lifeboats for everyone."

"This is a nice boat, and it's so big."

"Still it would be a small vessel in the big sea."

When the boat was full, it was lowered, but it slipped and hit the water, bow first. The passengers hung in their seatbelts. A crew member yelled an order to raise the boat again. Once they were level with the ship, Jurgen came and checked on them and the other people in the boat. "We're very sorry that the mechanism malfunctioned. Are you alright?" He helped everyone back on the ship and asked them if they were alright. Michelle and Vicky felt shaken but were unhurt.

"This time we'll lower the boat without passengers," Jurgen said. Vicky and Michelle looked on as the boat lowered evenly and hit the water on its keel. The boat's engine started and Jurgen was satisfied.

"That was a bad omen," Vicky said.

"Don't feel that way. I'm sure the problem is fixed."

"It wasn't bad this time but imagine what it would be like if it had happened in the cold North Atlantic at night and the ship was sinking."

People around them laughed and said they had enjoyed the drill. It was hot up on deck, probably well above 90 degrees, and the passengers were anxious to get back to the air-conditioned rooms.

"I need a drink after this frightening experience," Vicky said.

They walked back to their room to stow their life jackets and freshen up before heading for the bar.

"Wait for us, ladies," they heard David say. When they looked around, David and Jurgen came walking behind them.

"I'm sorry you were in the boat that upended. It won't happen again. That's why we have the drills," David reassured them.

"Why didn't we have a drill on the first voyage?" Vicky asked David.

"Because Captain Lowe didn't ask for one."

"Why don't you ladies go and have a cup of tea?" Jurgen asked.

"We were thinking about something stronger to calm our nerves," Michelle said.

"Well, we can take you to the bar, but we can't drink while we are on duty."

"I'm so glad my fiancée decided to join us on this voyage," Jurgen said as the four of them continued walking.

"Vicky will be at my table for dinner, and you, Michelle, will be at Jurgen's table, so we won't be eating together," David said.

"It's alright," Michelle said. "Vicky and I will be together during the day when you guys are working."

The two officers left Vicky and Michelle in the bar to talk about their future as sailors' wives. In the evening, they met new passengers at dinner. At the captain's table, David introduced Vicky to Europeans living in Dubai. At the chief officer's table, Michelle had the same experience. The dress was less formal than during the Maiden Voyage. The men wore tuxes or fancy suits and the women wore their hair in any style, and wore slim sheath dresses of various lengths. Only Muslim women wore dresses that covered their bodies. The menu showed no opulence. The diners could order their choice of meal, even vegetarian or vegan. "It will be more formal when we sail from Southampton," David said.

Both women were curious about what the Europeans were doing in Dubai. They were either businessmen or retired people who enjoyed warm weather and the luxury of domestic help. During the hottest summer months, they flew to Europe where most of them had second homes. Michelle met a man who was in the steel business and his wife an artist. The couple had lived in Switzerland for many years and had a summer home in Sweden.

The dancing in the ballroom after dinner was also less formal than earlier. At times, the music played rock-and-roll, and everyone seemed to enjoy it, whether they danced or not.

Chapter 48

Vicky and Michelle stood by the railing in the bow of the ship as it entered the Suez Canal. On one side they had Egypt and on the other the Sinai Peninsula. Both women documented their voyage, taking pictures and videos they would show to their students.

"Do you remember when pirates threatened the captain on an American ship in the Suez Canal?" Michelle asked Vicky.

"I remember. But I don't think anyone will attempt to raise a ladder up the side of our ship. It's too tall."

"You're right. Besides, David has arranged for security alerts as we go through the canal. I think I can see a guard by the railing from here."

"More guards are posted around the ship. They're all armed," Michelle said.

Their conversation was interrupted by the whirl of a helicopter above. An accented male voice boomed in the air: "We want to speak to the captain."

Vicky and Michelle saw the security guard aiming a gun at the helicopter. They could hear David's voice but didn't see him. "Get out of here. You're in restricted airspace. We have our guns aimed at you."

"If you know what's good for you, attach a bag of money to the line we're lowering now."

There was a pause before the first gunshot was heard. Michelle and

Vicky ran for safety and didn't see what happened next. The helicopter crashed in the water, and the Egyptian Coast Guard arrested the pirates.

"I think I got a video of the helicopter," Vicky said, her voice shaking. She showed it to David, who in turn showed it to the ship's owner, Mr. Cleaver.

Mr. Cleaver praised Captain Whitmore for the way he had handled the situation and said he would send the video to a news service. Several reporters interviewed David on secure lines, and the pirate attempt was broadcast on international television the same evening. The passengers flocked to the television screens on the ship.

"Our families must be in shock hearing about this," Michelle said to Vicky.

Relatives called them at once and talked to them on Skype. Ron Cosentino and his family were at home in Boston and wanted to make sure Michelle was safe.

"I hope nothing else will happen on this voyage," David said. "This is quite enough."

It was all people talked about during the dinner that night. Mr. Cleaver seemed to think that anyone else planning an attack on his ship would have been scared off. He proposed a toast to the continued safety of their voyage.

After the dancing in the ballroom, David invited Vicky to his captain's suite. Jurgen and Michelle stayed a little longer and talked about the day's incident. Michelle worried about future voyages. "Do you have to continue working on this ship, Jurgen?"

"I don't have a contract to continue after New York," he said. "But I wouldn't hesitate staying with this ship if David is the captain."

As David and Vicky entered the captain's suite, David took off his cap and placed in on a shelf before putting his arms around Vicky.

"I'm attracted to you, Vicky," David said, looking into her eyes.

"And I'm attracted to you," Vicky said, placing her arms around his neck.

"Are you ready for a relationship with a sea captain?"

"I would worry about you when you're at sea."

"If you sail with me, you don't have to worry. You're a good sailor. You haven't been seasick yet."

"I know, but I'm a teacher."

"Yes, I know, but that can change, can't it? As you know, I've been married before, and it's a lonely life. I've been looking for a wife for some time, and I think I found her. If it works out between us, I hope you'll be the one." He looked at her with loving eyes before their lips met in a passionate kiss.

"How long have you been divorced, David?"

"Five years, but we were separated two years before that. It's harder to be at sea when you don't have anyone to come home to."

"I had almost given up on finding a husband," Vicky admitted. "But there is something you should know. I was in a bad relationship years ago, and I'm cautious because ... because I was abused, both mentally and you know ..." She couldn't say it out loud. Her lip quivered.

"I'm so sorry, honey." David pulled her close and began to stroke her back. "I would like to try to erase those bad memories, if you'd let me."

"You're a gentleman, David, and I trust you."

"But you will be the boss, honey."

Vicky told Michelle about her amazing night with David the next morning as they stood by the railing and watched the ship moving up the Nile River. Michelle turned away from the arid view and jumped at Vicky's news.

"I'm so glad for you."

"David said that if it works out between us, he hopes I will marry him."

"That's wonderful, but I can see that you worry about something."

"My parents will want to put on a big society wedding with at least 500 guests. David only knows that my last name is Johnson. He doesn't know that I come from a corporate family."

"You should probably tell him."

"I know, but then he will start to wonder if he's good enough for me." Vicky frowned at the thought. "I'm the heir to a fortune, but possessions don't mean anything if I'm not happy," she said.

"I know, that's why you became a teacher. And David's love of sailing was probably what propelled him to enter the Naval Academy. From what I understand, David's ancestors owned real estate companies in New York and Boston, and his father owned a shipyard. David was never a poor boy like Jurgen."

"I didn't know that. He makes me happy and that's what counts."

"I'm sure everything will work out between you. It's getting hot out here. Let's go inside."

"Yes, I can't wait for us to enter the Mediterranean Sea, where it will be cooler."

"We'll soon be there." The two friends walked together to the Veranda Café. When they met David in his captain's uniform, he smiled and saluted them.

"It's too bad we can't show our affection for each other among the passengers and crew," Vicky said.

"Jurgen and I can't either."

When they had reached the Mediterranean Sea, David and Jurgen joined their fiancées on the bridge. David pointed to Mount Etna in Sicily. "It's the highest and most active volcano in Europe. Vesuvius is over there," he said, pointing to the mainland of Italy, "but it's not as high, and we can hardly see it from here. It looks like it's hiding in the clouds."

"I heard that Etna erupted recently," Michelle said.

"It erupts once in a while, but the last major eruption was in December 2015," Vicky said. She had read up on the history before the trip.

"Many poor immigrants came from Sicily to Boston. There was class distinction between them and other Italians," David said.

"I know because I'm partly Italian," Michelle said, "and my ancestor Roberto came from Genoa. I wish I could spot Genoa, but we're not sailing close to the coast, are we?"

"No, we're not," Jurgen said, "but you'll be able to see the city at a distance and the mountains in the background."

"How come we're not going into port for refueling?"

"Because this ship can sail two to three weeks without bunkering."

"My father visited Genoa and then went on to Rome and lived there for several months. That's where he began to write his book, My Life in Vietnam. He was a war correspondent in Saigon, and that's where he met Binh."

"It sounds like a fascinating story," Jurgen said. He turned to Michelle saying, "We could fly to Italy on our honeymoon if you like?"

"Oh, Jurgen, I'd love that."

"What is your ancestry, Vicky?" David asked with an inquisitive look at her.

"I don't know where the first Johnsons came from, but later we had Janssens in the family, and I believe they were Danish, but they could have been Norwegians."

"Then we both have Scandinavian ancestry. My Whitmore ancestors came from England, but my mother is Swedish. My dad has visited Sweden many times, and someday I would like to take you there, Vicky." He mouthed the word, *darling*.

"Sounds like a good idea, *darling*."

Michelle could see that David and Vicky were in love.

Chapter 49

Michelle had asked Jurgen to tell her when they came closer to Genoa, and lucky for her, it happened in the daytime. He picked her up in her room, and together they went to the starboard side of the ship, where Jurgen pointed to the north.

"Can you see the basin with the city built on the hillside?"

"Yes, I can see it. Oh my, this is where Roberto came from. I can see the Alps in the background. It's so exciting, Jurgen. I can't wait to actually walk on the streets where he walked. My father was here before he went to Rome. That was before he was married."

"Now, use these binoculars and you'll see more details."

"Oh my, I can see the harbor, churches, buildings, and streets."

Jurgen looked at Michelle as she spoke and squeezed her hand. "You can walk on those streets this summer, honey, right after we're married."

"Aren't you going back to work after we're married?"

"Not right away. I'll take some time off."

"I can't believe I will be back so soon, but I must film it because when we fly here, we won't have this view from the sea." She gave the binoculars back to Jurgen, aimed her camera at Genoa, and recorded a video. Then they stood by the railing and gazed at the coastline until Genoa disappeared from view.

While the ship passed through the Strait of Gibraltar, the two couples stood in the bow for the best view in all directions.

"Now, we're closer to shore," David said. "Africa is to our left and Spain to our right."

"Amazing," Vicky said, as she filmed both shorelines.

"Now, that we are entering the Atlantic, I'm afraid I'll be seasick again," Michelle said.

"To begin with, we'll have good weather," Jurgen assured her.

That night, Vicky and David talked about their future together, and Vicky said she wanted children. "I know that you already have a grown son, and you might not want a baby."

"I would love to have a child with you, darling."

"I'm so glad to hear you say that, but then I won't be able to sail with you."

"We'll work it out somehow. I could retire in a couple of years and do something else. But first we should get married. Will you marry me when we come back to the States?"

"Yes, I will, but I have to warn you. My mother is not going to be happy when she can't put on a large wedding."

"We won't have time for that. We are mature adults and can marry without telling your parents."

"Yes, that's what I'd prefer. My parents won't like it, but if they get a grandchild, they will forgive us."

"Tell me about your parents."

"Well, they are not the bigwigs at the top of the company, but my father works in the pharmaceutical business."

"Oh, those Johnsons."

"Yes, I have hundreds of relatives."

"That would be a big wedding." David looked perplexed.

"I hope it's not too shocking to you."

"I'm not marrying the company. I'm marrying you, and you're a grade school teacher. I just hope they will accept me as their son-in-law."

"They will. Remember that I'm almost 40, and they have waited for years to see me married."

"So, anyone will do," David joked.

"No, not anyone. Captain David Whitmore, the man I love. I have met your family and I like your parents very much."

"Should we get married by a judge, or do you have any preference?"

"A judge would be fine. I want Michelle and Jurgen to be our witnesses."

"Good choice. But in order to get married we'll need a marriage license, and for that we need our birth certificates. I don't suppose you have yours with you?"

"No, I don't. It's in Boston."

"So is mine. I also need proof of divorce, and that is in Boston as well. We need to fly to Boston as soon as soon we arrive. I'll order tickets."

"How long will Titanic Princess be in New York?"

"Because we expect a large celebration, we will be docked five days, and I hope it will be enough."

"If we're going to Boston, we should be married there with your family present, don't you think?"

"But what about your parents?"

"They don't live in Boston, so we'll skip them."

"I will have to send a wire to my dad and tell him that he and Mom don't have to come to New York."

"I'm excited already."

Vicky told Michelle about David's proposal the next morning and that they would be married in Boston.

"Great!" she exclaimed. "Perhaps we can have a double wedding."

"Are you going to Boston too?"

"Yes, we are. Jurgen is taking a leave of absence."

"I'm not telling my parents ahead of the time, because then pandemonium will break out. Mom would want a year to plan the wedding, and I want to marry now, asap, and start a family."

"Is David fine with that?"

"Yes, he is, thank God."

"I'm so happy for you." The two friends hugged and laughed until tears ran down their cheeks.

On Sunday, Mr. Cleaver announced that he would hold an interdenominational Christian service. Other religions had been invited to hold their services on Saturday or another weekday. Mr. Cleaver read the gospel for the day, gave thanks for a safe journey, and prayed the ship would bring all the passengers and crew to their destination safely. Three members from the orchestra jazzed up the hymns that were sung, and the worshippers clapped their hands in rhythm. Lastly, Mr. Cleaver invited worshippers to speak. The first speaker asked for a minute of silence in memory of those who had perished on the first Titanic. Another praised Mr. Cleaver for building the modern version of the ship and giving them all the experience of sailing on an ocean liner. Only one commented on the gospel text for the day and prayed. The service closed with the singing of *Nearer My God to Thee.*

As Vicky and Michelle left the service, Vicky said, "I thought the captain was supposed to lead the service."

"I think that Captain Smith on the Titanic led one service, but I don't know if it's a requirement. We'll ask David."

"It depends on the owner of the line and the contract signed," David said. "I certainly could have read the text for the day, but Mr. Cleaver offered to lead the service and it was fine with me."

As Michelle had predicted, she became seasick when they encountered heavy seas in the Bay of Biscayne.

"I mustn't be sick when we arrive," Michelle said with a worried look at Vicky.

"You'll be well again before then. I'm going to get some pills from David or Jurgen. Keep your head down as much as possible."

Wrenching in pain, Michelle held her stomach and aimed for the toilet, vomiting time after time until it felt like her stomach was empty. "Ugh, that was awful," she said to herself as she flushed the toilet and reached for a tissue to wipe her face. She hadn't seen Jurgen and Vicky coming into the room. Jurgen stood there with a roll of pills in his hand looking helpless.

"Sorry, darling, I should have given you these pills earlier. I'm not sure they will work now," he said.

Michelle grasped the roll and quickly freed a pill from the wrapping and popped it in her mouth. "Water please." Vicky handed her a glass of water that Michelle gulped down. "Slow down, you should only take a sip," Jurgen cautioned. As soon as Michelle stood up, she began to retch again.

"There goes the pill, down the toilet," Jurgen said.

"A sailor's wife should be able to stand up to the sea," Michelle said when she could talk again. She hid her running eyes and red face in a towel.

"So, so honey, once you're used to the sea, you won't get seasick." Jurgen stroked her back. "I got seasick too the first time I was at sea."

"So why aren't you sick, Vicky?" Michelle asked her friend with an accusing look.

"I don't know."

"Some people are more prone to seasickness than others," Jurgen said. "It's not so bad now with the modern facilities. Just think what the early emigrants had to endure in close quarters below deck with no water for cleaning up."

"My stomach hurts so badly." Michelle held her middle and bent over in pain.

"Yes, I know. I think you should get back to bed and stay there. Here are some paper bags that you can use, so you don't have to run to the toilet. Your stomach should be empty by now, and it's best that you don't eat anything until we come to Southampton. The sea will calm down by then. If you take another pill, you'll be able to sleep."

Jurgen led her to her lower bunk, tucked her in, and kissed her forehead. "I'll check on you soon. Vicky will be your nurse, won't you Vicky?"

"Of course, I will."

Michelle took a pill and slept the rest of the way to Southampton. Titanic Princess didn't make a stop in Cherbourg, France, like the original Titanic. The French who had booked passage to New York could take the Chunnel or fly to London.

By the time Titanic Princess sailed into Southampton, the recovered Michelle and Vicky stood on deck and looked up at all the cruise ships that towered over them. A towboat guided Titanic Princess into port, where the passengers were greeted by cheering people who welcomed them to Southampton. A band played, flags flew high, and it was all very festive.

Among the waving people was Dan Whitmore, the English cousin that Will Whitmore had met in London when they were both young. Dan had read in the papers that David Whitmore commanded Titanic Princess, and now Dan stood at the pier with his wife, Gloria, three children, and six grandchildren, waiting for a chance to meet Captain David. They would have to wait a long time.

David and Jurgen stood at the gangplank saying goodbye to the first-class passengers that would fly back to Dubai. Mr. Cleaver was the first to go ashore. At once, he was met by reporters and photographers. Dan and Gloria could hear him proudly telling how well the ship had performed. Then they had to wait for the rest of the first-class passengers to disembark, followed by the second- and third-class passengers. But the parade wasn't over yet. Crew members began to pass by. Dan said many of them would be replaced with new crew for the voyage to New York.

Chapter 50

Titanic Princess would be in port for a few days while the ship was thoroughly cleaned and made ready for new passengers.

"I'll leave her to you, Chief Jurgen, while Vicky and I go ashore," David said. "We'll be back tomorrow, so you and Michelle can go ashore."

"Ay, ay, sir," Jurgen replied, saluting his boss. "I'll see to that the new supplies are loaded."

David was dressed in his uniform as he escorted Vicky off the ship. When Vicky began the voyage, she could not have imagined that she would be by David's side in Southampton. She was dressed for the occasion in a light blue suit and felt like a princess as people waved to them. Having grown up in a well-known family, she was no stranger to public exposure, but this event topped everything she had experienced. A security officer walked ahead of them, scanning the crowds. Behind them, an aide pulled a cart with four overnight bags. The reporters that crowded around them were pushed away by the security guard, but cameras clicked and videos rolled. Vicky realized that the pictures would reach her family in America.

Dan saw his chance and called out, "Captain Whitmore, cousin David, I'm Dan Whitmore. May I say hello. We're related." David turned and looked at Dan.

"Are you the same fellow that my brother Will met here in London?"

"Yes, I am." The security asked Dan for an ID and then nodded to David.

The two men shook hands and Dan introduced his wife and pointed to the rest of his family. "We've been waiting a long time and really didn't think we would get a chance to meet you, but seeing the new ship was great."

"I'm glad you came. This is my fiancée, Miss Victoria Johnson. We're taking the train into London and will stay at a hotel at Trafalgar Square. Would you and your wife care to join us for dinner?"

"We would love to." Dan smiled and looked thrilled.

David asked the security guard to give Dan the information about the hotel, while Gloria and Victoria spoke briefly.

"See you later then," David said, saluting his relatives.

"Hope you don't mind," David said to Vicky.

"Not at all. I think it's fantastic that you can meet relatives here. I'll enjoy it, too."

"Our English relatives appeared to be a bit stuck-up when Dad was here, but when my older brother, Will, met Dan, they got along fine. They even flew to Sydney together."

As they approached pass control, the security guard took David's and Vicky's passports and told them to follow him.

"Welcome to the U.K. and enjoy your stay in London," the official said as he stamped their passports.

"Have you been here on stopovers before, David?" Vicky asked.

"Yes, but then I was alone. This is so much better. What do you want to do in London, honey?"

"Is it possible to tour one of the castles?"

"Yes, and that is something I've never done. I'll be glad to take the tour with you. That's probably all we'll have time for," David said as he helped Vicky board the train.

After they had checked into the hotel, David inquired about a tour to Windsor Castle.

"If you want to do the tour on your own, which is the fastest, it's best to take a taxi, and be there by 1 p.m. at the latest," the concierge told him. The security guard had to come along, of course. It was his duty to guard Captain Whitmore. David changed into leisure clothes so he would not be recognized, and Vicky changed to comfortable shoes. After a quick lunch at the bar counter, the guard had a cab waiting for them. Windsor Castle, located on the outskirts of London, was the home of Queen Elisabeth II and her family when she was not in one of her other residences.

At the castle, they saw the "State Apartments" used for state occasions and royal receptions. It was inspired by the grandeur of Versailles during the reign of Charles II. One ceiling painting portrayed his queen. Red flocked wallpaper covered the walls that were hung with portraits of former kings, and red carpet covered the floors. Ornate furniture, fireplaces, and works of art by European masters added to the grand décor. As David and Vicky left the castle, Vicky turned around and looked at the balcony that she had seen on televised episodes with the royals waving to their constituents.

"We have time to go inside St. George's Chapel, if you'd like," David said.

"Oh, yes, that's where Prince Harry will be married," Vicky exclaimed. "I can't believe I'm here."

"If we had gone on a group tour, it would have taken four hours including the chapel," David said, as they walked up the aisle on the black-and-white tiled floor. "It's so beautiful," Vicky whispered, looking at the pews that faced the aisle. The castle was magnificent, but this is breathtaking. Now I'll know exactly what it looks like when I see the wedding on TV."

David smiled, "I'm glad you are enjoying yourself, darling."

Back at the hotel, they changed for dinner. David wore a dark suit and looked like any other male diner. Vicky wore a sleeveless black dress and a pearl necklace. As they met Dan and Gloria in the lobby, David noticed Dan's oval Whitmore face that he had seen on many family portraits. The security guard selected their table by a wall and saw to that they were all seated before sitting down himself with the aide at the closest table to them.

David ordered champagne and they drank a toast to the Titanic Princess. Dan wanted to hear about the voyage, and Gloria asked how David and Vicky had met. After the main course, Dan asked about Will and his family. "He married the girl he met in Sydney! David said. I was there when they met," Dan said. "She was a pretty Norwegian girl."

"And a very smart girl," David added. "She is now a scientist." The time passed quickly until Dan asked for the check.

"No, Dan, this is on me. I asked you to join us and you are my guests," David said, handing his credit card to the server.

Having said goodbye to their guests, David and Vicky went to their room, and enjoyed being alone. The security guard and the aide stayed in an adjacent room.

"I feel like royalty," Vicky said. "Is this how it's always going to be if I sail with you, honey?"

"I don't think so. I don't have relatives in every port," David said with a grin.

"No, but there will be a guard and an aide present."

"As long as I am in command."

"What's the schedule of the ship after New York?"

"It's going to sail back and forth between Southampton and New York during the summer months. When winter comes, it will sail into the Mediterranean, to Dubai and warmer climates."

"Are you going to be on it?"

"Mr. Cleaver has asked me to stay on. If I take time off, he will get another captain and I might lose the opportunity. We still have time to get married in New York, and then you can sail with me as my wife, if you want?"

"Oh yes, but I need to have something to do on the ship. Otherwise, I'll be bored."

"If we had children passengers, you could arrange for daycare, but we usually don't have any children aboard now. What else could you do?"

"I could be a librarian if one is needed."

"I'll look into it."

"Now we are alone and I'm not on duty. No one will disturb us. He hung a "Do not disturb sign" on the door. Let's make the most of it, darling." He reached out for Vicky and took off her pearl necklace, then knelt before her and took off her shoes. He let one hand slide up her leg as he kissed her neck and lips.

It rained in the morning, so they ordered breakfast and stayed in bed until it was time to shower and get dressed to take the train back to Southampton and the waiting ship.

Chapter 51

The Voyage from Southampton and New York

The Titanic Princess sailed out of the Southampton port with much fanfare. The departure went smoothly. There was no near collision like when the first Titanic departed in 1912. Most of the passengers were from the U.K., but many Americans had flown in to sail to New York. The Titanic Princess also carried passengers from many different European countries. Mr. Cleaver had recommended period clothing for dinner the first day, but it was not mandatory. The meal would not have as many entrees as on the Maiden Voyage, but as expected the dinner was festive. The ship would sail directly to New York in seven days.

Once again, Vicky and Michelle stood on deck waving to the onlookers on the pier. Smaller vessels followed the ocean liner into the English Channel. Fog soon enveloped the ship, and the women retreated to the Veranda Café.

"This time, I'll prevent seasickness by taking the pill before we encounter heavy seas," Michelle said. I'm glad Jurgen is taking time off from work after we get to New York."

"David wants me to sail with him as his wife over the summer, but I'll probably go back to teaching in the fall," Vicky said.

"I hope to go back to teaching, too, but I might have to move to New York or New Jersey, so I'm here when Jurgen is in port."

"We both have to move if we're going to see our husbands between voyages." Vicky said. Her cell phone rang.

"Hello. Who's calling?"

"It's your mother. What's this I heard on TV about you being engaged to a sea captain?"

"It's true, Mom. His name is David Whitmore. He's a fine man and comes from a good family." Michelle saw how frustrated Vicky looked. She could hear the loud voice on the other end. Vicky stood up and walked out of earshot from everyone in the café. The conversation continued.

"It would have been nice to hear it from you, Vicky. We want to meet the man, of course."

"Mom, David and I are adults, and we don't need your permission to get married."

There was a pause on the other end. "Does that mean that you have already set the date?"

"The ceremony will be private. I'll let you know as soon as we're married, Mom."

"It's not what I had planned for my only daughter's wedding."

"I know, but I think you should be happy for me regardless."

"I hope you're doing the right thing. We have to talk more about it later. I can hardly hear you. Talk to you later then, hon."

Vicky said goodbye as the connection broke. Bewildered, she returned to the café and sank down in the chair with a big sigh.

"My mom is upset and disappointed, of course."

"I understood that much, but she'll probably come around."

"You are lucky, Michelle. Your parents have met Jurgen. I don't expect to see my parents at my wedding. It would be a big surprise."

"Well, you never know. Let's go to lunch." Vicky looked defeated.

"Do you want to attend the lecture this afternoon about the original

Titanic?" Michelle asked.

"No, I want to take a look at the ship library. I might be of help there in the future."

"Alright, I'll go with you then because I need something to read."

They were astounded when they saw how many Titanic books there were in the library.

"Here is one with the title, *Not my time to die: The Swedes on board*, that looks interesting," Michelle said. She leafed through it and said, "It contains survivor stories."

"And here is one titled, *A Night to Remember* that contains interviews with survivors," Vicky said.

There was no one there to help them check out the books, but they sat down and began to read. After a while, a woman came and apologized for being absent.

At once, Vicky offered to help. "I'm a teacher and I'm looking for something to do on the ship."

"I could use some help because I can see there are many people on board who like to read," she said, surveying the library room. I'll show you what to do if they want to check out books."

Vicky kept busy for the rest of the afternoon familiarizing herself with the books and helping customers find titles, while Michelle sat in a chair reading *Not my time to die*.

"This is fascinating," she said. "The book got its name because a young Swedish woman said it wasn't her time to die. The rest of a large group of people from her home area perished. The book is inscribed by the author as a gift to the ship's owner."

"You know, I'd be glad to volunteer here for the rest of this voyage, but in the future, I hope to get a chance to work here," Vicky said, looking up from a book.

"Oops, look at the time. We've to go and get dressed for dinner," Michelle said.

They dressed in long gowns that they had worn on the other voyages. Mr. Cleaver and a few other men wore tails. The dinner partners were new and interesting. Vicky took her place beside David at the captain's table.

"What have you been doing this afternoon, honey?" David asked.

"Michelle and I have been at the ship's library. David, I would love to be the librarian on the next voyage."

"I've already talked to Mr. Cleaver about it and he said it could be arranged."

"Oh, good." The man on her other side was a financier from London who talked to David about the stock market and business in general. David listened politely, then turned to the man on the other side of the table and asked him how he liked the voyage so far."

"It's wonderful. I think of the Titanic Princess as a floating hotel."

"I'm glad to hear it," David replied.

One man sitting at the middle of the table told jokes that made everyone laugh. Mr. Cleaver sat at the far end and told some good jokes himself. When he laughed his whole body shook. The earlier stiffness was gone, and everyone had a good time. The servers were busy changing plates and placing new dishes before them. The pheasant on the original menu had been replaced with chicken.

At Jurgen's table, the guests talked about whether airplanes emitted more carbon in the air than a passenger ship.

"In order to compare, you have to consider how many passengers we are carrying," Jurgen said. "An airplane would have to fly across seven times to carry as many passengers as we're carrying, and then we might come out the same as far as carbon imprint is concerned."

"We're using a lot of water with showers and all. Where is it coming from?" Michelle asked.

"We're converting salt water for our needs, about 630 tons a day."

"Bravo!" Someone said. "How fast are we going?"

"28.5 knots, or 33 miles per hour."

"It doesn't seem very fast compared to the speed we drive our cars," Michelle said.

"No, it doesn't, but the first Titanic could not move as fast as this ship."

When they finally broke up from the table, Jurgen said, "Don't forget to set your watches back one hour every night until we are close to New York time. Since we're moving slowly, you won't get jetlag."

Michelle didn't feel well when she woke up in the morning. Vicky was already up.

"I think you need to take a pill before you get up because the sea is choppy today," she told her friend. "Here, is a glass of water."

"Thank you, Vicky. You're a good friend. I'm not going to breakfast. It's best not to have food in my stomach."

"I'm going to the library after breakfast."

Michelle stayed in bed and thought about what her life would be like as Jurgen's wife. Was she making a mistake by marrying him? But she loved him and wasn't that enough? If she moved to New York, she would be away from her family and friends. Vicky would sail with David. Michelle contemplated what her future would be like as she dozed off.

In the ship's library, Vicky met many descendants of Titanic survivors who were interested in reading books about the Titanic's sinking. Descendants swapped survivor stories with one another. One told of a great uncle who had drowned and wondered if the library had any records of him. Vicky was kept busy trying to find the right book for each one and learned a lot in the process. When she couldn't help, she turned to the internet and searched for information. She handed a Swedish descendant the book, *Not my time to die*, and the woman was delighted when she found a detailed account of the person she was looking for. American first-class passengers on the ill-fated ship were well documented, for instance, John Jacob Astor, Isidor and Ida Straus, Benjamin

Guggenheim, and Molly Brown. Among the famous Brits were the White Star Line manager Bruce Ismay, fashion designer Lady Lucille Duff Gordon and her husband, and the Olympic athlete Sir Cosmos Duff Gordon.

Captain Smith perished, but the officers who survived became well known after they had testified at two inquiries. Colonel Archibald Gracie wrote a book with the title *The Story of Titanic*. Second-class passengers had also written accounts of their rescue, but it was harder to find information about Turks, Romanian, Poles, Latvians, Russians, Italians, and other nationalities traveling in third class. Names were too similar or spelled incorrectly. Birth dates could also be wrong. The people searching for information didn't always have the correct data about the original place of departure or the survivors' destination in the United States. Families were the easiest to locate, but also the saddest.

While having lunch with David, Vicky told him how excited she was about volunteering at the library. David said he had received several emails from his family telling him they had seen him and Vicky on TV walking off the ship in Southampton. "Here is one email I received from my Dad. I printed it for you."

It was good to see you and Vicky together and hearing that you're engaged. We can't wait to attend your wedding ceremony. Please cable us before the ship comes in, so we have time to plan for your homecoming and wedding. You have our warmest congratulations and best wishes.

I have just returned from a business trip to San Francisco. Henrik has so many orders that he has to start importing solar panels from China. He and Caroline broke up before they left Dubai, but Henrik is now in love with the girl he met in Sweden. Her name is Linda, and she stopped to visit him on a tour of the States. I met her and she's a lovely girl. If she is as good a match for Henrik as your mother was for me, Henrik will be very happy.

The letter continued with updates about all of David's relatives.

"You're lucky, David. You have an affectionate family," Vicky said. "I'll be glad to be a part of it."

Chapter 52

As Jurgen had predicted, Michelle slept through the storm. When she woke up, she asked, "Where are we?"

"We're out on the ocean, but it's calmer now. I want to see you walking before I leave," Vicky said.

Michelle took a few stumbling but necessary steps to get to the bathroom and called out, "I'm fine." But Vicky waited until she was back in bed before leaving. "I'm not as strong as I thought," Michelle admitted.

When Vicky returned, Jurgen was with Michelle. "How's my patient?" he asked.

"Much better," Michelle tried to smile.

"Vicky has a tray of light food for you, sweetie."

"Thanks, Vicky."

"Many other passengers were sick during the storm. The dining rooms were almost empty last night," Jurgen said.

"So, you didn't get to dance with the lonely ladies?"

"No, the ones who were on their feet didn't feel like dancing."

A little later, David shared his concern with Jurgen about a particular passenger.

"I have noticed one dark-bearded man," David said. "He was especially noticeable yesterday during the storm. He wasn't sick but seemed awfully nervous."

"Yes, I noticed him, too," Jurgen said. "We have to keep an eye on him."

"I have notified security. A guard will shadow him." David changed the subject.

"What is this I hear that you won't be sailing with us after New York, Jurgen?"

"It's true. I want to marry Michelle and fly to Europe with her. It will be our honeymoon."

"I'll miss you, but I'm glad you can do that. I'm afraid I would lose my position if I did."

"It will be better for Michelle if I sail with a ship out of Boston. Then she can be with her family while I'm away and she can continue to teach. Since she gets seasick, I couldn't ask her to sail with me."

"Will you have a big wedding in Boston?"

"Just her family. Mine won't come all the way from Philadelphia."

"And Vicky isn't inviting her family to come to ours, so it will be only my relatives."

A security guard came running toward David. "Come with me, sir," he said. As they hurried away, Jurgen wondered what the problem could be.

Michelle felt well again as she dressed for the evening's dinner. "What are you going to wear when you get married, Vicky?" she asked.

"One of my long gowns. I'm not wearing white."

"We have enough dresses to choose from. I'll ask Jurgen which one he wants me to wear."

"I guess we won't have a double wedding after all."

"No, it would be too difficult to coordinate especially since David and I will have only five days to get back to the ship."

Both Michelle and Vicky could feel the tension during dinner. David and Jurgen exchanged glances and there were security guards in every corner of the room. The servers took their plates before the guests were finished eating and quickly brought the next dish. Before the dessert, David and Jurgen excused themselves saying that duty called and escorted their ladies away from the dining room. "There won't be any dancing with us tonight," David said.

"Why not?" Vicky asked. "What's going on?"

"I'll tell you when we get to my cabin." He walked so fast that Vicky had trouble keeping up with him.

"You are making me nervous," she said.

"It's nothing for you to worry about," David said as soon as he had closed the door behind them. "Sit down, honey," he said, although he didn't sit down himself but paced back and forth.

"We will probably arrest one of our passengers who has acted suspiciously, but first we have to check his background. You can't say anything about this to anyone, not even Michelle, understand?"

"I understand, but are we in danger?"

"No, darling. It's just that we have planned to have a memorial ceremony and lay a wreath tomorrow at the location of the Titanic sinking, and we don't want any disturbance. Therefore, it's best that the suspicious man is detained. I'll take you to your room now, because I'll be busy, but Michelle can keep you company. Don't worry about anything darling."

He hugged and kissed her and then quickly put his captain's hat on again and opened the door for her.

Jurgen had not told Michelle that much, only that there were some concerns about having the memorial ceremony. "We're arriving at the site earlier than expected and we have to plan for the event," he said.

"I think it's nice to honor all those people who gave their lives," Michelle said to Vicky.

"I do too, but since we are having an early night, I'm going to read one of the books I borrowed from the library. Do you want one, Michelle?"

"Yes, I might as well read," she said.

They took off their gowns and dressed in robes before curling up on the sofa, one in each corner. Vicky had a hard time concentrating on her book about the Titanic. She really didn't want to be reminded of the sinking at this time. She put away the book with a yawn and said, "I'm tired, I think I'll go to bed." Michelle continued reading a wedding book.

After a restless night, Vicky woke up with an uneasy feeling. There was something different about the ship. It felt like it had slowed down. She saw that the sea was calm, and it hardly looked like they were moving at all. "We are slowing down because we don't want to arrive too early at the memorial site," she said to Michelle, who had just begun to stir.

"Well, we can't be slowing down because of icebergs when there aren't any," she answered, looking out the window. The sun was rising behind them and lit up the calm sea. "It's so beautiful," she said.

They looked in awe at the sight. "We're heading home," Vicky said dreamingly.

"It will be good to get home. Cruises are nice, but I'd rather be on land," Michelle sighed.

At breakfast, it was announced that there would be a memorial ceremony on deck at 4 o'clock in the afternoon. Vicky couldn't find David before it was time for her to go the library and hoped that he would look her up. He came at 10 o'clock and motioned to her to follow him into the corridor. "Everything is alright," he said. "We have the man. See you at the ceremony." Vicky drew a long breath of relief and returned to the library.

There was a flower shop on the ship, and Michelle went there to get roses to throw into the sea at the memorial service. She saw that the florist was busy decorating a wreath and asked if it was for the ceremony.

"Yes, it is," he said. On the way out, she met Jurgen in the hallway. "I see that you bought roses, and I think I know what they are for," he said. "I was going to buy one for you."

"I bought one for Vicky too. She's working, you know." Michelle breathed in the aroma of the roses while looking at him. "You remind me of our wedding day. Do you want roses in your bouquet?" he asked.

"Yes, as long as they are not too prickly."

"We have so much to look forward to, you and I." Jurgen looked relaxed and happy. "I love you," he whispered. "I love you, too," Michelle whispered back.

Chapter 53

The prisoner moved restlessly in his small cell and sweated profusely when the two security guards came to interrogate him.

"What's the matter. Don't you like the accommodations?" the guard named Rob asked.

"You have to let me out," the prisoner said, shaking the bars.

"Not yet, we are checking your background for terrorist activities."

"I'll confess if you let me out." He was clearly very agitated.

"No, you have to confess now. It's clear to me that you're afraid of something.

The man looked at his watch and his chest began heaving. "There is a bomb close to us, and it will explode," he gasped.

"Where?"

"Over there, under the cover."

The second guard, Ben, ran for help while Rob peeked under the cover.

"How long until it goes off?" he asked.

"Half an hour."

"Can you defuse it?"

"Yes, yes, if you let me out." His eyes were wide with fear, and he jumped up and down in his cell.

"We have to wait until my partner comes back." The minutes ticked away as did the timer on the bomb.

"After you have secured the bomb, you are going back to your cell."

"I know, but I want to live."

"How much damage could this bomb do?"

"It could sink the ship."

Rob was clearly shaken but asked, "Why would you do something so horrible?"

There was no answer as Captain Whitmore arrived with two security guards.

"He has planted a bomb, but he'll defuse it we let him out," Rob said.

"How long before the bomb goes off?" the captain asked the prisoner.

"I'm not sure, maybe 15 minutes, maybe less."

David barked out an order to the guards. "Draw your weapons, and give me the key. Who has the key?"

"I have it," Rob said, fumbling for the key on a chain that hung at his waist.

Captain Whitmore put the key in the lock and turned it while the guards pointed their guns on the prisoner.

"Go and render the bomb safe, for God's sake," the captain roared.

The prisoner's hand shook uncontrollably as he bent down to defuse the bomb. The guards began to sweat and David felt the blood rush to his head but kept quiet while the prisoner tried to steady his hands. Looking at his watch, David prayed they weren't too late.

Finally, the prisoner stood up, saying, "It's safe now. It won't explode."

The prisoner seemed to have relaxed, so David had to believe him.

"Get back in the cell," he commanded. The guards held their guns on the man and he had no choice. Rob went over to the bomb and determined that it was no longer active. "All clear," he said.

"Do you have accomplices on board?" The captain's voice was stern but steady as his eyes bored into the prisoner's.

"No, I did it alone."

Turning away from the prisoners and addressing the guards, David said, "Put extra chains on the cell door and a pad lock. One of you has to guard the prisoner night and day until we reach New York. You'll take the first pass, Ben. Turning to Rob, he said, "You did a good job."

David motioned to Rob and the other two guards to follow him to a place where the prisoner could not hear them. "I will notify the FBI. No one can mention to anyone what has happened until after the FBI has taken over. The bomb has to be put behind lock and key. I leave that up to you, Rob. The FBI will take possession of it, I'm sure. We have to assume there is an accomplice, who has to be apprehended. Now, Rob, I trust that you'll lock up the bomb."

"Ay, ay, sir."

"What did the prisoner say to you when you were alone with him?"

"He said that the bomb could sink the ship."

"Then a colossal tragedy has been averted."

David felt shaken but relieved as he departed the scene with two security guards accompanying him. He realized he would not have any privacy for the rest of the voyage. It would be a small price to pay considering what could have happened.

At 4 o'clock in the afternoon, David stood by the railing on the boat deck ready to lower a wreath into the sea. The ship slowed down. A large group of passengers had gathered. The orchestra was present and so was Mr. Cleaver. David gave a short memorial speech.

On this spot, more than 106 years ago, the newly built Titanic, the largest ship built up to that time, foundered and sank. More than 1,500 passengers and crew lost their lives among the icebergs. Only about 700 were saved by another ship, the Carpathia, and its commander Captain Rostron, who responded to Titanic's call for help and steamed forward among the icebergs, unfortunately arriving too late for the poor people for whom there were no lifeboats. The Titanic had gone to the bottom of the sea. The Carpathia picked up the helpless people in the lifeboats and returned with them to New York, although he was headed for Italy. Today, we honor all the victims with a minute of silence, after which we will lower the wreath into the water. If you brought flowers, you may toss them over the railing. The orchestra will then conclude the ceremony by playing the Navy hymn, "For Those in Peril on the Sea."

David had selected the Navy hymn because he knew everyone on board the Titanic Princess had been in great peril as recently as that morning.

Many tears rolled down the cheeks of those present as they bowed their heads in silence. Michelle thought about her ancestor Roberto saving himself by jumping into the sea and also saving the life of David's ancestor, Anna. When the wreath had been laid, Vicky and Michelle went up to the railing and tossed their roses over board. Their eyes followed the wreath floating away.

"How do you know this is where the ship sank?" Vicky asked David as she caught up with him.

"It's marked on the sea map. I'm sorry, but I cannot see you in private for security reasons."

"I understand. Be careful." Vicky suspected it had something to do with the suspicious man. David had said she had to trust him on that, and she did. He would tell her later.

As they approached New York, Vicky and Michelle stood in the bow and sighted the Statue of Liberty and Ellis Island. Vicky, like most Americans, had ancestors who had come to America on a ship. David had told her not to hurry off the ship, but wait for him and Jurgen, so they stood there while Titanic Princess glided into port. Large crowds had gathered at the pier to welcome the ship and everyone on board. In the next moment, the crowd was pushed back as several police cars with emergency lights and sirens drove all the way to the gangway. Men carrying weapons emerged from the cars and boarded the ship.

"They must be coming for the suspicious man," Vicky said. "I wonder what he's suspected of doing?"

"So, there is a valid reason why David and Jurgen have been so secretive and David has been so heavily guarded," Michelle said.

They stood as in trance waiting for the officers to return with the prisoner, but there were actually two. "So, he did have an accomplice. I think we have had the thrill of the day," Vicky said. "I can imagine the press that will show up. I'm afraid David will not be able to make our flight to Boston."

"I talked to my dad on Skype, and he said Binh would meet the ship in New York, but how's that little man going to be able to see anything in this crowd?" Michelle said.

"Has he become famous like your dad predicted?"

"He has been on television in New York, and the newspapers have featured his story. That's all I know," Michelle said. Vicky's cell phone rang. "It's nice to be back in civilization again," she said, as she retrieved it from her purse. "It's David."

"Where are you?" he asked in a low voice. "You should know that security is listening to us."

"Really. Michelle and I are standing in the bow. We saw the officers entering the ship and returning with two prisoners."

"Don't be alarmed. Everything is fine, but do not talk to anyone about this. I just want to say that I have a meeting with Mr. Cleaver. I'll call you as soon as the meeting is over."

"Okay," was all she could say.

"Can you believe that, Michelle? Security is monitoring his calls."

"It must be more serious than we thought." Next, it was Michelle's phone that rang and Jurgen calling her.

"Honey. I'll escort you and Vicky off the ship and we'll be driven to the airport. You should go to your room and get your hand luggage ready. Everything else will be taken to the airport. David will meet us at LaGuardia. He might be a little delayed."

"Is someone listening to us?"

"No, my darling. I'm not as important as David."

"You are important to me."

"You and Vicky can wait for me in your suite. Do not talk to any reporters. See you soon, sweetie."

"We're supposed to go to our room and wait for Jurgen. He will escort us off the ship and to the airport. David will meet us there. We cannot talk to any reporters," Michelle told Vicky.

"Alright. Let's go then."

It was difficult to move against the stream of passengers who wanted to get off the ship, but the two friends made it to their suite. There was nothing to do except wait. Michelle decided to call her sister Caroline, and they talked for a long time.

When the call ended, Michelle turned to Vicky saying, "Caroline is going steady with a former employee, named Harold. She had a crush on him a couple years ago. Harold now works for another company, and they feel free to date. She said this time it's serious, and I'm glad for her."

After a while, two porters came and picked up their packed suitcases. When Jurgen finally came, the rest of the passengers had left, and they could get off the ship without waiting in line. A security guard cleared their way through Immigration and Passport Control. At the airport, Jurgen attracted attention in his uniform. Reporters swarmed around them and the security guards were busy turning them away. The television screens blasted scenes and reports of the docking of Titanic Princess, the FBI agents, and a story about an attempted terrorist attack on board.

"Terrorist attack!" Vicky's face turned pale. She looked at Jurgen and asked, "Is David alright?"

"He is fine. Mr. Cleaver will talk to the reporters."

When David arrived, he was escorted by two security guards. He hadn't had time to change out of his uniform and naturally attracted a lot of attention. The reporters wanted his story about what had happened but wouldn't get it from him.

David, Jurgen, and their ladies were escorted to a lounge where they could be alone before boarding. The pilot was holding their plane as requested by one of the security guards until Captain Whitmore, his party, and their luggage were on board.

"Here is the good news," David said. "Mr. Cleaver has given me time off with pay for the way I handled the threat, actually two threats. I don't have to report to duty until the ship leaves for Southampton next time."

"That's wonderful news, David," Vicky said. "But why were the two men arrested?"

"I'll tell you when we are alone, honey. Not now."

"Let's fly home to Boston," Michelle said. "My family is waiting for me and Jurgen."

"And my family is waiting for Vicky and me," David said. "I just have to call my father and tell him we are safe. We'll be met by security at Logan Airport and driven home."

Binh stood on the pier waiting. He couldn't see the ship for all the tall people who stood in front of him. Finally, he said to the Chinese lady who accompanied him, "Let's go home, honey, and watch it on television."

The Whitmore Fictional Characters

First generation

Anna Olson Whitmore, b. 1890, adopted by Martin and Ellen Olson, biological daughter of Henry Addison and Brita Erickson. Sailed on the Titanic in 1912, rescued by Roberto Cosentino.

- married John Whitmore in 1912

s. Henry William, b. 1913

d. Kristina, b. 1919, not married

Second generation

Henry Whitmore, b. 1913, son of Anna and John Whitmore, became an architect

- married Sharon, born in Canada

s. Henry W. Jr. (Bill), b. 1938

s. Norman, U.S. Airforce captain killed in Vietnam

Third generation

Bill Whitmore, b. 1938, son of Henry and Sharon Whitmore, became a manufacturer of sailboats

- married Stella in 1963, b. 1937 in Sweden

s. Michael Henry William (Will), b. 1964

d. Lisa, b. 1966, residing in Sweden

- married Göran, professor

s. Mattias

d. Emma

s. David, b. 1970. Sea captain, chief officer on Titanic Princess, promoted to captain.

- married Judith, b. in Australia. Divorced.

s. Matthew, b. 1999

s. Christopher, b. 1975, died the day he was born.

Fourth generation

William Whitmore (Will), b. 1964, son of Bill and Stella Whitmore, became a professor in San Francisco

- married Amanda**Iversen, b. in Norway, professor in San Francisco

s. Henrik b. 1992

s. Michael b. 1997

**Amanda's family includes parents: Iver and Marita Iversen of Stavanger, Norway; brothers Bjarne and Olaf. Bjarne married Siv and had two sons, Thord and Johan. Olaf married Camilla and had two daughters, Sonia and Stine.

Fifth generation

Henrik Whitmore, b. 1992, son of Will and Amanda Whitmore, became a manufacturer of solar panels in San Francisco

- not married

The Cosentino Fictional Characters

First generation

Roberto Cosentino, b. 1888 in Genoa, Italy, reporter, d. 1925

Sailed on Titanic in 1912, rescued Anna Olson

- married Julia Nicolo of Italy. Journalist and newspaper owner, remarried.

s. Joshua R. Cosentino, b. 1920

Second generation

Joshua R., b. 1920, son of Roberto and Julia Cosentino. War correspondent in London during WWII, newspaper owner/publisher

- married Vanessa, b. in England

s. Ronald J. Cosentino, b. 1947

d. Rachel, b. 1949, corporate secretary

- married Pascal of Dutch descent

Third generation

Ronald J. Cosentino, b. 1947, son of Joshua and Vanessa Cosentino. War correspondent in Vietnam, newspaper owner

- Brought a Vietnamese orphan, Binh, to the U.S.

- married Anita Benson, book editor, New York

s. Sean, b. 1982. U.S. Army Captain, d. 2010 in Afghanistan

- married Jenna

s. Justin, b. 2010

d. Michelle, b. 1985, teacher

d. Caroline, b. 1992, corporate financial officer

d. Lauren, b. 1997

The End.